Praise for Laurelin Paige's
Star Struck

"The chemistry between her and Seth is like a match to dynamite, instant and incredibly hot."

~ *RT Book Reviews*

"Heather and Seth are extremely likeable, have great sexual chemistry and cherish each other in the most unique ways."

~ *Harlequin Junkie*

"She has quickly become one of my favorite Hollywood romance authors, and I continue to anxiously await what she will come up with next!"

~ *The Book Pushers*

"What do you get when you put a snobby actress from the wrong side of the tracks and a super-hot alpha guy that's good with his hands together? Perfection, if you're reading *Star Struck* by Laurelin Paige."

~ *Smut Book Junkie*

Look for these titles by
Laurelin Paige

Now Available:

Lights, Camera
Take Two
Star Struck

Star Struck

Laurelin Paige

SAMHAIN
PUBLISHING

Samhain Publishing, Ltd.
11821 Mason Montgomery Road, 4B
Cincinnati, OH 45249
www.samhainpublishing.com

Star Struck
Copyright © 2014 by Laurelin Paige
Print ISBN: 978-1-61922-561-9
Digital ISBN: 978-1-61922-096-6

Editing by Holly Atkinson
Cover by Lyn Taylor

First Samhain Publishing, Ltd. electronic publication: June 2014
First Samhain Publishing, Ltd. print publication: June 2015

Dedication

To all the loves of a former life—the Thespians, theater geeks, drama queens that surrounded me in my days of plays and musicals. The dreams we dreamt together were grand and inspiring. You taught me so much that translated into my new life, making my new dream possible. In every way, you are my foundation. Thank you.

Chapter One

Heather Wainwright rolled the straw of her drink between her plump raspberry coated lips, her iced skinny mocha now mostly just watered down espresso.

"Do you want me to stop for another?" Lexie asked, eying her sideways from behind the wheel of the BMW Active Hybrid, her short black hair bobbing with the subtle movement.

"No. Just next time get me a bigger size to begin with." Heather dropped her empty cup into the holder in front of her and stuck the nail of her thumb between her teeth. She was anxious but unable to identify the source of the emotion. With as often as she'd felt that way lately, she should have been getting used to it.

Should have been were the key words. More and more, her anxiety interfered with her daily activities. She'd even started to get a reputation on some of her sets as a diva. Maybe she should take Lexie's advice and give herself a vacation. She'd certainly earned enough clout in Hollywood to take a break without losing any career footing.

She sighed. Even if she wanted to take a break, she couldn't. Not now. She was booked almost solidly for the next year and a half with various film projects. Even if she could get out of some of her obligations, she wouldn't. It was too much like quitting, and Heather would never be called a quitter.

"At least you had a few days off." Lexie seemed to sense the source of Heather's sigh. "Maybe I shouldn't have signed you up for this. You could have used the three solid weeks."

"No, it's fine." Her tone came out whinier than she'd intended. Yes, she could have used the rest, but she'd never pass up an opportunity to help the Urban Arts Partnership, and Lexie knew that. That was why Lexie had proven herself as the best assistant Heather had ever had—she understood the actress in a way few people did. In fact, after working together for two years, Lexie was more of a friend than an employee. "I'm sorry I'm being a bitch about it. I want to do this."

Heather had only gotten back to L.A. five days before, having just completed a six-week shoot in Colorado. She hadn't even finished buckling her seatbelt in the car outside LAX before Lexie'd delivered good news and bad news. The good news was her next film had encountered a significant delay in production, giving her an extra three weeks before she'd have to start filming. This meant she'd have time to rest but, more importantly, it meant she was available for the annual 24-Hour Plays, a charity event that benefited the Urban Arts Partnership. Heather had been disappointed when she'd thought she wouldn't be available for the event—she tried to never miss it.

The bad news was that the 24-Hour Plays' usual spokeswoman, Rosie Barrett, had fallen on the set of her own movie and broken her leg in three places severe enough to require surgery. At the last minute, Montblanc, the sponsors of the event, were scrambling for a replacement. Without any consultation, Lexie had volunteered Heather for the job.

Heather rested her elbow on the window ledge and glared at her driver. "But tell me again why you thought I'd be up for taking Rosie's place?"

It was Lexie's turn to sigh. "Because you're an avid supporter of Urban Arts and you are a born schmoozer. It's a perfect gig for you." She glanced in her side mirror, avoiding Heather's piercing stare. "At least I didn't sign you up for that interview that Jenna Markham's people have been bugging you about."

"If you'd done that, I would have fired you."

Jenna Markham was a cross between an investigative reporter and Barbara Walters. She dug up the deepest darkest secrets of her subject's past and then made him or her get all weepy about it in a televised interview. Heather had managed to keep most of her roots buried. She was not about to blow that with a bare all interview.

"See? I know that. Which is why I told her no and I told Urban Arts yes. Because you want to help Urban Arts." Lexie bit her lower lip. "Besides, though I still think you need to take some time to chill, now is not necessarily the best time to do so. You need something to keep your mind off of Collin moving out."

Heather flung her hands in the air in frustration. "I don't need anything to keep my mind off of Collin! This isn't a devastating breakup. I'm fine. How many times do I have to say it?"

"It doesn't bother you at all that he's been sleeping with someone else for the past who knows how long? That he's moving in with her?"

Heather dropped her hands to her lap and shrugged. "Eh." She couldn't explain her feelings about her on-again, off-again boyfriend, Collin Satchel. While his decision to move out left Heather alone in her twenty thousand square foot Bel Air house, she didn't feel any lonelier than she had when he was living there. Their entire relationship had been based on sex and playing a mega Hollywood couple for the media. Truthfully, the sex hadn't been all that fulfilling.

"I slept with other guys too," Heather admitted now. "Don't look at me like that. Collin and I had an understanding. The only rules were use protection and keep it on the down-low." Not that any of her trysts had gotten her off the way she'd needed. What was she missing?

"Well, even if you really are fine, which I doubt, the press is going to say otherwise. Unless you're out in the world, being seen, showing how fine you are without him. Hosting the plays is a perfect opportunity for that."

"You're right, you're right." Heather could improvise anything, schmooze anyone. So what was her hesitation about hosting the 24-Hour Plays?

It was the importance of the event—that was what. Of all the causes and funds Heather championed, this one truly mattered to her. Acting had been the only thing that had pulled her through her childhood, and the Urban Arts Partnership was all about keeping the arts in underprivileged schools. She was afraid she couldn't do it justice, that she'd do more harm than good.

But the event needed a spokesperson. They'd thought of her and Lexie had accepted for her. Backing out now would definitely hurt the success of the plays. "You're right," she said again. "But you have to write every one of my spokespersonish speeches, Lex. And if there's any other extra work to do, I'm throwing it to you."

"Of course. That's my job. Anyway, the only thing really extra is tonight. It's casual, so no biggie."

The *tonight* Lexie referred to was where they were currently headed—the Meet and Greet for all the behind-the-scenes people. There would be reps from Montblanc and Urban Arts, as well as the backstage crew managers. Heather just had to share a few drinks, laugh at a few mediocre jokes and smile for a few pictures. Then she'd be out of there—free and clear until the official start the next evening at nine.

"What time did this start?" Heather asked, noting the dashboard clock read *7:27.*

"Seven. So you are sufficiently late."

Heather never arrived anywhere on time—another attribute that gave her diva status in the eyes of the press. It wasn't that she always wanted to make an entrance as many gossip columns surmised. She'd simply discovered that arriving late guaranteed she wouldn't be waiting alone. Fans were less intimidated to approach her when she was by herself. There was safety in numbers.

"Do you want me to come in with you?" Lexie asked as they neared Drebs, the location of the get-together.

"No." Heather leaned forward, trying to estimate how much trouble she'd have getting into the swank bar without being mauled by fans and press. Drebs should have been a low-key spot, but word must have gotten out that this meeting was taking place there. She could already spot a few cameras in the small group gathered outside the doors. Maybe it would be easier to get through if Lexie was with her. "Yes." But would she look even more like a diva if she paraded her assistant along with her? "No," she said finally.

Lexie chuckled, seeming to understand her thought process. "I'll be in the lot outside. I won't use valet so you can make a quick getaway if you need to. Sound good?"

"Yes, thanks." Heather flipped down the shade above her to give herself a quick look in the mirror. She looked good, even with her casual makeup and her long dark blonde hair free of product. She was made-down enough that with her sunglasses on, she might be able to slip in unnoticed. Though wearing sunglasses in the evening was a red flag of a celebrity in itself.

"They're going to spot you," Lexie said pulling into the valet station. "But it will be fine. Just let the valet open the door for you and rush in. Don't stop for autographs. Get inside, skip the host and head straight for the private room. You know where it is."

Heather appreciated the pep talk. She let out a deep breath and took another in as the valet opened her door.

"Text me if and when you need me," Lexie called as Heather stepped out of the BMW.

"It's her!" someone called as soon as the door shut behind her, followed by a scream of recognition. Another scream followed by shouts of her name.

Then so many voices were screaming and shouting, she couldn't distinguish what any of them said. The crowd pressed around her, pens and napkins and body parts thrust in her direction. She pushed her shoulder through the bodies, but was stuck.

Shit. She should have brought a bodyguard.

She turned back to tell Lexie to stay, but Lexie had already pulled through the valet station, too far to see Heather's distress.

Panic rushed through her.

The doors of the bar swung open and a hand reached through the crowd toward her. She grabbed for it before looking up to see the owner, letting the strong arm pull her safely inside.

"I'm so sorry, Heather," said Patrick Atlas, the executive from Montblanc and the source of her rescue. "Someone tipped off the press."

She swallowed the anxiety that had nearly overtaken her and pasted on a smile. "No worries. I'm used to it."

Patrick kissed her cheek then led her farther into the bar toward the private room, holding her hand the whole time. She hated how comforting his hand felt around hers. She shouldn't have let the crowd get to her like that.

Heather watched the back of Patrick's head as they walked. She'd known him for as long as she'd been involved with the 24-Hour Plays. He'd come on to her often, even though she always turned him down. Right now she was grateful for the familiar face—or familiar brown head, rather—though she normally would be more reserved around him, not wanting to lead him on. He was attractive and wealthy and powerful, but his charm was too smooth. Sweet nothings and soft caresses did nothing to fire up her libido. Truthfully, she couldn't say what it was that fired her up, but she knew it wasn't Patrick.

Patrick opened the doors of the private dining room and gestured to the large rectangular table in the center of the room. "I've saved you a seat at the end by me," he said. "I'm just going to let the hostess know that our party is complete and I'll be right in. Oh, the waitress has already been by—can I put in a drink order for you?"

What she wanted was a mug of beer, but her next movie featured her in a bikini so extra calories were out of the question. "A glass of White Zin, please."

"Got it."

She heard him shut the doors behind her as she surveyed the room that bustled with chatter and the clinking sounds of glasses and bottles. There were nearly thirty people there, many that she recognized. She spotted a few members of the Urban Arts Board of Directors at one long end of the table.

For a long moment, she stood watching the group, unseen by anyone. Usually she was the center of attention. It was both odd and surreal to be in a room unnoticed. And also awfully nice. Like a slice of heaven.

But in her experience, heaven never lasted long. Neil Phillips, the coordinator of the plays, saw her and waved her over, prompting a few of the people sitting next to him to look up. "Heather!" he exclaimed, standing to give her a hug as she approached. "I hear you're taking Rosie's place last minute."

"Like anyone could take Rosie's place," she said.

"If anyone can, it's you."

Heather gave him her first genuine smile of the evening. Of the many people who had worked with her on stage and film, Neil was one of the few who saw past her "difficult" status. He'd never done anything but bolster and uplift her and she had nothing but respect and admiration for him.

After Neil sat back down, she greeted his assistants and a few of the other people she recognized as stage crew. Then the Urban Arts crowd had to say hello. Finally, after greeting nearly everyone, she moved to the empty chair.

"Here, let me." The man sitting next to her spot stood to pull out her chair for her.

"Thank you." She sat down then shifted to face the man as he retook his own seat. Her breath caught.

God, he was gorgeous.

Not pretty-boy-leading-actor gorgeous like the men she worked with, but rough-rugged-muscular-man gorgeous. His dark blond hair fell high on his forehead, giving a perfect view into his light blue eyes that twinkled in the low light of the room. She guessed he was her age—her real age of thirty-three, not the twenty-nine all her online bios stated. But then he smiled and the creases at the edges of his eyes suggested he might be older, or that he had spent a lot of time smiling. Either way, the laugh lines made him all the more handsome.

As if her eyes had a mind of their own, they traveled lower, past the well-groomed scruff that covered his face to the T-shirt that hugged his bulky chest and thick biceps. Even through his clothes, she could see how muscular he was. This guy was strong. The kind of guy who could pick her up and swing her over his shoulder with one easy movement. The kind of guy who either worked out religiously or had a job that kept him in the best of shape.

The kind of guy who'd probably be a little rough in the bedroom. Not too rough. Just rough enough.

Her core clenched at the thought.

A blush crawled up her face. Why was she thinking like that? Sure, she hadn't had any in...she quickly did the math. Though she'd tried to hook up with Micah Preston, a costar in her last film, he'd turned her down, leaving her sexless on that six-week shoot. Before that, Collin had been on location in Italy. And before that, she'd been in Australia filming...

Damn. It had been over eight months. No wonder she felt horny.

"You're trying to figure out what role I have in all this." The man's deep voice poured over her like a glass of Merlot, warming her head to toe.

"What? Oh, sorry. Yeah." She fell into his statement, using it as an excuse for her staring. "Hmm..." She pretended to try to figure it out, still too stunned by his beauty to actually put together real thoughts.

"I'm not going to tell until you guess. If that's what you're waiting for."

"No. Though it's not fair that you know who I am and I have no idea who you are."

Jesus, she was flirting. With a stranger.

Not a problem. She flirted with everyone. He didn't know she actually felt what she promised in her seductive tone.

"Who says I know who you are?"

Her mouth opened but no words came out. She'd assumed he'd known who she was because, well, everyone knew who she was. And now she'd made an ass of herself.

He laughed. "I'm kidding. Even if I didn't know who Heather Wainwright was, I'd guess you were the actress spokeswoman. You ooze celebrity."

Was he making fun of her? She couldn't tell. Except the way his mouth twisted up in a small smile suggested he was playing with her. No one ever played with her. They kowtowed and charmed and kissed her ass. His obvious indifference to the Hollywood rules made her tummy flutter. Were those butterflies in her stomach? How long had it been since she'd had butterflies for a guy?

Trying to ignore her squirmy insides, she played back. "And you ooze..." She scanned him again. What he oozed was sex.

Pure, hard, all-male sex. But she was trying to guess his role in the 24-Hour Plays, not define what he did to her physically. Besides, she was sure he already knew.

"I ooze....what?"

"I'm not sure."

"Nothing bad, I hope."

"No. Good things." Definitely good things. And she'd just said that out loud.

Though they'd maintained eye contact for most of the conversation, he caught her eye now with such intensity she had to look down, her face warm. "Let's see..." She skimmed the faces around them, attempting recovery. "You're sitting with Neil. So I might assume crew."

Please, God, don't let him be stage crew. She couldn't keep flirting with him if he was crew. Could. Not.

It wasn't that she was stuck-up—no, that was exactly what it was. She was totally stuck-up. Not a quality she was necessarily proud of, but it had gotten her where she was today. For that reason alone, she embraced it.

But this man exuded something more superior than crew. She already had identified all the crew heads, so what on earth would he be in charge of? He certainly didn't read as one of the Urban Arts reps. They all huddled together at one side of the table, a bunch of modern day hippies.

Maybe he represented the venue—the Broad Stage. He could be in charge of the coordinating volunteers.

But his well-sculpted body, his confident demeanor said differently. He didn't sit at a desk. He had strength and power. He had to be with Patrick. There was no other answer. "You're also sitting near Patrick's team. And your jeans and T-shirt are designer. I'm going to have to say you're a Montblanc Exec."

"You peg me as an exec? Okay." He chuckled. "But my ex-girlfriend picked the clothes out. So maybe that shouldn't be a factor in your concluding thoughts."

"*Ex*-girlfriend?" Shit, she was so obvious.

"Yes. Ex. I'm single." He took a swig from his beer, mesmerizing her with the way his lips circled the bottle. "As are you, if I'm to believe what I read standing in line at the grocery store."

"Very single." She might as well have invited him to her bedroom. What the hell was she doing? She knew nothing about the man. Nothing beyond the fact that he was H-O-T hot.

As if reading her thoughts, he held out his hand. "Seth Rafferty."

His name sounded familiar, but she couldn't place it. She was horrible with names anyway. She gave up trying when his firm grasp closed around her fingers. His touch shot sparks of bliss up her arm and straight down to the warm spot between her thighs. "A pleasure to meet you."

He held her hand longer than he needed, his rough thumb grazing back and forth against her soft skin. "Not to sound too cliché, but the pleasure is all mine."

"Good, you've met Seth."

Heather pulled her hand into her lap as Patrick took his seat on the other side of her, setting a glass of wine in front of her as he did. "I was afraid the waitress would take too long to get in here, so I just ordered at the bar."

Heather barely heard Patrick's explanation of his delay or how her wine had arrived. What she focused on was his first line, his acknowledgment that he was glad she'd become acquainted with the yummy specimen sitting next to her. That practically confirmed Seth was with Patrick's team. Not a crewmember then. Thank the Lord.

"Yes, we just met." She lowered her head, fearing her cheeks were coloring yet again.

If he noticed her blush, Patrick gave no indication. "Have you told her?" He directed his question to Seth.

"Uh, no." Seth shifted in his chair. "I was leaving that for you."

Heather's brow furrowed, confused by the vague exchange between the men.

"Well then," Patrick said, his eyes lighting up. "Heather, we're doing something new this year. You know that all the plays performed in the event are written and put together in a twenty-four hour period. This year, instead of just using a projected graphic background, we are also adding set. Whatever pieces can be constructed in the same twenty-four hour period."

Heather's brow crease deepened. Set construction? How exactly would that work? Like one of those home improvement shows where a carpenter built items within a limited time? And even if that could work, who would be...

Oh God. No.

But before Patrick continued she knew. She knew and she wanted to die.

"Seth here is going to be building all the pieces for us. It's very exciting, isn't it?"

No, it wasn't exciting. Seth wasn't a member of Montblanc or Urban Arts. He wasn't from the Broad Stage. He was a crewmember after all.

Heather Wainwright, Hollywood A-list actress, had been flirting shamelessly with a carpenter.

Chapter Two

Celebrities held no special interest for Seth Rafferty. They were simply people. People he worked with. Nothing exciting. Their shit stank just like everyone else's. His job kept him in close proximity to them on a daily basis and, while that part of his occupation was what interested his friends and family the most, he'd become immune long ago.

Which was why he hadn't been prepared for Heather Wainwright.

He first spotted her when she'd entered the private dining room. She'd stood alone, watching the group at the table, not knowing that she'd caught his gaze. She was pretty, yes. All right, she was goddamn beautiful. And sexy. Her legs were long and lean under her knee-length skirt and her breasts pressed nicely against her low sleeveless shirt. But she was a megastar—those qualities were standard package.

Except there was something about her that Seth hadn't expected—a vulnerability he'd rarely seen in other actresses. A bewilderment at her place in her world. A softness that he'd thought must be impossible to maintain in Hollywood.

She pulled it all in when she'd been called out. Seth watched her out of the corner of his eye as she put on her celebrity façade and greeted the others at the table.

But when she'd sat next to him and they'd talked, he saw glimmers of it again—pieces of a fragile soul he sensed she kept hidden from other people. A longing to drop the *I-got-it-going-on* persona and instead let someone else take charge.

And oh, what he'd do to her—*for* her—if he was in charge of her. His pants had tightened at the thought.

It wasn't just a sexual attraction. He'd also enjoyed the conversation, even though they hadn't talked about anything important or of consequence. There was something in her easy tone that made him feel like he could keep talking to her forever. About nothing. And he could certainly keep looking in the deep chocolate pools of her eyes forever.

Prepared for her or not, Seth Rafferty was star struck.

Then she found out what he did for a living—or what she *thought* he did for a living—and everything changed. The playful sparkle in her eyes vanished while the color drained from her face and her smile curled downward into a look of disgust.

And Seth was struck again, this time with disappointment.

"So what do you think?" Patrick asked, eager for Heather's reaction to the new event format.

"Hmm," she said as if trying to decide how to phrase her response. Seth sensed her delay wasn't about the format at all. She was grappling with the realization that he wasn't an exec for Montblanc. That she'd been conversing with someone *beneath* her.

He shook his head slightly trying to shake off the fascination he'd had with her, disappointed to find she was one of *those* actresses. One with an ego as big as her reputation proclaimed. Too much of a diva to even recognize the names of prominent crew members like himself. What a shame.

He'd been with her type before. His ex-girlfriend—ex-fiancée. Erica. She'd been the type who only cared about him when his status proved worthy. It was bullshit, and he'd changed the way he dated after her, careful to only involve himself with women who liked him when they didn't know dick about what he did for a living.

After more hemming and hawing and three sips of wine, she spoke. "Actually, Patrick, I think the idea's terrible." And once she'd found her voice, she couldn't stop. "I mean, a set? For the 24-Hour Plays? Why? The lack of a set—the impressionism of the whole situation—that's part of the beauty of it. Why would you change it? What do you hope to add with this element?"

Patrick's eyebrows rose. "Oh, well, we just…"

"No offense to you, Seth." She glanced toward him, not really looking at him and he winced at how arousing it was to hear her say his name. "I'm sure you're amazing with a hammer and everything. But…it's just…it's wrong."

He shrugged, not daring to talk. He was too appalled and pissed and turned on to speak. Anything he said would just get him in trouble, and not the good kind of trouble.

"I'm so sorry to hear you feel that way, Heather."

Seth sneered inwardly at the sincerity of Patrick's amends. Patrick held power in this situation. Why did he feel he had to smooth over the ruffled feathers of some snotty actress? What she needed was a good spanking.

And then thoughts of her creamy skin turning pink under his hand had him needing to adjust himself under the table.

Settle down, boy. She's not worth it.

"Does Rosie know about this?" Heather jutted her lip out in challenge.

If she'd jutted that lip out to him, Seth was pretty sure he'd have to bite it. *Not worth it, remember?*

"Yes, and Rosie was completely behind it." Patrick took a swallow of his martini— more of a gulp. "In fact, Heather, you're the first person who's opposed it."

"Maybe you aren't asking the right people. I'm sure people like Seth here are all for it because, you know, set construction is his thing and all."

Set construction really wasn't Seth's thing. Not anymore. He'd moved beyond that years ago, but for some reason, he was strongly opposed to letting Heather know that. She'd probably calm down and relax if she realized his true occupation. She might even pick up the flirting again.

Laurelin Paige

The thought sickened him, mostly because that led to other thoughts of how far their flirting could go. And, to quote Heather, that was *just wrong*. He had standards. He didn't need Heather Wainwright. He didn't need to be a star fucker.

No, it was better that she thought he was a carpenter—a nobody in her world. That way it would be easier to keep her out of *his* world. He had no interest in such blatant snobbery.

Except Patrick was about to spill the beans. "Actually, Seth's more about the big picture," Patrick said. "You know he's a—"

Seth cut him off before he could say more. "Maybe Heather has personal issues that have influenced her opinion."

Heather's head swung to face Seth, daggers shooting from her eyes. "I'm not sure what you mean by that, but my opinion is influenced by the fact that I've done the plays for five years in New York and three years in L.A. and they've been fabulous as is. I don't understand the idea of fixing something that isn't broken. But you're probably a fixer type."

She crossed her arms, increasing the abundance of her cleavage and he corrected his earlier thought—her breasts were above standard package. Way above.

It didn't matter. Beautiful tits did not make up for a holier-than-thou attitude.

"Patrick, I'm sorry to interrupt." Janice Shafer, Patrick's sidekick from Montblanc, leaned in from the other side of him. "We're having a small issue with the Urban Arts scholarship performer. Would you mind giving your opinion?"

"Excuse me a moment," Patrick said to Heather, and Seth detected relief in his voice, as if he were grateful for the chance to end the conversation. Patrick turned his chair toward Janice and the Urban Arts rep who sat beside her.

Seth listened halfheartedly as the rep explained that the teenager scheduled to sing at the plays had a problem with her guitar and that it might not be ready for the show on Saturday and did Patrick have any suggestions for getting a replacement.

But his mind was on the blonde beauty next to him and the tension rolling off her body in thick waves. Her tension fueled his irritation. First, he was just irritated at himself for being reeled in by her, for believing he'd seen something different in her. Then he was pissed at his Johnson for still being very interested in the woman despite her pettiness.

But the more he thought about it, the more he was furious at her. Was she really that shallow? Or was he reading her wrong?

He shouldn't say anything. He should just let it lie.

But he had to know. "You're not upset about using a set, are you?" He kept his voice down so that only she could hear him. "You're upset that you were flirting with someone who builds sets."

Heather's mouth dropped open. "I was not..." She lowered her voice to a tense whisper. "I was not flirting."

"You most certainly were too." Seriously? How could she deny it?

"I was not." She stabbed her index finger into the table as if to enforce her point. "I was talking to you like I talk to everyone. I'm very charming."

"You're not that charming."

"I am so charming." She shifted in her seat and he could see her anger revving up. "How dare you, anyway?" She hissed. "You don't know. You don't even know me."

He wanted to say that he did know her. He knew her type. Conceited, arrogant. She expected the world to fall at her feet, and when it didn't she demanded an explanation as to why. Wasn't that what she'd just done with Patrick?

But he couldn't bring himself to be that honest. It was too cruel.

Laurelin Paige

Still, he couldn't drop the conversation. Not yet. Not when she'd played with him like she had. "I know that you didn't flirt with anyone else who talked to you here tonight."

She sat back, her eyelashes fluttering. "Were you watching me? Are you, like, obsessed with me?" She huffed out a thick breath of air. "Typical."

"And I know your reputation does not label you as charming." It was a low blow. Everyone truly in the Hollywood realm knew reputations were often a bunch of bullshit. But he was pissed.

"My reputation? That's...you can't believe..."

He had her where he wanted her—flustered and out of defenses. He went in for the kill. "And wasn't it funny how your charm went away the minute you discovered what my involvement with the plays was? When you figured out you were flirting with a crewmember."

"I have nothing against crewmembers."

"Then it's just carpenters."

She rolled her eyes. "God, this is ridiculous. You're totally twisting this around to be about something that it's not. You're taking my opposition to using a set and making it about you. Self-centered much?"

Fuck polite. She'd gone cruel first. "Well, isn't that the pot calling the kettle black. Stuck-up, much?"

"Asshole."

"Bitch."

Her eyes blazed with indignation. Then she scooted her chair back and stood with a *hmph* before escaping to the corner of the room, phone in hand.

He felt better having spoken his mind, but also worse at the absence of her warmth. And while he'd wanted to slap her with his words, which he had effectively done, another part of him wanted to follow after her and wrap her in his arms.

What the fuck was that about?

26

For the second time that night, he shook his head. He'd have no sympathy for her. He'd come from nothing, had built himself up from the ground. It had been tough and he wouldn't wish it on anyone, but he'd never forsake his roots. That was why he'd been so impressed with the Urban Arts Partnership. They respected the less fortunate and gave kids a chance to shine through art. Art had been his own savior in his early years. It was why he'd approached the organization and offered to contribute a set. So he could give back, could be a part of the good they did.

Heather Wainwright represented exactly the opposite of what he was hoping to accomplish here. He'd made the mistake with Erica, trying to hide his past, but he'd learned. Now he'd rather be associated with the *underlings* than the highbrows any day.

He took a long pull of his beer and made up his mind to remain anonymous in the production. He needed to get Patrick on board. He focused on Patrick's conversation, which seemed to be nearing an end. One of the Urban Arts reps had volunteered to find a music store to donate a guitar for the event. Problem solved.

When it seemed like a good moment to cut in, Seth scooted over to Heather's seat. "Hey, Patrick." He waited until the exec had excused himself from the others and gave Seth his full attention. "I wanted to ask a favor."

"Shoot."

Seth leaned in so he could talk quietly. "I'd rather you didn't tell anyone that I'm the one donating the materials for the set or that it was my idea. I'd prefer it if everyone just thinks I'm a carpenter."

Patrick raised a brow. "Well, well. Successful and humble to boot?"

"No, I'm not humble." He couldn't make himself a hero in this. That was going too far. He also couldn't explain to Patrick about his interaction with Heather. "You know how it is. If everyone knew my job title, they'd want me to hire them, all that. It's best to remain low key."

Patrick nodded. "I'm with you. Actually, this is easier for me. Because, and I hate to admit it, I still don't really know what a movie production designer does."

Seth chuckled. "No worries. Not many people do." Then, realizing Patrick was waiting for an explanation, he went on. "I'm in charge of everything visual. The costumes, the set, the make-up—the entire aesthetic of the film."

"Wow. Big job. I heard you could be up for an Oscar nom."

"I'm not getting my hopes up." Though he was an early front-runner.

But, while an Oscar would be very exciting, he didn't need it to feel validated. It was one of the top jobs a person could have on a movie and he'd worked his way up from carpenter to set decorator to set designer to art director before finally landing on production designer. He loved every aspect of his job. He loved working with the director to determine how a movie was supposed to look and feel, then creating it from scratch. He loved overseeing the set and costume design and working with the director of photography to make sure Seth's vision would show up the way he wanted on film.

He loved that he got to select and hire all the people to get it done right—the make-up artists, the costumers. The carpenters.

"Well, good luck," Patrick said. "I'd love to see you win a big award. I could say I knew you when. And don't worry, mum's the word."

The sound of a woman clearing her throat drew Seth to look up behind him. Heather stood with arms crossed and a glare on her face. Had she overheard his conversation?

"You're in my seat."

No, it didn't seem she had. He imagined she'd be the type to throw the information in his face if she had.

She raised her eyebrows as if prompting a response.

"Yep, I'm in your seat." Seth scooted back to his own chair. "And now I'm not."

Heather slid into her chair and Seth didn't miss that she inched it away from him as she did.

That was fine. He didn't want to be sitting next to her either. The sooner the evening was over, the better.

Heather seemed to feel the same. "Patrick, I'm leaving in twenty. If you want me to be here for intros, you'd better do it now."

Everything on her time schedule. Total diva.

Patrick glanced at his watch. "Yes, that's a good idea." He stood and got the room's attention by tapping his drink with a spoon.

Seth barely listened as Patrick introduced himself and welcomed everyone to the event. Then it was time for introductions, starting with Heather.

Heather's speech was modest, stating only her experience with the 24-Hour Plays and not reciting her long resume of films and television appearances. She didn't need to. Everyone knew who Heather Wainwright was.

When she sat, everyone clapped. Except Seth. He wasn't trying to blatantly be rude—he just couldn't bring himself to acknowledge anything about her.

He stood for his own intro. "I'm Seth Rafferty. It's my first time at the plays. I'll be building the set, a new element of this year's production." He caught the eye of Neil Phillips, the only other person in the room who knew Seth's real job experience. "I've, uh, been working on film sets for nearly twenty years now. That's about it."

It wasn't a lie; he didn't say he'd been *building* film sets for twenty years, just that he'd been *working* on them. From Neil's nod, he could tell he got the message across. Neil wouldn't give him away.

Seth sat back down, pleased with himself. This was good. Heather would avoid him because he was only a carpenter and he could focus on his job.

And maybe he'd have to whack off a few times to get her lush lips and orange blossom scent out of his head, but he wouldn't be the first guy to pleasure himself with Heather Wainwright on the brain.

Somehow, that thought only made him tense up again.

Yeah, the next few days were going to be a bitch.

Chapter Three

Heather watched out the tinted passenger window of the BMW as an up and coming director walked into the Broad Stage with his assistant. A few feet behind him was a writer she recognized as well.

"It's five 'til nine. I guess I got you here too early," Lexie said. "Do you want me to drive around?"

"No. I want to be on time. But only just on time. So let's sit a couple of minutes. At least until another one of the actors shows up." Heather heard how she sounded, how her arrival rules seemed like a game. She wished for the millionth time she didn't have to be like that.

But then for the millionth time, she reminded herself that this had been the life she'd wanted. The fame and the fortune didn't come free.

"You never told me how last night went." Lexie pushed the recline button on her seat. "Since we have a few minutes."

Heather groaned. When she'd left Drebs after the intros, she'd been in no mood to talk. Her encounter with Seth Rafferty had left her furious and frustrated. Sexually frustrated. To the point that even her favorite pink vibrator wasn't able to ease her need.

More than twenty-four hours later, her anger had softened, but her confusion had increased. Maybe talking about it would help.

Problem was, where to begin? "It was terrible." Seth wasn't the guy she thought he was. The realization had come with Patrick's ridiculous announcement. "They're changing the format. They've added a set to the show to be constructed in the same time frame."

"That might be cool."

Heather gave Lexie her best *seriously?* look.

But in the privacy of her car with just her assistant, she allowed herself to give it some real thought. "I guess it might be cool. But it's totally unnecessary."

"And?"

Lexie had worked with Heather long enough to tell when she was holding something back. Sometimes it was a good thing. Sometimes not so much. "And the guy who's building the set is an asshole."

"Is he?"

"He totally called me a bitch."

"Just out of the blue?"

"Sort of." No, not out of the blue. That was why she hadn't wanted to talk about it. Because she'd probably deserved what he'd dished and she didn't want to admit that.

She pressed her face against the window, remembering how into Seth she'd been before...well, before. How into him she was after too. Even though she was pretending like hell that she wasn't. "He's also really, really hot."

"Oh."

Her head snapped toward Lexie. "What is that supposed to mean?"

Lexie fiddled with her nose ring and shrugged. "It means, oh." Heather continued to stare at her friend until she sighed. "It means I understand your frustration. He's cute, but you would never fool around with a guy like that."

"A guy like what?" Heather held her breath, half dreading, half hoping Lexie would confront her on her shallowness.

"An asshole."

"Right." Heather nodded, accepting the lie. "That's exactly the problem."

"What else would it be?"

But of course, that wasn't what Lexie had meant *by a guy like that*. She'd meant that Heather would never date a blue-collar type of guy. She'd meant it was beneath her. If Lexie had been brave enough to say it, Heather couldn't have denied it.

She was so fucking petty it made her sick.

But she couldn't change how she felt. A lifetime of hard knocks had tattooed her soul and her conceit was born of her attempt to leave that part of her behind. Heather didn't talk about it much, but she'd shared bits and pieces of her past with her assistant. Though she didn't have to explain, she was flooded now with the need to be understood—to validate her emotions, to maybe come to some understanding herself.

"Do you know what my father said to me the day he kicked me out?" Heather looked straight ahead, afraid of the intimacy of eye contact. "I was sixteen. I'd told him he was a piece of trash. He said, 'Trash breeds trash, baby doll. That's all you've ever been, that's all you'll ever be.'"

Her eyes stung with the memory. Her mother passed out drunk on the beat-up loveseat they'd covered with a ratty mustard-colored quilt, her father buzzed from coke, smelling like old food and sweat—the scent he always bore after finishing his shift as a dishwasher for a local restaurant. Heather had gotten home late after a show she was in at the community theater and he'd gone off on her, complaining that she didn't pull her weight around the house. He told her she had to quit all that "acting stuff", drop out of school and get a real job.

And in retaliation, she'd told him she wasn't going to give up her future just because her parents were trash.

He'd laughed at her. Told her she'd never amount to anything.

Then he told her to get her things and get out.

So she had. And she never looked back.

Well, maybe she did look back. More like kept peering over her shoulder. The past found a way of slamming into her from time to time and keeping an eye out for it at least helped her prepare.

Now, Heather bit her lip before any tears could fall and was surprised when Lexie's hand landed firm and comforting on her thigh.

"But you're not trash," Lexie said. "And you never were. Even if you messed around with a guy who reminded you of the trailer parks, it wouldn't mean you're living up to your daddy's prophecy."

"I know." But didn't Heather sort of believe exactly that? That if she didn't rise above her past in every area of her life that she would have proven her father right? Even now, as successful and rich as she was, she always felt like she was just one wrong choice away from being right back where she came from. "I know," she said again. "But I don't know. You know?"

"I know."

Heather returned her gaze out the window and saw an actor she knew entering the Broad Stage. "There's Matt Shone. I should go in."

She reached for her oversized bag, but the strap caught on her seatbelt latch and the whole thing tumbled forward, the contents spilling on the car floor.

Heather cursed as she began shoving items back in her bag. This was totally a sign that she should clean out her purse more often. Did she really need three packs of gum and four different flavors of lip-gloss? Not to mention the random papers and trash and empty pill bottles.

Her hand closed around her birth control pills container—her *empty* birth control pills container—and she cursed again.

"What's wrong now?" Lexie asked, pointing her cell phone light toward the floor so Heather could see what she was doing.

Heather held up her pill container. "I was supposed to pick up my refill today and I forgot. Can you go?" She'd already missed starting her pack by a day. Maybe two. She didn't quite remember. Mostly she used them to regulate her period these days anyway, since sex wasn't in her recent repertoire.

"Of course. At your pharmacy back in Bel Air?"

"Yeah. Do you mind?" Heather felt awful. It would be more than an hour round trip. "I'm really sorry."

Lexie shrugged. "No problem. Can you manage the check-in without me?"

Heather considered. "I'm sure I can figure it out. Just be back to pick me up when we're done with the intros, which should be around eleven."

"Then I'll see you at eleven."

"Cool." Heather opened the door and stepped outside of the car, slinging her purse over her shoulder.

"Don't let anyone call you a bitch," Lexie called after her.

Heather rolled her eyes but smiled before she shut the door behind her.

At the entrance of the Broad Stage, she was greeted by a member of the stage crew she recognized from previous years, though she couldn't recall her name. The tag on her breast pocket displayed it as a reminder. *Oh, Vera.* That was it.

Vera led Heather through the sign-in process. First, she took her picture against a black backdrop for the programs and together they composed a short bio. Then there was the equity paperwork that, had she been there instead of driving off to Bel Air, Lexie would have filled out. Heather struggled through it herself, asking for a new form when she'd written down the real year she'd been born instead of the one she kept on file with Actor's Equity. It was pathetic how much she relied on her assistant.

Throughout check-in, Heather kept her eyes on the people roaming the theater. Though she wouldn't admit it aloud, she was searching for Seth. His call time had been earlier and he was likely already there, probably backstage. Still, she couldn't stop hoping he'd pop up in the lobby. She wanted to see him again in the worst way. Wanted to see if that weird attraction she had for him was really as strong as she remembered, or if she'd heightened its intensity in her mind.

But the only people she encountered were writers and directors and actors signing in, as well as the stage manager's crew who were leading them.

When Heather's paperwork was completed, Vera gathered a few of the actors and gave them a tour of the stage while she went through the familiar spiel of how the next twenty-four hours would work. "You have ten minutes until intros start. Everyone will be there and you'll get matched up with the writers and the directors. There's six of each. After your intros, the writers will have all night to write their plays, about fifteen pages—fifteen minutes—in length. They'll include info from your intros in the plays they write, so if there's something you really want to do on stage that you've never done, that's the time to mention it."

Heather bumped hips with Angie, one of the other actresses. "I know you've always wanted to smack me. Now's your chance."

Everyone laughed.

"Exactly," Vera agreed. "The writers have until six in the morning to hand in a finished draft of their play. The directors will arrive at seven. They'll meet with their crews at eight to discuss tech, blocking, and this year, set construction."

Heather's heart skipped a beat at the mention of set—at the thought of Seth. She barely heard Vera continue with her speech.

"At nine, rehearsals start. You'll rehearse all day until the show goes up tomorrow night at seven. The whole shebang will be over by nine p.m. Then we party."

"What will they do with the set pieces after the show?" Matt Shone asked.

Good point. Just more proof the whole idea was a waste of resources.

But Vera's answer surprised Heather. "They're auctioning them off next month to raise more money for Urban Arts. You can't imagine how much some people will pay to sit in a chair that was sat in by Heather Wainwright."

Heather smiled weakly. It was true—her discarded trash made tons of money on eBay. Selling the set pieces was a great idea. An excellent idea. Maybe she'd judged the concept too harshly.

Of course, she already knew it had been the guy not the idea that had her in a dither the night before. He'd even rightly called her on it.

"And what do we do with the props we brought?" This was Matt's first year at the event and he'd been asking a lot of questions. He was younger than Heather and didn't run in her circles, but she'd met him a couple of times before.

She shook off thoughts of Seth. "Share your prop at the intros," she told Matt. "Then the writers will add them into their plays somehow. It's wicked funny."

"What did you bring?"

"Uh, uh. You'll find out when everyone else does."

The props were Heather's favorite part of the intros. Some of the items she'd brought in the past included a clown suit, a Chiquita Banana hat, and a large wooden moose. She'd had to make-out with the moose in that play. It had been the hit of the night. This year, she'd brought fur-lined handcuffs. It was sort of on the tame side as far as props went, but a good writer could make something awesome with it.

Except, now that she thought about it, she hadn't seen the handcuffs when she'd been stuffing her contents back into her bag after spilling it all over the car.

She slipped away from the group into the vestibule at the back of the theater. Dread began to rise as she rooted around through her purse, searching for the prop. Then dread turned into panic when she confirmed its absence.

Dammit!

She pulled her phone from its pocket on the side of her purse and pushed the speed dial button for Lexie. Before her upbeat voice could get out a proper greeting, Heather jumped on her. "Did I leave my cuffs in the car?"

"What?"

"My handcuffs. My prop for tonight. Did they fall out of my purse when I dumped it?"

"I don't see..." Heather could hear Lexie moving around in her seat and silently prayed her searching didn't cause an accident. "Oh...wait. I do see them." It only took half a second before she understood the problem. "Shit! I can race back, but I'm thirty minutes away."

"That isn't soon enough. They're starting in ten minutes. I'm going to have to find something else."

She hung up on Lexie mid-sentence and began rummaging around in her bag again, this time searching for a substitute. But everything in her purse was mundane and ordinary. Nothing that would even show up on stage from the audience.

For a brief moment, she considered going without a prop. What would they do? Kick her out of the plays? She was the spokeswoman.

And that was exactly why she couldn't go without a prop. She was supposed to be the pro, the actress all the newbies would look to. The prop was one of the most important elements. She had to find something.

She stuck her head in the restroom next to the vestibule. Nothing. Not even a plunger. Then she scanned the empty security desk by the back entrance. Again, nothing. Maybe the small trash container under the desk would work. She kept it as an option but wasn't ready to end her search.

She crossed the corridor to the workroom at the side of the theater and looked around.

Bingo.

The entire back counter had an array of tools—hammers, saws, screwdrivers, and tools she didn't know the name of. This was where Seth would be constructing the set pieces. These must be his tools. He'd touched these tools, used them.

She put her hand out and brushed the items as she walked along the counter, enjoying the rush that came from knowing they belonged to the sexy carpenter. Images of him using them filled her mind, turning her entire body to warm mush.

She let her hand settle on an electric drill. It felt strange in her grasp, not an item she'd ever find herself in contact with. She wasn't even sure she knew how to use one. It was perfect— an unexpected prop and one that a writer could have a lot of fun with.

But she couldn't take it...could she?

She heard voices from the stage and could tell the group was gathering. The intros were about to start. She had no time. She glanced around to see if she had any other options and spotted an older, more worn drill on the counter. Black sharpie marked it as *"Property of Broad Stage"*. This drill was better. Bigger and more awkward, but she'd feel less guilty about borrowing it. Without another thought, she picked up the old drill and began wrapping the cord around its body.

"Did you get lost?"

She spun around at the sound of the familiar voice—the voice that made her slippery in her silk panties—and clutched the drill behind her back.

Seth stood in the doorway, one arm propped against the frame, his blue eyes freezing her to her spot. He wore a plain burgundy T-shirt and carpenter jeans. She hadn't imagined the intensity of her attraction to him—it was real. Just looking at him now made her chest tight and her lungs struggle for air.

Realizing he'd nearly caught her in the act of "borrowing" a tool, she threw her shoulders back and put on her best innocent look. "No, I was...just...trying to find some place I could be alone." She could feel her eyelashes fluttering as she spoke, as if they had a mind of their own. Whether they were trying to hide her guilt or flirting, she wasn't sure.

God, she was pathetic.

Seth narrowed his eyes and approached her with long slow steps, each making her heart beat faster. "There are lots of places in the theater to be alone. This isn't one of them."

It certainly wasn't. Though she was alone with him. His words pretty much acknowledging that fact made her lightheaded.

He kept coming toward her until he was right beside her. "Aren't you supposed to be at the cast Meet and Greet?"

"Aren't *you* supposed to be there?"

"I'll get there eventually." He leaned against the counter and gestured at her with a nod. "Whatcha got behind your back?"

His scent, a mixture of soap and sweat and cedar, wafted from his skin, making her weak in the knees. "Nothing." *Yeah, that didn't sound childish.* "I mean, none of your business." *Oh, much better.*

Why did speaking to Seth always get her so flustered? He wasn't supposed to talk to her, anyway. It was a rule all the crew was given—only talk to the actors when necessary for the show. That was the assurance given to protect the stars' privacy. She clutched onto that rule now like a life vest. "You aren't supposed to talk to me."

"Whoops."

Obviously, Seth didn't care too much about following rules.

And if he was going to be that way, she wasn't going to feel bad about borrowing a drill. She just had to figure how to get out of there with it. Glancing around, she spotted another exit just behind her. If she walked backwards, she could make it to that door without him spotting the drill. She had to try.

"Well, since I'm essential out there, I better go." She took one cautious step away from him.

"You mean as opposed to me being unessential."

She hadn't meant for that to sound so snotty. "No." But it was true. The Meet and Greet was about the actors. The set was completely unnecessary. "Well, yes. But..."

"Don't fret it, princess. I knew what you meant."

His tone reaffirmed that he'd already made up his mind about her. He thought she was stuck-up, and wasn't she? But he didn't have to parade his disgust for her. "Whatever."

She took another couple of steps backward, but the cord slipped from where she'd wrapped it around the drill. Before she realized it, the heel of her sandal caught on it, throwing her off balance. She cast out her arms, trying to stop her momentum, but she only managed to postpone the inevitable fall.

Thankfully her plummet was stopped by strong, fast arms that circled around her waist in a firm grasp.

"Whoa." Seth held her, his face inches from hers, concern in his eyes mixed with something else. Desire? "You okay?"

She stared into his face, at his lips so close she could kiss them if she lifted her head. She *wanted* to lift her head. So bad. "I'm okay." Her voice was a whisper. "I just tripped."

His eyes scanned her face, lingering on her mouth. Then moved lower to her breast line. She felt her skin warm and redden under his gaze. When his stare found its way back to hers, he unwrapped an arm from her waist and brought it between them.

She tensed, waiting for his touch. Longing for his touch. Would his hand trail up her arm? Or caress her cheek? Or,

41

Laurelin Paige

though highly inappropriate, brush her breast? She let out a shaky breath at the thought.

But the touch she longed for didn't come in any form. Instead, he pulled the tool she still clutched from her grasp and curled his lip. "If you needed a drill, princess, all you had to do was ask."

Disappointed and embarrassed, she pushed out of his arms. "Don't call me that."

"Do you need a screw as well?"

"Stop it, okay." It surprised her how near tears she was. "I needed a prop. Are you happy? I knocked over my purse in the car and my handcuffs must have fallen out and my assistant is clear out in Bel Air picking up my birth control and she won't be back in time for the Meet and Greet, even if I manage to go last and I was desperate so I came in here to look for something I could use and this was the first thing I found." Her words tumbled out in a rush.

He chuckled in a way that both irritated and excited her. "Handcuffs? Birth control?"

Her face warmed from equal parts frustration and humiliation. "Can I just...can I use it?"

"Can you use what?"

"The drill, Seth."

"Of course. I told you all you had to do was ask." His eyes sparkled with amusement. "But here—" He exchanged the theater's drill for his own still on the counter. "Take mine instead. No one will know who it really belonged to or that you came unprepared. Now, wasn't it a good thing that I was around?"

He held out the drill to her and she took it, brushing his fingertips as she did. The touch shot a surge of electricity through her body. Still, she said, "This doesn't make us friends."

42

His hand sprang out and grabbed her arm just below her elbow. "Do you really think I want to be friends?"

Confused by the roughness of the action and the delight of his fingers on her bare skin, she didn't know if she should pull away or lean in farther. "I...I don't know what you want," she managed to stammer, realizing she didn't know what she wanted either.

His grasp softened slightly and he drew her closer. For the second time that night, she thought—no, wished—he would kiss her. Instead, when his head bent toward her, it stopped near her ear. "Isn't it too bad that you won't let yourself find out?"

His husky whisper sent a serious shiver through her body. For one minute she believed she could let herself find out. That she could forget her past and everything that Seth represented to her. That she could fall into his arms and let his mouth and body erase every bad memory and association she had with people who performed manual labor for a living.

But she'd spent too many years believing just the opposite. The walls she'd have to break down to let someone like Seth in were pretty sturdy.

When she spoke, her voice didn't sound like her own. The tone was meek and unsure and breathy. "I have to go."

"Yes, you do."

He released her and she turned and walked away on unsteady legs. And just like when she'd left her trailer house at sixteen, she didn't look back.

He was like her past. She didn't need him. She didn't want him.

This time, though, the effort to not look was excruciating.

Chapter Four

At nearly one o'clock in the afternoon, Seth was exhausted and grumpy as fuck. He'd been busting ass on set pieces since he first saw the scripts at six-thirty that morning, not even stopping to eat breakfast with the cast and crew. He couldn't spare the break, but more importantly, he was certain if he saw Heather, his focus would be shattered.

Not that his focus was any good having not seen her. He'd been working with a semi all morning. Every time he reached for his tools, every time he drove in a screw, he couldn't help but remember his interaction with her the night before. She'd looked so damn sexy with her scarlet red nail polished fingers clutching his drill. How gorgeous her hands would look wrapped around his cock.

His dick leapt just thinking about it.

But her attitude was still not worth it, he reminded himself. There were enough beautiful women in the world. Why he was so hard-up over such a bitch was beyond him.

Seth wiped a layer of sweat off his brow with the back of his arm and placed his sander on the ground. He removed his safety glasses and gloves, then ran his hand across the arm of the wooden deck chair he'd just finished. It was smooth enough. As smooth as it was going to get with no time to varnish, anyway.

His ears perked at the bustle of changing casts on the stage next door. Each of the six shows had only one precious hour onstage, the rest of their rehearsals taking place in outlying rooms, and he'd tried to complete construction for each show as they arrived on stage. The deck chair was for the play scheduled to rehearse now—Heather's show. He'd likely see her when he delivered it.

He took a deep breath and hefted the chair over his shoulder to carry it out to the stage. One step onto the wing, though, and he nearly dropped the piece. He'd known he'd encounter the bombshell, but there was no way he could have prepared himself for the sight that met him.

Heather, apparently not yet needed onstage, was practicing in the wings. On her knees. Wearing nothing but a skimpy yellow polka-dot bikini. Straddling the drill. His drill.

Fuck, if she wasn't every man's wet dream come to life.

His cock instantly grew from semi to raging.

Realizing she hadn't noticed him, he adjusted the chair on his shoulder and continued his task. Instead of going around the actress in his pathway, he stepped over her with one long stride.

Yeah, he was asking for trouble. Somehow he couldn't resist trouble when it took the form of Heather Wainwright.

"Hey!" she screeched as he passed.

Ignoring her, he walked onto the stage and set down the deck chair near the back, careful not to disturb the actors rehearsing.

"Damn, Seth!" Mardi, the director of Heather's play, exclaimed from the audience. "That's perfect! Thanks!"

He smiled and nodded toward her.

"Let's start from the top now that we have the real chair," Mardi said to her performers as Seth returned back to the wing. Back to Heather.

Again, he didn't alter his path, but stepped over the actress in one stride.

"Do you mind?"

He turned back to face her. "I should be asking you the same thing. You're in my space, after all."

"This is not your space. This is the wing. Where actors wait for their entrances."

"By all means. Go back to your waiting. Don't mind me."

She glared a delicious glare that caused his cock to pulse. Then she lowered her head and returned to practicing with the drill.

He folded his arms and leaned against the wall to watch her. She recited her lines quietly so he couldn't quite make out what she was saying, but from her actions, he understood the gist. Heather's character was attempting to drill into the sand at the beach. For what reason, he could only imagine, though he could tell the bit would be funny as she struggled, with the heavy drill, straddling it to get a better grasp.

It would also be goddamn sexy as hell. Just ask the straining bulge in his pants.

He let out a laugh, disgusted with his body's reaction.

"What?" Heather's head snapped toward him.

"None of your beeswax." He'd be damned if he let her know what she did to him.

"Then can you give me some space here? Remember you're supposed to leave me alone."

"You started talking to me first, princess." He stepped toward her. "And this is my territory."

She dropped the drill and stood. "Stop calling me that!"

"What? Princess?" He felt the smirk on his face. "I just call things as I see them. Sorry if it hits too close to home."

Her brown eyes widened. "Why are you such an asshole?"

"Why are you such a bitch?" A bitch with fuckably pouty lips and soft, luscious curves.

"I'm only responding to my environment. You're so mean to me. What did I ever do to you?"

What did *he* do to *her*? He almost laughed out loud. As if she was completely innocent in their feud.

He couldn't take it anymore. Forget keeping his reaction to her a secret. She asked and he was so turned on by her that his body moved of its own accord. Grabbing her by the waist, he pushed her into the wall behind them and pressed full against her. Damn, she felt better than he could have ever imagined. Her full breasts rose and fell with her heavy breaths, her nipples standing through the flimsy material of her suit, begging him for attention, begging him for more contact.

"That's what you do to me, princess." He nearly growled the words as he ground his erection into her pelvis.

She drew in a sharp breath, such a sexy sound he nearly exploded.

His brain screamed at him to stop. He shouldn't be doing this, shouldn't be touching her. Not just because she was a snotty bitch, but because of their roles in the showcase. His behavior was incredibly inappropriate.

But he couldn't help himself. When he registered the desire that mirrored his in her eyes, he couldn't stop himself from leaning in to take her plump lower lip between his teeth, nibbling softly before thrusting his tongue into her lush mouth.

He'd barely gotten to taste her, to lose himself in the wonder of her warm lips, before her palms landed on his chest and shoved. Hard.

Her delicate stature was no match for his muscled frame, but he pulled away, as horribly painful as it was to do so.

She slapped him.

"What the fuck do you think you're doing?" Her eyes were dark with fury.

Well, he deserved that.

He brought his hand up to rub the sting from his cheek but was startled from the action when Heather grabbed fistfuls of his T-shirt and pulled him back to her. Back to her sweet mouth.

He was so astonished that it took him half a beat to react to the rough sweep of her tongue. Then he did react, with plunging strokes of his own, sucking her lip deep into his mouth, his fingers winding tightly into her ponytail. He couldn't get close enough to her, couldn't get deep enough inside her.

Her fingers dug into his chest as he pushed closer, and he groaned. She met it with a low, needy moan, the sound vibrating through Seth so completely he could feel it in his balls. He increased the depth of the kiss, stealing her breath until they were both panting as his hand circled her plump breast and squeezed. She cried out softly against his lips, spurring him on, driving him further into her embrace.

He pulled the cup of her bikini down to expose her nipple and lowered his head to take it into his mouth. He bit and sucked, letting out the aggression he'd felt toward her over the past two days. He was rough and abrasive and from the sweet gasps that escaped her mouth, she loved it.

Damn, could she be any sexier?

Pure lust enveloped him and he knew nothing could tear him from her—not her attitude, not his past experience with Erica, not his conscience telling him he knew better. Nothing.

Except the sound of her name being called from the stage behind them.

"Goddammit," she hissed, pulling up her swimsuit. She brushed past him, not giving him a second look as she retrieved the drill and headed toward the stage.

Whether she'd been pissed about their encounter, about missing her cue, or about being interrupted, he didn't know. What he did know was that the snotty princess had gotten under his skin. Big time.

Yep. Goddammit was right.

Heather went through the rest of rehearsal on autopilot. If she let herself think at all, her mind would journey right back to the heated moment backstage with Seth—the brusque way he'd thrown her to the wall, his rough mouth on her breast, his cock pressed hard against her. And those thoughts were not ones she could grapple with easily.

Particularly difficult to digest was her reaction to him— she'd wanted him so damn much. More than she'd wanted a man in a long while. His lips on her had ignited such an intense blaze of wet desire, she was certain everyone could tell through her skimpy bikini bottoms. She would have given him all of her if they hadn't been interrupted.

Thank God they *were* interrupted.

Because what she would have done and what she should have done were so not the same. Even if she could get over all that he was and represented in her life, she still detested the man. Why she was so turned on by someone so insolent and mean was a question for her therapist and she had no appointments set for the near future.

Lunch followed her cast's stage time, bringing relief. The concentration it had taken to remain in character had given her a headache which she hoped food and downtime would ease.

But, having her mind free of lines and blocking, she now had to face what had occurred with Seth. It weighed on her as she made herself a plate from the catered buffet and then looked for a place to sit among the tables the crew had set up in the docking area.

Seth's work area.

Just being among his tools and unfinished set pieces made her heartbeat pick-up. Where was he, anyway? She pretended not to look for him as she navigated her way to a table of actors and sat down.

Only half aware of her peers' conversation as they commented and compared their scripts and rehearsals, Heather said little, focusing instead on chewing and swallowing her fruit salad. Those were appropriate things to do with her mouth. Not kissing and nibbling and licking the salty skin of the tasty carpenter.

She went hot, thinking again about Seth's demanding mouth.

As if summoned by her thoughts, he was standing in the doorway when she glanced up. Their eyes locked and her blush increased. Jesus, just seeing him across the room turned her on.

And the gleam in his eyes said he knew exactly what he did to her.

Dammit.

She had to squash this now. She closed her eyes to break the contact. When she opened them again, he was at the buffet table. Alone. Now was her chance.

She stood and pulled down the cover-up she had donned over her bikini costume.

"Finished already?" Matt asked.

"No, I just want some more..." She looked down at her barely eaten food. "A bottle of water." Yeah, that was good. "I'll be right back."

She hurried over to the buffet and stepped as close to Seth as she dared. Even inches away, she felt heat emanating from him, causing her hairs to stand on end. She reached past him for a roll she wouldn't be caught dead eating—refined carbs...not a chance—and ignored the way her nipples perked up at the brush of her arm against his. Leaning into him, she lowered her voice and said, "Before never happened, okay?"

Seth didn't look at her. Didn't even acknowledge her.

He moved farther down the buffet table. She put the roll back and scooted after him. "Did you hear me?" she asked a little louder this time.

He lifted his head up. "Are you talking to me? Cast and crew aren't supposed to fraternize."

"No, the crew isn't supposed to..." Oh. He was mocking her. She narrowed her eyes. Of course he wouldn't make this easy. Irritation ran through her veins which, oddly enough, increased the ache of desire in her lower belly. "God, you never quit, do you? Such an asshole."

"You keep saying that. But you also plunged your tongue into my mouth. You know how they say actions speak louder than words—"

Mouth gaping, she pulled at his arm and dragged him through the doorway and around the corner to the security area.

His lips curled up in a half-smile. "What? Round two already?"

"Keep it down!"

The smile disappeared. "I see. You're worried about your precious reputation. Whatever, princess. Stay out of my way and I'll stay out of yours."

He turned to leave.

"Wait." The request was out of her mouth before she could stop herself.

"What?"

She peered at the open door to the loading dock behind him. They weren't really hidden from the cast and crew, but she wanted—scratch that—she *needed* to have this conversation. She stepped around an outcrop by the exit and gestured for Seth to follow.

With a sigh, Seth set his plate of food down on the desk and joined her in the nook. He leaned his arm against the wall, trapping her in the small space. "What?" he asked again.

She was dizzy with his smell, a combination of fragrant wood shavings and sweat and soap. She had to force herself to focus. "*You* plunged your tongue into my mouth first."

"A mistake I won't be making again." But his eyes lowered to her lips.

51

She was perplexed by his words which contrasted so starkly with the hunger in his eyes. Did he feel as much conflict about her as she did about him? And if so, why? No way to know unless she asked. "Why did you do it?"

"Do what?"

"Kiss me."

He took a step toward her. "Are you asking me to kiss you?"

She stepped back, shaking her head. "No."

Another step forward. "Are you sure?"

"No." Another step back.

Seth grinned.

"I mean, yes, I'm sure. You're confusing me. I'm asking why you kissed me."

"Are you suggesting that you didn't kiss me?"

"Oh my God." She was against the wall now. She couldn't retreat any farther. "Talking to you is impossible."

He took a final step, closing the last amount of distance between them. He was so close that it would take no effort to reach up and claim his lips. Again. "Then maybe we shouldn't be talking."

"I'm sorry, I'm not interested." But her voice was shaky, his accusation so right on she couldn't lie about it. World famous actress that she was, she couldn't give one simple line. Pathetic.

She wanted to look away from his piercing gaze, but with him so near, there was nowhere else to look. "Are we done here? Because I need to finish my lunch."

He chuckled, a sound full of incredulity, but God, didn't it stir something in her core. "You pulled me back here, remember?" He leaned toward her and she pressed her palms against the wall behind her for support. How did he keep getting her trapped like this? And why did she go crazy with the anticipation of what she hoped he'd do next?

But he didn't kiss her, just kept his face inches from hers. "I'm done if you are."

"Good. I am." She waited for him to move out of her way. When he didn't, she said, "Excuse me."

"One more thing."

"What?"

"I kissed you for the same reason you kissed me."

She had kissed him because she couldn't *not* kiss him. His pass at her had been startling and improper, but it also awakened her to the depths of hunger she felt for him. Compelled her to seek more. Even now she wanted more.

Still, her brain tried to protest. "Well, it never happened."

"Fine. Do we have to pretend this time never happened either?"

Before she could fully register what his words meant, his mouth crashed against hers. Her lips parted and instantly his tongue was inside, swiping across her teeth, before dueling with her own tongue with thick, luscious strokes. His kiss was deep and demanding, washing her with waves of lust and need and relief. Such relief.

He pressed his body tighter against her and her hands flew around him, digging into his back to steady her weakening knees. As if he understood her sudden inability to stand, Seth tugged at her thigh, urging it up and around him. She wrapped one leg around him and then his hands were at her ass, holding her so she could wrap the other around him as well, the short cover-up crawling up to her hips.

In this position, she could feel his erection ridge across her crotch—so near to her throbbing center, yet so far. She squirmed against him, trying desperately to relieve the ache, not able to get the friction she needed with her bikini bottom and his damn jeans in the way.

Seth met her fidgeting with a firm thrust as he bit down the side of her neck. In some far away recess of her mind, she remembered how hard it was to cover hickeys with make-up while another recess reminded her that stage make-up hid more than film make-up, and the most dominant part of her mind said, "Who the fuck cares?" She wanted him to suck her and bite her and pinch at her skin until he'd marked her completely. Until he'd demonstrated his desire on every inch of her.

Using the wall to leverage her body, Seth removed a hand from her ass and untied the shoulder strings of her cover-up. It fell, bunching between them at her waist. Then he pulled at the string behind her neck, releasing her breasts from captivity. She was proud of her breasts—they were one hundred percent real and amazingly firm. Not that she wouldn't get surgery the minute they began to fall, but so far they'd held.

And from the look on Seth's face, he appreciated how well they'd held. He leaned back to gaze at them, a wicked smile sliding into place. After what seemed like an eternity, he bent to lick first one nipple then the other. Then he leaned back again and blew a stream of air across them, seeming to admire how they puckered even more tightly.

Heather moaned, needy for action, not his eyes.

He understood, returning his mouth to her breast, he sucked her taut bud into his warmth, and lowered his hand to the place where she needed him most, pressing his thumb through her suit into her aching clit.

"Fuck, yes!" she growled.

This was happening. She was in Seth's arms, in his mouth, and she didn't care anymore who he was or where he came from. Only cared about where he was going and whether or not he'd take her with him.

Except, there was just one thing that niggled at her. One thing that kept her from giving herself over to him completely. "So," she panted near his ear, "then you do like me?"

It was ridiculous to ask, but it mattered to her in an insane way. Almost as intensely as she needed him inside her, she needed his approval, his understanding. His acceptance of her perma-bitch attitude with him.

He closed his teeth around her nipple and bit hard. She yipped at the wonderful mixture of pleasure and pain. When he let go, he pulled away and looked her in the eyes. "Are you still embarrassed by me?"

One word and he'd take her. She knew it, could feel it in her bones.

But just as she had no understanding of why she needed his acceptance, she understood that he needed hers.

And she couldn't give it to him. She answered with silence.

"That's what I thought."

Her cover-up fell to the ground as he lowered her, gently helping her stand without him. Too gently. Already Heather missed his forcefulness.

"No, princess." He found the strings of her bikini, pulled the suit up over her breasts and tied it around her neck. "I don't like you. I'm disgusted with myself for being so stupidly attracted to you."

His words hurt like a van smashing into her. But she understood far too well. "You can't possibly be as disgusted as I am."

He laughed. "I'm sure that's true. Thank you for reminding me." He shook his head and she could see in his eyes a self-loathing that mirrored what she felt inside. "I'll go out first so you can pretend this whole mistake never happened."

But as she watched him leave, she knew she couldn't forget. Not just because he'd left her horny and yearning and blue-clitted, but because their interaction revealed so many things about herself she didn't want to deal with.

She retrieved her cover-up from the floor and slipped it over her head, wishing the cotton material could cover up more than just her near-naked body. She wished it could cover up Seth's bite marks and her flushed face and her trailer park past and her pathetic excuse for a soul that never let her move anywhere beyond white trash.

Chapter Five

The rest of the day flew by at breakneck speed. More rehearsing, tech rehearsal, and a quick dinner that she barely touched. Then it was show time. Though nervous, she adored the rush she got from performing live. As a film actress, she rarely got to experience those jitters that came from knowing her performance wouldn't be edited or perfected in post-production. Whenever she did, she embraced it, cherished it. Even conflicting thoughts of the sexy carpenter somewhere out in the house watching the show weren't enough to distract her from her high.

Heather's play, third in the line-up, had a great placement. The audience was already warmed up and her bit as a dumb blonde trying to drill for oil in the sand at the beach brought roars of laughter. She almost wished the performance was taped so she could see it played back later. Except that was one of the great things about the 24-Hour Plays—they were one time, and one time only.

Normally she'd steal up to the balcony with the other actors when her piece was completed so she could watch the rest of the shows. But this year as the spokesperson, she also had to announce the Urban Arts Spotlight performer and give a speech after intermission highlighting the charity and its many accomplishments. In her speech, she also introduced the new element of the night—the set built by carpenter Seth Rafferty that would be auctioned off the following month. The audience clapped with approval.

Yeah, she'd been wrong about the set. It had definitely added to the plays and would benefit the Urban Arts program significantly. Not that she'd ever admit her change of heart to Seth.

She missed watching the final show from backstage so that she could take a quick shower and primp. She changed into a black and white striped maxi with a scoop neck and elastic criss-cross back. It fit the casual mood of the after party but didn't skimp on the sexy.

Then the show was over and it felt like her work was just beginning. Immediately, she was ushered to the foyer by Patrick to be introduced to important donors. After posing for pictures and signing autographs, she was shuttled to the hotel where she had to endure an hour long press junket before finally making it into the cast party. She gave a final speech at the party to thank the cast and crew and her duties as spokesperson were officially over.

With a giant sigh, Heather collapsed on a couch next to Lexie by the pool and sipped at her Tequila Sunrise while trying to decide if she had enough energy to join her costars at karaoke in one of the poolside hotel rooms. The need to rest her aching feet outweighed her adrenaline pumped desire to sing old 80s hits, so she settled for just listening.

"You did good, chicka," Lexie said, raising her glass in a toast. "I call the evening a success."

"And your opinion's the only one that matters." Though that wasn't true. Heather cared way too much about what other people thought of her. She'd tried to move past it and after years in the media spotlight she should have grown a thicker skin, but she was sensitive by nature. Always looking for the approval her father never gave her.

But yes, the event had gone well. She expected positive reviews in the papers the next day. The 24-Hour Plays were low-key, so the coverage would be minimal.

Heather scanned the pool area. She hadn't seen Seth all evening—not that she'd been looking. Maybe he didn't do parties. Or maybe he was avoiding her.

Or maybe she just hadn't looked hard enough. Because there he was in the back corner with Neil, chatting around one of the appetizer buffets. Seeing him, she instantly felt bathed in a flash of warmth and the fire pit seemed to suddenly blaze hotter. He'd changed into clean jeans and an olive button down shirt that she knew would bring out the green specks of his eyes.

Why on earth was she thinking about his eyes?

"Who ya staring at?" Lexie followed Heather's gaze. "Oh, yum! Who's that?"

"The asshole I told you about."

"The one who called you a bitch and built that amazing furniture that's going to sell for thousands?"

"Yeah." The thoughts she'd buried all evening flooded her now—she'd said she didn't want him, but she did. Very much so. But the things he'd said, the horrible truths he'd revealed about her...

Seth Rafferty had done quite a number on her. He'd left her dazed and confused and horny as hell.

And ashamed. He'd left her that too.

Curling her feet underneath her, Lexie eyed Heather as though trying to read her mind.

"He kissed me," Heather admitted as casually as she could.

Lexie's jaw dropped. "And you're just telling me this now?"

"A lot was going on." Heather had wanted to tell her earlier, had needed a confidant. But also, she hadn't wanted to say a thing. Her interactions with the man had been very personal.

"Nothing's going on now. Spill it."

"I slapped him." She'd been proud of that actually. "But then I kissed him back." More than kissed and more than once. Details.

"He's certainly not a bad choice for rebound."

"He's a terrible choice. He's..." A slew of adjectives describing Seth ran through Heather's head, none as demeaning as she'd like. "I don't even like him. He's a total ass."

"A total hot ass."

Heather sighed. "Yes."

Silence settled over them and, as the tequila made its way through Heather's veins, she began to relax for the first time in two days.

After a while, Lexie sat forward and looked around. "The party seems to be winding down. I'm going to head out. Do you need anything before I go?"

"You got me all checked in?" Knowing how beat she'd be after the night was over, Heather had opted to rent a room in the hotel.

"Yes. Your luggage is in your room. Room 417." Lexie dug into her purse and pulled out a hotel key that she handed to Heather. "Here's your key card."

"And I'm in the spa tomorrow?" Had her words sounded slurred? She probably should have eaten something.

"Yes, booked all day." Lexie eyed her suspiciously. "Are you okay?"

"Yeah, totally." She stretched. "I'm just really tired."

"Then relax and enjoy tomorrow. I don't want to hear from you until at least late afternoon."

God, Lexie was an assistant sent from heaven. She pictured Lexie with angel wings and started to giggle.

"Maybe you should call it a night now. You're starting to get loopy. You didn't eat anything today, did you? Do you need me to help you to your room before I leave?"

"Nah, I got it."

Lexie stood then leaned down to give her boss a hug. "Say your goodbyes and get to bed. And if you end up in bed with that carpenter..."

Heather rolled her eyes. "Stop it. I'm not going to bed with him." But she couldn't shake the feeling that she and Seth had unfinished business. Maybe she'd talk to him one more time. Make sure he'd gotten the drill she'd left on the counter in the loading dock. Maybe give him kudos for his set pieces. Maybe give him a piece of her mind.

Or a piece of her body.

But maybe first another drink.

Seth had managed to avoid Heather since their hot make-out session at lunch. It was obvious there wasn't a worse match for him than the feisty blonde, but God, he hadn't met a more responsive woman. The way her mouth had opened to him, the feel of her sexy legs wrapped around him and her gorgeous tits pressing against him. She was so damn hot.

He'd been so consumed with her, Seth had almost missed out on the satisfaction of a job well done. Almost, but not quite.

"The Urban Arts program is going to make out on that auction next month," Neil said, handing Seth another beer. "The general feedback is very favorable. It was a great suggestion. Maybe we'll even add it to the New York plays in November."

"Thanks, man. I feel good about it." He'd feel even better if he hadn't nearly molested the spokeswoman for the event in the back of the theater earlier in the day. Twice. Actually, the thing he felt the worst about where Heather was concerned was not finishing what he'd started.

"You should feel good. You are totally invited back next year. If you don't mind me asking, though, how come you didn't want anyone to know you donated the materials?"

Seth hesitated. Neil was a good guy, real down-to-earth and a major supporter of bringing Seth's set idea to life. He popped the top off his beer—his sixth in an hour. "Truthfully," he said after taking a swallow, "I don't really care who knows. As long as Heather Wainwright doesn't know."

"Heather?" Neil's eyes widened in surprise. "Why... Actually, don't answer. I have a feeling I don't want to know."

"Maybe I'm being a dick." No maybe about it, he was being a giant dick. "But she's stuck-up. And this whole project—the Urban Arts, the 24-Hour plays—is about helping the less fortunate. Not about alienating or demeaning people who are considered beneath you." Though he wouldn't mind being beneath Heather. In the physical sense, anyway.

"I get it." Neil opened his mouth to say more and then stopped himself.

"Go ahead. Say whatever you want. I probably need to hear it."

"It's just that I've worked on the shows for as long as Heather. She can come off as a real snob. At heart, she's not like that. She believes in the project and the work we do. I think there's something personal about it for her."

Seth rolled his bottle between his palms, wondering if he should slow down. "I suspect you're right. But it's personal for me too." He used to deny and hide his past. Then he learned the hard way that he couldn't run from who he was. That was when he realized that he wouldn't be where he was today if it hadn't been for where he came from. If Heather had a similar story, then she needed to embrace it as well.

Just his personal opinion.

"Speak of the devil," Neil said, his eyes pinned to a spot behind Seth.

Seth turned to see what Neil was looking at. There was Heather, heading straight toward him, her sexy sway accentuated by her hip-clinging dress. If he wanted to continue to avoid her, he needed to go now.

Or he could just stay right where he was and see how things played out.

The latter option certainly seemed more fun. Okay, he'd definitely had more beers than he should have.

And the way Heather was weaving suggested she might have had a bit too much to drink herself.

He excused himself from Neil, who gave him a knowing grin and stepped out to meet her approach. A good idea, since, when she was only few feet away from him, she stumbled. Setting his beer bottle on the table next to him, he caught her at the elbows to steady her and tried not to notice how her soft skin pimpled into goose bumps under his fingers.

"Hey, you don't need to catch me all the time."

Her breath was a warm breeze on his face twisted with the fragrance of alcohol and orange juice. Yep, she'd definitely been indulging.

"Then quit falling all over me." It took all his strength to not pull her closer to him. Even drunk, she was tempting and sexy as fuck.

"You wish." She shrugged out of his grasp. God, if his hands didn't feel empty without her in them. "I need to say something to you."

Seth chuckled. "Of course you do."

She placed her fists on her hips, attempting—he suspected—to look threatening. Instead she looked even more adorable. He wanted nothing more than to throw her across the buffet table and ravage her. Not stand and take whatever insult she planned on dishing out next and pretend that each curt word didn't make his dick harder.

He retrieved his bottle from the table and prepared himself with a long swig.

"You are such an arrogant...Wow! Ipswich Ale. I'm impressed."

"What? Did you expect me to be drinking something domestic like Coors or Bud? Because if that's what the bar had, I'd be just as happy with one of those."

She scowled. "No. Ipswich is just one of my favorite beers." Her words slurred together. "God, do you really think I'm that shallow?"

Yes, he did.

Or maybe he didn't. She certainly had a superiority complex, but she also had that vulnerability that kept appearing under her mask of self-confidence. He'd glimpsed it that first night he'd met her, then again when she'd asked for his drill. And every time he'd kissed her.

And when she'd practically begged for him to say he liked her.

Especially then, and he'd done nothing but disappoint her.

Thinking about that made his head swim. Or the ale did. Either way, he pushed the thought aside. "What did you have to say to me, Heather?"

She frowned as she tried to remember. Then her eyes lit up and she pointed a long finger at him. "You are a fucking arrogant asswipe..."

His cock strained against his jeans. "You'll understand if I don't want to stick around for this." He brushed past her, needing to get away from her before he acted on his drunken desire, but unable to do so without touching her one last time.

"Don't interrupt my apology."

Apology? He turned back to her. "This is an apology?"

"It might be." Her eyes clouded. "If I can remember my next line..." Leaning against the table with one hand, she brought her other hand up to rub her forehead.

Shit, she really was drunk. Moral duty burst through his foggy brain. "Heather, how are you getting home? You aren't driving, are you?"

She looked at him, uncertainty in her eyes. After a minute, her face cleared. She reached into the cleavage of her dress and pulled out a key card.

Yeah, that wasn't hot at all.

She waved the key in front of his face with triumph. "I'm staying in the hotel."

Thank God. There was no way she'd make it farther than that without causing a scene. He didn't even know if she could make it inside the building in her current state. "Do you need help getting to your room?"

"Are you offering to take me?" She smiled mischievously, and grabbed his shirt collar. "Because if you're trying to get me in bed, all you had to do is ask."

His cock leapt at her husky throwback to the line he'd given her the night before. Why did she have to be such a damn sex kitten? He'd thought he couldn't resist her when she was a mega bitch. If she was going to play seductress, he had no chance.

Except, sexy as she was at the moment, she was also drunk. Taking advantage of inebriated women was not his style.

It would be easier to keep that thought in his head if he wasn't intoxicated himself.

He covered her hands with his and gently pulled them off him. "I'm more concerned about you making a fool of yourself. You seem to care a lot about your reputation."

"A fool of myself?"

"Because you've had too much to drink."

"I've only had two." She wrinkled her forehead in thought. "Maybe two and a half."

"Have you eaten anything today?"

"Um...I don't...I can't remember." She swung to look behind her. "Did I, Lexie?" She continued her circle. "Lexie?" When she'd made it back around to Seth she was dizzy and wobbling. "Oh, yeah. Lexie's not here."

Sighing, he set down his beer bottle and grabbed her firmly by an elbow. "Come on, princess." He had a feeling he shouldn't be doing this, but he couldn't reason out the harm.

Glancing around to make sure no one was watching them, he escorted her to the nearest doors leading inside.

"Where we going?"

"Your room."

"How exciting." She giggled, and his chest ached at the sweetness of the sound.

He led her to the elevators and pushed the call button before he realized he didn't know where they were going. "Tell me your room number."

"You're so bossy." She sidled closer to him. "It's really sexy."

His dick twitched eagerly. What had he been asking her about? Oh yeah. "Your room number, Heather."

"417," she said just as the elevator doors opened. "I have no idea how I remembered that."

"Get in." His voice sounded as strained as he felt. He was wound up so tight over her that he wasn't sure how much longer he could resist.

And he was taking her to her hotel room. What the fuck was he thinking? Or maybe it was the alcohol thinking for him. He was too fuzzy to be sure.

Thank God they were alone in the elevator. As soon as the doors shut, Heather threw her arms around Seth's neck and pressed against him.

Shit.

"Seth," she sighed into him. "I'm so tired. I'm just going to rest my eyes for a minute."

"No, no, no, princess. Keep your eyes open. We're almost there."

But his words were in vain. She was already slack in his arms when they arrived on the fourth floor. Cursing under his breath, Seth lifted her and followed the arrows looking for her room. He passed it twice before he made it there. He'd lectured her, but now that he thought about it, he hadn't had anything to eat before those beers either. No wonder he wasn't thinking straight.

At her door, he set her down on the ground, keeping a firm arm around her to keep her upright. "Heather? Heather, sweetie? Where'd you put your key?"

When she didn't respond he realized he'd have to find it himself. She didn't have a purse so she'd either dropped it on the way to her room or she'd put it back where she'd been keeping it.

Only one way to find out.

"Don't get too excited, buddy," he said to his cock, then slipped his hand down the front of her dress to search for the key. If his fingers lingered a little longer than necessary after he'd found the card, well, could she really blame him?

He slid the key card into the slot and prayed it was the right room. When the light went green and the door clicked open, he let out a sigh of relief.

Now to get her inside.

He patted her face. "Heather?"

She opened her eyes. "What happened? Where are we?"

"You passed out. We're at your room." He should leave her there at the door, but he found himself saying, "I'm going to help you inside. Is that okay?"

"Yeah."

She had wakened enough to stand but still needed support walking. He led her through the suite to her bed and sat her on the edge.

"Are you good?" He kept his hands on her shoulders, holding her in a sitting position.

"Yeah, I think so." She looked up at him with a smile that made his pants feel tighter.

Christ. What was he doing here?

"Let me help you with your shoes." Not a good move. But he bent down, ignoring the sway of the room as he did, and unbuckled her strappy sandal. He slid her dainty foot out of one shoe then repeated the process on her other foot. He kept his face down, aware that if he met her eyes, she'd see the effect the intimate act had on him. Seriously, he wanted to do some pretty kinky things to those lovely feet. It took a shit load of strength to not suck on each pink-tipped toe.

His hand dallied on her ankle, as he indulged in the feel of her silky skin.

"Thank you, Seth."

He looked up now, the sound of his name on her tongue causing his chest to squeeze all the air out of his lungs. With great effort, he stood. He wasn't sure she was ready to be left alone—or, rather, that he was ready to leave her alone—but he realized a quick escape was essential. Though he couldn't just dump her and leave, could he?

Yeah, he could. He should.

Except he found himself asking, "Would you like me to get you a bottled water before I leave? I can grab one from the mini-bar."

"That would be nice. Thanks."

After assuring she was okay on her own, he left her bedroom and returned to the outer room of the suite. He took a deep breath, rubbing his hands over his face. God, what had he gotten himself into?

Nothing, he'd gotten himself into nothing. He was merely helping a pretty lady who needed help.

Yeah, right.

As he grabbed two bottles of water from the mini-fridge, he spotted himself in the wall mirror. "Give her the water and get out," he told his reflection. "Don't be a dick. Don't think with your dick. Just get in and get out."

Feeling confident he could accomplish his mission, he returned to the bedroom. "Here you go, I'm leav—"

But he never finished his sentence. He couldn't. The sight that met him in the bedroom stole all possibility of speech.

Because Heather lay on the bed, her torso propped up on her elbows, her mouth twisted in a sexy smile.

And she was stark naked.

Chapter Six

Holy fuck...

Heather Wainwright—naked. Though he couldn't give a shit about her celebrity status, Seth suddenly understood why she'd made the 50 Most Beautiful People list three years running. She was absolutely breathtaking.

He'd already viewed her tits—gorgeous tits that had surprised him with their authenticity—but finding her spread out naked in front of him was a sight to behold. Though her breasts were still a highlight, she had other truly beautiful features—taut long legs, curvy hips and a stomach so flat he could eat on it. Except if he was going to be eating, it would be lower, on the nearly bare stretch of area that peeked out between her soft supple thighs. His mouth watered with the desire to taste her.

As if controlled by something outside of him, a magnetic force drawing him to her, Seth took a step toward the bed. He was vaguely aware of an alarm going off in the back of his head, his conscience reminding him something about getting in and getting out.

Oh, he'd get in and get out all right. In and out all night long if she'd let him.

But wait—this wasn't right. Of all the times in his life that his gentlemanly side had abandoned him, it had to go and show up now when he'd be perfectly happy to be a man without morals.

With a sigh, he closed his eyes so he could concentrate without the distraction of the beautiful unclothed body in front of him. That was better. He could control himself now. Could remember why he needed to leave.

He opened his eyes, keeping them pinned to the abstract painting on the wall above the bed. "Heather." He was surprised he could talk so naturally. "What exactly are you doing?"

"Seducing you." Her words came out in a purr, soft and sweet with a frequency that seemed to be tuned right to his dick.

He was in so much trouble.

"Very funny." *Get in and get out.* "Here's your water." Not daring himself to have any contact with her, he kept his eyes averted and moved to the nightstand, planning to drop the bottles there and leave. He managed the first step, but moving so close to her was a big mistake. Because now he was within her reach.

Not even a second passed between the moment he let go of the bottles and the moment Heather grabbed his shirt. She'd moved to the edge of the bed, up on her knees. "What's so funny about it?"

Damn, for a woman who'd had too much to drink, she could move.

But she was still drunk. He had to remember that. "Heather, you're not in any condition for this." He couldn't ignore her bare skin now that it was pressed up against him, no matter how hard he tried. At least he couldn't see her as well in this position.

Her response to his statement was to kiss along the underside of his jaw.

Keep focused. "And if you remember correctly, we don't really care for each other. Despite being attracted to one another..." More than attracted. He was goddamn ready to spill his load simply from what she was doing with her mouth on his neck. *Imagine if her mouth was elsewhere...*

Focus! "But you probably don't remember that we hate each other because, as I said before, you're drunk. And I'm drunk." He brought his arms around her with the intention of pushing her away, but didn't seem to be able to do anything but stroke the silky skin of her backside with his palms.

She kissed up to his ear. "I'm not that drunk."

"You passed out in the elevator." Oh God, her tongue in his ear…

"I'm a good actress."

"You're not that good of an actress." But he found himself questioning whether or not she was really as drunk as he'd first assumed. Had the whole thing been a ruse to get him to her room?

As if reading his mind, she asked, "Are you sure?"

Yeah, he was sure she was drunk. If she wasn't, she would have defended her acting. There were other signs. He could still smell the liquor on her breath. She'd been dead weight when he'd carried her—she couldn't have faked that. Her discarded panties were still wrapped around one ankle as though she may have had trouble getting out of them. And sweet as her kisses may be, they were also sloppy.

Definitely drunk.

Question was, did he care?

"I do not take advantage of drunken women." There was no pretending his words were for her. He was reminding himself. Fat lot of good his self-scolding did—his hands had already made their way down to caress her fine ass.

Her hand lowered as well, clutching his hard as fuck dick through his jeans. "It seems like I'm the one taking advantage of you."

The sirens in his head increased. He was seconds from disaster and if he had any hope of walking out of this, he had to assume control of the situation. Now.

In one swift movement, he threw her down on the bed, his body pressed against her so that her hands were pinned over her head. "Heather, stop!"

But now she was where he dreamed of having her—naked and underneath him, her sexy body soft and submissive.

And when she stared up at him under hooded lids, desire brimming in her eyes, the battle was lost. With a growl that was half frustration, half lust he said, "When I fuck, I take the lead."

His mouth came down hard against hers, devouring her lips with a frenzy he reserved for more serious relationships. He usually liked to ease into rough play, but this woman brought it out in an abundance that surprised him.

Heather, however, didn't seem offended, but delighted. She matched his tongue's frenetic strokes, gasping as he licked deeper into her mouth. When he'd claimed her lips at the theater, the kisses had been stolen—he'd taken what he wasn't sure she was willing to give. Now, though, his assurance of her willingness gave him free reign so he took and took and took.

Her wriggling underneath him reminded him she had more body to explore. He licked along the trail of bites he'd left earlier. He couldn't deny the burst of satisfaction he felt from their presence on her otherwise flawless skin. She might not be his by any stretch of the imagination, but for today—and for as long as her skin remained red from his marks—she couldn't dispute that he'd been there. And now she was allowing him more.

At her breasts, he began his feast.

Her nipples stood at perfect attention, calling to him. He took one spire into his mouth, drawing in as much of her plump breast as he could. He sucked and pulled at her tender skin until she cried out. Then he repeated the action on her other breast. Fuck if her cries didn't drive him to pull further, to suck harder. The woman seemed to enjoy it. So many women wanted to be treated delicately, and he often had to hold back.

Heather's body, though, begged for it—craved it. He could smell her desire wafting from her pussy, and the way she shivered and arched her back into his lips, he knew she loved it.

He lingered over her tits until they bore marks that would likely still be there in the morning. Then he slipped his hands underneath her slim thighs and pushed them forward, her panties falling off her foot from the movement. She squealed as he bent her knees into her chest opening her to him. Just him.

Jesus, her pussy was gorgeous.

She had one tiny strip of short hair that covered her clit and trailed down to her hot opening. He stared at the beautiful sight for several heated seconds. He could have stared longer, but Heather's fingers found their way into his hair and shoved him down to her core.

"Come on," she mumbled. "Need you."

His conscience screamed at him, trying once more to convince him that going any farther would be utterly unscrupulous, but the buzz of his own desire drowned it out. He was too eager, too lost in his lust-filled haze to do anything but give in to Heather's request.

He propped one of her long legs over his shoulder then lowered his mouth until he was almost touching her. "Is this what you want?" He swiped her strip with one slow brush of his tongue.

"Yes! Please!"

His eyes teased her as he lifted her other leg to drape over his other shoulder. "Should I give you more?"

"Yes, yes! Please, more!"

He adored her pleading, wanted to hear her beg for his cock. But first, he'd ease her longing. Show her he could be sweet when he wanted to. He licked her again then zeroed in on her clit, which was swollen with want. Swirling his tongue around her bud, he alternated with light and rough pressure until she was trembling beneath him. Then he went in for the kill. He plunged two fingers deep into her wet hole as he sucked her clit into his mouth with the same intensity he'd applied to her breasts.

"Fuck, yes!" Her breathing was ragged. She was close.

He couldn't wait to see her orgasm. He knew it would drive him insane. He'd have to have her after that, have to bury his dick into the warmth of her body.

She thrust her hips upward and he plunged his fingers in again, this time crooking them to hit against the sensitive sides of her walls. He paired this latest assault with a nip of her clit.

With a violent cry, her thighs went rigid. Hot fluid spilled onto Seth's hand as Heather rocked her hips against his mouth.

"That's it, princess," he said, consuming the sight of her coming apart. It was beautiful. So goddamn beautiful it made his balls ache.

He continued to lick at her tender area until her body went lax and her breathing evened out. Gently, he lowered one leg off his shoulder, then kissed along the underside of her thigh to the back of her knee before setting it on the bed. Then he repeated his kisses on her other leg before kissing up her body toward her face where he planned to kiss her fiercely, share her taste with her, stir her up again so that next time he could come with her.

And next time wouldn't be so gentle, but it would be oh so nice.

Except at her lips he discovered her deep breathing wasn't a sign of her post-orgasmic state of relaxation.

It was a sign she'd passed out cold.

He tapped softly at her cheek with the back of his finger. "Heather?" But she didn't respond. She was sincerely out. Already a gentle snore accompanied her inhales.

Dammit.

He'd known she was drunk, but had let her convince him that she was up for sex. He was an idiot. A fucking horny as hell idiot. Add intoxicated to that list. There was no way he would have gone so far if he'd been sober.

At least, he hoped he wouldn't.

Honestly, it was a miracle from the gods that she'd passed out. Otherwise, he probably wouldn't have been able to stop himself, and that would make him an even bigger asshole than he already was. Besides, she would easily explain their fucking as an error in judgment made while intoxicated. When he took her for real—which he would eventually; he had no doubt of that after he'd had a taste of her—he wanted her to have full control of her actions. There was no way he'd let her dismiss their time together as a drunken mistake.

As for now, he could only blame himself for his painful erection. For half a second he considered pulling out his dick and whacking off while he could still drink in the view of her lovely naked body. Thankfully, a moment of clarity hit him and he realized he was a creep for even thinking it. He didn't need another reason to be disgusted with himself.

Instead, he swept one more gaze down her splendid form, putting it to memory so he could take care of himself later, alone. He had a feeling this memory might take him days of beating off before he even scratched the surface of his lust.

He rolled off the bed and let out a frustrated sigh, her scent still on his breath causing him to let out another. Then, in attempt to be a gentleman, he tugged the covers out from underneath her and pulled them up over her naked body. Wrapped in warmth, she curled up on her side, a content smile pasted on her sleeping face.

At least she'd been satiated. Maybe it would earn him points with her in the future. Though, now that he thought about it, their paths weren't likely to cross again. That wasn't something Seth could live with.

He looked down at her, scrutinizing. Sure, she was the most beautiful woman he'd ever seen. But his attraction to her was more than that. And seeing her like this, asleep and peaceful, he remembered what it was—her hidden layer of vulnerability that he yearned to expose, itched to impose on. If she opened up to him like he thought she could, he would wrap himself around her fragile side and make her forget all those things he suspected she'd buried deep inside.

At least, he'd like to give it a try.

He rearranged his stiff bulge in his jeans in an unsuccessful attempt to ease his discomfort, and opened the drawer of the nightstand in search of hotel stationary and a pen. When he found what he needed, he scrawled a quick message to Heather and left it next to her phone. He'd give her a chance to take the next step.

If she didn't, he'd take the next step himself.

A repeated buzzing drew Heather out of a deep sleep. Not yet ready to open her eyes, she became aware of two things— she had no clothes on and her head was pounding.

Oh, and there was a buzzing. Somewhere nearby. A familiar buzzing.

Her phone.

Still not opening her eyes, she reached her hand out to the nightstand and felt around for the cell she suspected was there. When she found it, she opened one eye just long enough to read the name of the caller. *Lexie*. Why was Lexie calling her so early? Though, it might not even be early. Heather had yet to determine what time it was, but it felt early.

She pushed the talk button. "What?"

"Heather?"

"I said what?" Goddammit, her head hurt. She vaguely remembered drinking a bit too much. And eating practically nothing. That explained the gurgling in her stomach.

Relief filled Lexie's voice. "Thank God I got hold of you. I was worried. The spa called and said you didn't make it to your appointment and you didn't answer my calls."

"Oh, fuck." Heather sat up and opened her eyes, noting the vicious sway of the room as she did. "Hold on a sec." She pressed the phone to her chest while she gathered her thoughts, remembered where she was. Oh yeah, the hotel. She was supposed to spend the day in the spa.

She glanced at the clock on the nightstand. 11:42. Her appointment had been at eleven. Raising the phone back to her face, she said, "I didn't ask for a wakeup call or anything. Can I get in later?"

"Yeah, you prepaid for all day so whenever you want to show up is fine."

"Awesome." Because as soon as she got over her raging headache, a full body massage would be exquisite. Heather lowered the phone again and grabbed for one of two bottles of water on the nightstand, noticing a packet of pain relievers there as well. She tore into them, hoping they'd work quickly.

When she put the phone back to her ear, she realized Lexie had been talking. "...glad you got to sleep in, at least. You needed it."

"Yeah, I did need it." She couldn't even recall what time it was when she'd made it back to her room. Or how.

Then in a series of embarrassing flashes she remembered—Seth, her throwing herself at him, her naked. And one glorious orgasm. "Oh...fuck..."

"What's wrong?"

"I'm hung over." She shifted and realized her upper thighs were sticky. "And I think I had sex last night."

"Oh my God! With the carpenter?" Lexie's excitement was evident.

It aggravated Heather's head. She lowered the volume on her phone several notches before answering. "Um, yeah."

"Well? How was it?"

Truth was, she had no idea. She remembered getting naked, remembered Seth doing amazing things to her body. She looked down at her breasts and noticed they were dotted with hickeys. Yeah, she remembered that. She'd practically released from that alone.

But past that, she recalled little. "I don't know. I think I passed out."

"That's all sorts of wrong."

It *was* all sorts of wrong. She'd had sex with an amazingly attractive man and she couldn't remember any of it. God, how was it that Seth, who reminded her too much of her past as it was, could—in an instant—turn her into the slutty girl her father always thought she'd be?

That was why she had known she shouldn't get involved with him. Yet here she'd gone and ignored her own advice.

Stupid, stupid, stupid.

Lexie's voice pulled her back from her self-reprimanding. "You used a condom at least, right? Because you missed a couple days on your birth control, remember."

A condom? "Fuck! I didn't even think about that." Had they? She closed her eyes and fought against her pain to try to remember details. "I'm sure we did." They had to have. Right? "Hold on." She got up and began searching the room, looking in the empty trash cans and on every surface she could find. She even looked under the bed and through the bed clothes. Nothing.

"Shit, Lexie, I don't see a condom wrapper anywhere."

"Are you sure?"

"Yes! I've looked everywhere. There's nothing!"

"Don't panic." Lexie's calm voice was a stark contrast to Heather's racing heart. "Morning after pill. I'll arrange to get one for you."

"No! I can't."

"Why?"

Heather rubbed a hand across her aching forehead and sat heavily back on the bed. "It's like abortion. I'm Catholic."

"You are not." Lexie laughed. "You haven't stepped foot in a church since I've known you. And Catholics are against birth control in general."

"But birth control is not the same as killing a baby that might already be in the process of..." She let her voice drop off with a sigh. How could she possibly explain this? When she'd left the trailers, left who she was, she developed a short list of values. Things she'd never back down on, no matter what. Like, she wouldn't do full nudity onscreen. She'd never sleep with a guy to get a role. And no abortions or morning after pills. She didn't want to spend any part of her life in regret, and she had a feeling that erasing a would-be person could lead to some serious regret.

But she didn't expect anyone else to understand. She sighed again. "I know, it sounds ridiculous, Lexie, but I just can't do it. I can't explain it."

"You don't have to. I get it."

Had she mentioned in the past twenty-four hours how much she loved her assistant? She should send Lexie to the spa in her place. Or just buy her a day of her own.

Meanwhile, Heather had to face the possibility that she might be pregnant. Except...had she and Seth actually had sex? God, she wished she could remember. "Maybe I won't even need it. I don't even know for sure if we had sex."

"You don't know?"

"I passed out." She cringed at how slutty her words made her sound. Knowing Lexie wouldn't judge her, she forced herself to go on. "But I was naked and coming on to him...he couldn't have resisted, could he?"

"Do you feel sore?"

Heather did a few Kegels, feeling for any sort of tightness. "Not at all. But I took Advil when you called."

"Maybe he was small."

No way. She'd felt his erection through his pants. More than once. "I don't think that's it. God, I wish I could remember! The last thing I can recall is an incredible orgasm." Incredible was defining it lightly.

But then he'd left. "And he wasn't here when I woke up."

"Asshole."

"I told you." Heather glanced down at the folded hotel stationary she'd seen next to the Advil. Now she picked it up. "Just a sec, Lex. He left a note."

The ball's in your court, princess. If you want to see where this could go, give me a call.

She read it several times before she spoke. "He left his phone number. I could call him."

"But you won't."

Heather thought about it. Part of her really wanted to call him, wanted to see him again, wanted to see where things could go between them.

But another part of her, the bigger part of her, was scared. Scared of what Seth reminded her of. Scared of what Seth brought out in her.

"I won't call him. He shouldn't have bailed. And he shouldn't have fucked me without a condom!" If they'd fucked at all, which Heather was beginning to doubt more and more. Doubting made her angry. Sure, he'd left a note. And water. And Advil. And maybe hadn't taken complete advantage of her while she was naked and vulnerable. Though she'd been in the wrong state of mind to consent, he had given her a mind-blowing orgasm. Now that she thought about it, it seemed she'd seen him drinking an awful lot too. And had she thrown herself at him, or was that just a bad dream? Memories of lying naked and in wait for him tugged at the edges of her consciousness. Had she really done that?

Perhaps Seth Rafferty wasn't the asshole she kept making him out to be.

But if he wasn't an asshole, then she'd have to face the fact that she really was a bitch.

And that wasn't happening. Not today anyway. "I'm done with Seth," she told Lexie, mostly to convince herself. "And I'll be glad to never see him again."

"Sounds like a plan. But keep his number in case you need to contact him for a paternity test."

"Please don't even go there," Heather groaned. "But I'll keep it."

After Heather ended her phone call with her assistant, she grabbed a pair of sweats and some underwear from her luggage with plans to shower before heading to the spa. But first, she folded Seth's note into a small square and stuffed it into an empty pocket of her suitcase.

Maybe, if she buried it deep enough, she could forget about the hot carpenter and the myriad of confusing feelings he imposed upon her.

Except she knew that wasn't likely. Especially if she already had a permanent Seth reminder growing in her belly.

Funny how that thought didn't freak her out as much as it should have.

Chapter Seven

Seth stared at his Google calendar and cringed. It was completely blank. Blank for the next three months. The movie he had been booked to do had suddenly been postponed a year. Such postponements weren't uncommon in Hollywood, but often it was a sign of other problems with the film. The delay gave him an out in his contract, if he wanted it. He'd have to look more into the situation before he made a decision.

Meanwhile, his calendar was empty. First thing on his day's agenda was to find a project to work on. Not that he needed the money, but he didn't enjoy being idle. He'd been idle the two days since the 24-Hour Plays ended and was already about to go insane. All he could think about was Heather Wainwright.

Figuring out what to do about Heather was the second thing on the day's agenda. He'd known she was a big barrel of badness from the beginning, and he wasn't changing his mind about that theory. But since he'd had a taste of her, both in the literal and figurative sense, he had to have more, barrel of badness or not. She was like a good malt beer—he shouldn't have as much as he wanted, but he could rarely stop after only one glass. Everything about her turned him on: her eyes, her breasts, her silky skin, her pouty lips. Just thinking about her gave him a giant hard-on. A giant hard-on that had been impossible to relieve no matter how guilty he felt for taking advantage of her drunken state or how many times he stroked himself.

What sort of magic spell did this woman weave?

Even her stuck-up attitude, which had initially been a turn-off, had become one of the things that made him hornier than hell. The sass that came out of her lovely mouth... He never knew what to expect next, half of her words making his hand itch with the need to spank, the other half making his cock twitch with the need to bury inside her. A fair amount of what she said made him want to do both.

Yes, he'd have to find a way to see her again. And soon.

After he worked out how to see her again, he'd have a big decision to make. Tell her the truth about his career or continue to let her think he worked in Hollywood as a carpenter?

He glanced over at Erica's sketch of his favorite spot in the San Gabriel Mountains that he had pinned on a bulletin board above his desk, the only remnant of his time with her. He should've thrown it out ages ago, seeing how it always brought up a painful ache when he looked at it. But, besides the fact it was a damn good piece of art, it served as a reminder of a dream he hadn't yet fulfilled. One day he intended to build a cabin on that land. It was supposed to have happened with Erica. Now...

Now the plan had to wait. He couldn't even think about it. Not while the sketch still held so many memories of his past, promises of a future that didn't come to fruition.

He closed his eyes and let thoughts of her settle on him. *Erica.* She'd been an artist—a painter mostly—that he'd hired for a film he'd designed. It wasn't love at first sight, but their feelings developed pretty quickly. He'd thought at first that her interest in him might be solely based on the fact that he was her boss—that he could get her places. Then they grew closer, eventually moving in together. Finally, he proposed.

He hadn't set out to hide his past from her—it just never came up. How did you tell a woman that your father was in jail? That you had your own juvie record? He didn't like to talk about it back then, so he didn't share it with her. After they were engaged, and they began working on guest lists for the wedding and she wanted to know whether to include his parents, well, he had to tell her.

And she'd left. Because, as she had said, "Children follow in their father's footsteps. How could I possibly have children with you?"

Funny, he thought he'd turned out pretty damn fine.

But he wasn't going to hide his past from a woman again. It was who he was, what made him. Maybe he was going too far in hiding his present from Heather, but he didn't trust as easily as he used to. His trust had to be earned.

Okay, maybe he was making excuses for himself, but he never said he was perfect.

His cell phone rang and he didn't hesitate to grab it from the corner of his desk. He deflated when he looked at the caller ID. *Joe Piedman.* Not Heather. He'd suspected that she wouldn't call him, but he still hoped, jumping every time his phone rang, and swallowing the disappointment when he realized it wasn't her.

Though he was disappointed this time too, a call from Joe might help him with his empty calendar. A fellow project designer, Joe was a good friend as well as a colleague. Often they'd throw work each other's way when one of them was too busy to take a great offer. Hopefully that was why Joe was calling now.

"Joe, just the guy I wanted to hear from."

"Oh, really?"

"I'm hoping you have a line on a job. I have a hole in my calendar."

Joe chuckled. "That's too bad. Something fell through?"

"Postponed. It's a downer, but what can you do?"

"Just go with the flow," Joe said. "Well, I do have a job, but not for you. Maybe you know someone who can fill it for me?"

Damn. Seth pinched the bridge of his nose. Back to square one on the job front. "What's up?"

"I just took over as Production Designer on this film midway through pre-production. They had this guy before who completely screwed the whole job. Missed all his deadlines, hired flakes—I hear he had a coke problem, but that's gossip so don't go spreading that around. Anyway, they fired him, pushed out the schedule a few weeks and I took over, and what do you know? The lead carpenter was friends with the guy. He took his crew and bailed the minute he found out his bud got fired. So now I have a film that starts shooting in two weeks, no carpenter, no crew. My usual guys are already tied up. Do you have anyone you can recommend?"

Seth worked with a couple of crews on a regular basis that he suspected were probably free. The one he recommended to Joe would depend on the scope of the work. "What's the movie?"

"Working title is *Girl Fight*. It's a comedy. Don Frazier is directing. Stars Natalia Lowen and Heather Wainwright as these chicks fighting over a guy. Almost one hundred percent on soundstage so the—"

Joe kept talking but Seth's brain was stuck back on the name *Heather Wainwright*. Instantly, he knew what he could do. What he shouldn't do, but *why* shouldn't he? He'd been lead carpenter on sets before, after all, and had been damn good at it, if he did say so himself. Getting a crew together shouldn't be a problem. And his calendar was open.

Did it make him borderline creepy? Yeah, maybe. But he'd never claimed he was a saint.

"Joe," he said, trying not to sound too eager. "I think I may have the guy for you."

"Hey, Heather!"

Heather looked behind her as she walked through the sound studio toward her trailer and saw her costar Natalia jogging after her. Heather halted until Nat caught up.

"How do you think today went?" Nat's bright blue eyes sparkled with enthusiasm.

Heather shrugged. "I've had worse first days." How long had it been since she'd been excited about a first day on set? She couldn't even remember.

"Totally." Natalia twirled a strand of her recently dyed blonde hair around her finger. "But the scenes went well, don't you think?"

Seriously? They were going to discuss the shoot like a bunch of amateurs? "Yeah, they went fine." They'd been better than fine considering how preoccupied Heather had been all day. How preoccupied she'd been for the past two weeks. Every time she had a moment to think, her thoughts wandered to her belly and what might or might not be growing inside. She was hyper-focused on her body, wondering if every minor breast pain or belly cramp was proof that a pee test would scream positive.

When she wasn't thinking about her possible pregnancy, she was thinking about the cause of that possible pregnancy. Seth Rafferty had gone from someone she wanted nothing to do with to someone who might be a very big part of her life. And she wasn't that upset about it. In fact, she wanted to see him again. So much so that she'd even considered calling him. Many times.

But what would she say if she talked to him? *Did you use a condom when you screwed me 'cause I might be pregnant* just didn't seem like a conversation to have over the phone. The other things she could say to him—*Can I see you again? Do you even want to?* Those things took more courage to say. More courage than she had.

Yep, secret was out: Heather Wainwright was a big fat chicken.

So she hadn't called him, leaving her distracted by him at the most inconvenient times. Like in the middle of filming.

And now, when she should be paying attention to her costar.

She glanced at Natalia out of the corner of her eye and noticed she seemed deflated. Shit. She'd wanted reassurance and Heather hadn't given it. Sometimes she forgot that she was the old pro in the biz, that other people wanted her approval.

She pulled out her best smile for her costar. "Today was good, actually. You did good. Really good."

"Thanks." Nat beamed at the compliment.

Then she continued past her own trailer, following Heather to hers. Dammit.

Problem with being nice was people mistook it for friendship. All Heather wanted was to get into her trailer, change out of her costume, and get in a hot shower. Nat, on the other hand, wanted to be buddy-buddy. She leaned against Heather's trailer, making herself comfy. "That's too bad about the old Production Designer. But the new P.D. seems to be on the ball. My camera tests were really well organized."

Don't be a bitch, Heather told herself. *It won't kill you to be friendly.* "Yeah, mine too. I've worked with Piedman before. He has his shit together."

Anyone who knew Heather and Natalia personally would laugh at the characters they'd been cast. Natalia's personality more closely fit the sweet girl-next-door that Heather was playing. Heather's diva reputation matched Natalia's snotty character to a tee. Sometimes Heather found herself wishing she was more like Nat in real life—nice, kind, genuine. But that would require knocking down a bunch of walls and letting people in. How did Nat do that? Remain so unguarded and unaffected while working in Hollywood. She was a lot newer to the biz than Heather was. Perhaps that was it.

"It must be nice to be back on a sound stage after your last film. Weren't you out in the mountains?"

Heather's last film had been a modern day western, most of it shot near Golden, Colorado. She'd hated nearly every minute of it. The city had been so small that there'd been nothing to do off set. She'd been lonely. Collin hadn't visited at all. Lexie had taken the shoot off to help her mother through breast cancer treatments. Then, when she'd turned to her costar, Micah Preston, for comfort in the carnal sense, he'd brushed her off.

Of course, a week after the 24-Hour Plays, she'd discovered with the rest of the world that he'd had his eye on someone else during that shoot. He'd announced his love for her on America's Choice Awards, of all places. So it wasn't like a real rejection when he'd blown off Heather. He'd simply been taken. Still, thinking about it stung, so she shook it off and focused on the question Nat had asked. "It's so much nicer to be shooting in a studio instead of on location." She couldn't remember, or didn't know rather, if Nat had ever shot anywhere but on a set so she added, "Location gets old fast. It's lonely and lacks amenities."

Nat nodded again. She nodded so often and so enthusiastically Heather decided to nickname her Bobblehead. In her head, of course. She'd never say it to Nat's face.

Also in her head she imagined smacking herself for her constant rude inner-dialogue.

"Our set looks awesome too," Bobblehead said, unaware of the less-than-nice thoughts running through Heather's mind. "I can't believe they built it under pressure. And the crew..." Natalia leaned in, lowering her voice. "There's at least one hottie."

"You mean a carpenter?" Did her nipples just perk up at the thought of a hot carpenter? *Down girls—fat chance it's Seth.*

"I don't know. Whatever they call those guys with all the tools."

Normally Heather would have made some snarky comment about Nat's naiveté, at least to herself, but the idea that it could be Seth had her distracted, scanning the set behind them for anyone that might be a carpenter. She spotted someone with a tool belt. Not Seth. Not really hot either, but maybe Nat's thing was the uniform, not the actual man. Heather nodded her head toward him. "That guy?"

Natalia nodded her head in another direction. "That one."

Heather followed her gaze.

And nearly peed.

Was loss of bladder control an early sign of pregnancy? Or was it just a sign of pure and utter shock at realizing the hot carpenter was *her* hot carpenter?

She didn't mean to stare, but she couldn't help herself. He looked even yummier than he had at the Broad Stage—he hadn't worn a belt then, she hadn't gotten to see him use his tools. Now, he stood behind a set piece, securing a loose board with a nail gun. Why the sight had her rubbing her legs together like a cricket singing a lullaby, she had no idea.

And as if he could hear her cricket song, he turned his head and stared directly at her, his eyes nailing her across the distance as efficiently as he'd nailed his set piece. Even if she wanted to look away, she couldn't. She was glued to him, the world seeming to disappear around them as his lips slowly curled into a sexy grin.

Then he was walking toward them, closing the space between them with sure-footed steps that exuded nothing but pure male confidence. She was heady from his stride alone. When he was near enough for her to catch his scent, her knees wobbled. Holy shit, what the man did to her...

Natalia's eyes flitted back and forth from Seth to Heather. "He's coming over here," she whispered with an excitement that made Heather oddly pissy.

"Yeah, I know him." She meant her words to claim him. Though she was in no way *with* Seth, it didn't make him free game to anyone else. As if that made any sense.

"Lucky," Nat said under her breath as Seth reached them.

He crossed his arms over his chest—had his arms always been that buff? It was sort of disgusting in a totally hot way. "Heather," he said with a nod.

Did the sound of his voice turn everyone to jelly or just her?

"Seth. Fancy seeing you here." Her voice was terse, but his smile widened anyway, increasing her pissyness. Why was he here? On *her* set. And why did it make her so damn unsettled?

"I don't think anyone's ever said fancy in reference to me before."

"I imagine they haven't." In direct contrast to Heather's acerbic tone, Natalia's dripped with sugar and honey and all those sweet girly things that a woman put in her voice when interested in a guy.

Heather didn't hide her eye roll. "Seth, this is Natalia Lowen." As she made the introduction, Heather felt a sharp pain to the chest that she didn't quite recognize. Maybe it was indigestion. Didn't pregnant women get all sorts of heartburn?

Seth took Nat's outstretched hand. "I know who you are, Natalia."

Heather wrapped her arms around herself, trying to warm up from the sudden chill that passed through her coincidentally at the same moment that Seth's gaze had left her for Nat.

"You do? I'm flattered...Seth, was it?" Did Nat just thrust out her chest? Oh God. She was already buxom. She didn't need to thrust to flaunt it.

"Yeah. Seth Rafferty." He winked at the young actress. "Nice to meet such a wonderful up and coming star."

Nat blushed.

But before Natalia could respond with an equally flirtatious line, Heather cut in. "I'm going in my trailer. Interesting seeing you again, Seth. Nat, see you tomorrow."

Heather opened the door to her trailer and climbed the stairs, forcing herself to not look back. And not to make too much from the fact that neither Seth nor Nat had acknowledged her departure. Inside, she quickly stripped out of her costume, stifling a scream of frustration that would surely be heard if they were still outside making eyes at each other.

What was with that anyway? Winking and smooth talking. Did Seth come on to every actress he met? He probably did. Isn't that what any normal guy in his position would do? He was a tradesman working around beautiful rich women. A hot tradesman who turned Heather into a big doughy pretzel on the inside.

But that was beside the point. The point was she wasn't special to him. That was fine. Seth wasn't special to her either. Not in the least.

Except, if she had his baby…

Fuck it. She wasn't thinking about that anymore. She'd deal with that if it turned out she was pregnant, not before.

She stripped down to her underwear then wrapped her silk robe around her, knotting the belt. Then she gathered her costume up to hang outside her trailer. If she didn't, a costume assistant would likely come by knocking on her door while she was in the shower.

Or maybe that was just an excuse to see if Seth and Nat were still outside getting friendly.

She opened her door and found them where she'd left them. Neither of them looked up as she hung her costume on her door. They simply continued giggling and winking. Well, Nat was giggling, twirling her hair around her finger while Seth winked and nodded.

It was gross. Like, *make Heather puke* kind of gross.

Also, it made her indigestion worse, or whatever that sharp pain in her chest was.

And before Seth went spreading his seed with her costar, he should probably know about the seed he'd possibly implanted in her. Yes, she'd decided she wasn't going to think about the pregnancy prospect, but she had a right to change her mind. It was a service to her fellow actress. Besides, she still hadn't figured out why he was there. It seemed like a rather odd coinky-dink.

Without a second thought, she said, "Seth, can I talk to you?"

"Sure." He didn't move.

"In private." She gestured inside her trailer behind her.

"I need to get changed, anyway," Natalia said. "See you around, I hope."

"I'm sure you will," Seth said and an unexpected urge to kick him in the nuts washed over Heather.

She stepped inside and out of his way, holding the door open so he could walk past her.

"If you wanted me in your trailer, Heather, you know all you had to do was ask."

She let the door slam, ignoring how giddy it made her to hear her name on his lips and paced back and forth a few times before turning and leveling a stare at him. "What are you doing here, Seth?"

"You said you needed to talk." He leaned against the counter across from her as if he felt completely comfortable in her private space.

"I mean, on the set of this movie." She forced herself to keep her eyes on his face and not on his thighs bulging through his tight jeans. His fucking gorgeous thighs.

93

"Working, princess. Just like you."

And just as she'd been giddy at him saying her name, the return of his god-awful nickname for her made her slaphappy like a drunken teenager. She refused to let him see his effect on her, though, and kept focused. "But on *my* movie? That can't be a coincidence."

"It can't?" Seth scratched behind his neck. "Hollywood isn't really that big of a town."

Of course he'd evade her. Like always. Talking to Seth was like playing a game of Ring around the Rosie. He liked to force her to be blunt. "I'm just going to come right out and ask—are you stalking me?"

"*Stalking* you? God, I forgot how high and mighty you were."

"It's a reasonable question." Had he averted his eyes when he answered? Maybe that was her imagination. "Look, I've never seen you before in my life and suddenly you're everywhere."

"I'm not everywhere. Add drama queen to your list of personality traits."

"Whatever."

"If that's all..." He straightened.

"No, wait. That's not all."

"What?"

"I have something to... Did you...I mean..." She stumbled over her words. As many times as she'd practiced this conversation, none of her lines seemed right. She put a hand to each temple and closed her eyes. "I wasn't on birth control," she spat out. She opened her eyes slightly, peering at him like she'd peer at a bad accident—not wanting to see, but needing to all the same.

"Okay." Seth drew the two short syllables out, as if he didn't know how to react to her statement.

"That night. At the hotel." Was he purposefully making this difficult?

He nodded once, leaning back onto the counter. "I figured that's what you meant." His hand came up to rub his chin, which was stubbly from a long day on set. "What I can't figure out is why you're telling me."

"Are you kidding me?" He *was* purposefully making this more difficult. He had to be. But if he wanted her to spell it out for him, she could do that and still keep her head high. Maybe.

"Seth, when a woman isn't on birth control, other precautionary measures are needed." She spoke slowly, as if explaining to a child. When he still registered no understanding on his face, she rolled her eyes. "I'm asking if other measures were taken."

Seth laughed. A deep belly laugh that Heather felt vibrate in the center of her womb. Her face flushed, partly from embarrassment, partly from frustration. Partly from desire. God, this man was such an incredible ass. She'd been worrying and fretting about being pregnant for two plus weeks and here he was laughing at her.

And her stupid body couldn't respond in any way but to want him.

Dammit, Seth had made her life such an incredible nightmare. If he wasn't going to answer her, was just going to laugh at her, then she wanted him to go. Then she could cry out her humiliation in private.

She opened her mouth to tell him to leave, but he spoke before she could. "I shouldn't be laughing."

Relief swept through her. Thank God, he had a decent bone in his body.

He frowned. "I should be offended." Her brows rose in startled confusion. "I just don't know if I'm more offended that you think I wouldn't use a condom or that you think we had sex that you can't remember." Before she even had time to register what he was saying, he backed her up against the stainless steel refrigerator, caging her with his body. His voice was gravelly, his breath hot on her face. "Because if we did fuck, princess, you'd remember."

Her mouth fell open as she tried to sort out what he meant. "But I remember..."

"Yes, I went down on you." His eyes darkened. "And you enjoyed it. And it was incredibly beautiful. Then I left."

He left. Huh.

A sickening feeling rolled through her as she realized he hadn't even tried to get on her.

"I left because I'd had too much to drink and you were passed out. Not because I wasn't interested. I was trying not to be a total douche."

She licked her lips. "But you were interested, though." Why did she even give a shit? She should be celebrating her not-a-chance-she-was-pregnant status and move on. Instead, she was practically begging for him to validate his attraction to her.

"I left frustrated and hard as fuck. About as hard as I am now." He pressed his body against hers, demonstrating his state of hardness.

She let out a moan. She hadn't realized how much she'd yearned for that contact, to feel him and his desire tight against her. It was both heavenly and aggravating all at once. Like scratching at an itch that could never quite be satisfied. If he kissed her, that would help. She looked up at him, pleading silently for his lips.

He bent closer but stopped just inches from her mouth. "Frankly, princess, I'm frustrated now for other reasons too. I gave you my number. You thought you could be pregnant. Why didn't you call me?"

She had no idea how to answer, her brain barely working with him so close to her. She struggled to form words. "I...don't know."

"Because you're stubborn, that's why." He circled her nose with his own. "Maddeningly stubborn. You know what I think might help cure you of that?"

"What?" It came out as a whisper, anticipation stealing her voice.

"A good old-fashioned spanking."

Chapter Eight

A spanking? Seth couldn't be serious. How dare he patronize her like that? Like she was an insolent child.

Yet, at the same time, the thought wasn't unappealing. In fact, a warm pool of moisture had gathered between Heather's legs and her heart pounded loudly against her ribcage. Her sudden increase in desire had her tongue-tied and shaking.

"Bend over the table."

Seth's rough command didn't irk her as it should have. Instead, she found herself moving to the round dining area as if under a trance, and bending over with her rump in the air.

"That's my girl." She gasped as she felt his warm touch on the back of her bare thighs. His hands snaked up her legs under the hem of her short robe until they cupped the cheeks of her behind. "Stretch your arms out and grab the other side of the table."

She did as he said, her robe pulling up farther as she stretched her body across the table. His fingers curled under the band of her bikini panties and pulled them down. Then he flung the bottom of her robe up around her waist so that she was completely exposed.

He inhaled on a hiss, running his strong hands over her bare skin. "Fuck, Heather, your ass is gorgeous. I could spend hours with you in this position alone."

Her stomach twisted in excitement.

Then she panicked.

Her heart thudded wildly in her chest, her hands felt clammy as they gripped the table. She barely knew the man who had her in this very vulnerable position. Though he really hadn't taken advantage of her while she'd been drunk, that didn't mean he couldn't now. What would he do to her if she let him? And could she even stop him if she wanted to?

"Seth..." she called out to him, not knowing how to express her sudden anxiety. She hated this feeling of uncertainty. Especially when it was mixed with piercing pangs of yearning. She was a mess—bewildered and out-of-control. She didn't know what to do to make it go away, how to calm down. All she knew was that she didn't want Seth to stop.

As if reading the volumes she spoke in the single utterance of his name, he assured her with a husky voice. "I'm going to give you what you need. Let go and give in. Trust me, princess."

That was all she needed. Permission.

She sighed and rested her head down on the table in front of her, allowing herself to relax under his strong hands as they massaged her cheeks. She did trust him. Incredibly, insanely—stupidly, perhaps—she trusted him implicitly. Even more, she wanted whatever he planned to give her. Suspected he might fulfill her in ways that she'd never been fulfilled before.

The first strike came without warning. She let out a cry as the palm of his hand smacked across her tender skin, her eyes blurring from the pain. Immediately, he followed by gently kneading the area until the burn turned into overwhelming pleasure. Oh God, the contrast—the sting then the soothing touch that came after. Like sweet and sour all at once. Like soaking in a steamy hot tub in ice cold weather. Like nothing she'd ever experienced. The sensation was incredible.

And incredibly hot. She was drenched with desire.

He struck a second time, on the opposite cheek, and this time as he rubbed away the pain, she moaned. He repeated the pattern, striking and kneading, burning then soothing her until her knees were so weak that she wouldn't have been able to stand without the support of the table under her.

"That's enough, I think," he said after the sixth strike, and she bit back the urge to cry out again in both relief and disappointment. His hands continued to caress away the last of the sting, leaving no spot on her backside untouched. She'd never been touched like that—with such force and care all at the same time.

Her body had completely relaxed when one of Seth's hands journeyed lower, past the curve of her behind to the slick opening between her thighs. He groaned. "I think you liked that almost as much as I did. You're dripping wet." He slipped his fingers through her folds to the taut bud of nerves hidden within. Applying perfect pressure, he circled the spot with his thumb, teasing her to the brink of orgasm. "You know what this means, don't you?"

She could barely concentrate. "What?" She had no idea what anything meant anymore. All she knew was an intense ache of need. A need that only Seth could fill.

"You have to make a decision now." He continued to massage her nub and she bucked her body against his hand, wanting more, more, more. The light in the trailer seemed dimmer. She was close, so close.

"Do you want me to go?" Seth asked. "Or do you want me to stay? If I stay, I'll fuck you, and you'll remember it. You have to decide."

She'd have to decide? She felt like she'd already conceded all her power to the man behind her, and now he was saying the decision was hers? A tiny voice in the back of her brain reminded her that letting him stay would erase all the distance she'd put between her and her past.

But the hum of her body, still singing from his hands on her behind and so on the verge of climax, drowned out the sound of resistance.

It also made speaking impossible.

"Heather, I'll give you whichever you want but you have to tell me. Go or stay?"

"I...I..." Why couldn't she just say it? Yes, she was distracted with pleasure. But also, he had been right—she was maddeningly stubborn. Not even allowing herself to give into what she so desired.

"If you can't say it, I can't stay." Seth pulled away, the sudden departure of his hands leaving her pussy throbbing.

"Don't go!" It was a desperate cry, a sound she didn't even recognize as her own.

Seth returned to his position over her, his hand finding its way back to her core. He pressed himself against her back, covering her body with his, the hard length of his cock digging into her hip. His breath, hot at her ear, sent a shiver down her spine. "What is it you want, Heather? Ask me."

"I want you to fuck me." She said it. The words tumbled out of her mouth as though they could no longer be contained inside her, and with them came her climax crashing through her with acute ferocity.

"You have no idea what hearing you say that does to me."

While she trembled through the remainder of her orgasm, she heard his zipper then the distinct sound of a condom wrapper being torn. He had a fucking condom. Thank the fucking Lord.

She was still inwardly praising the miraculous invention of prophylactics and that Seth had one with him when he plunged inside her. "Oh God!" she screamed. Jesus, was the man hung or what? Because she hadn't yet gotten a peek at the goods, but damn, did he fill her. Filled her so full, she felt like all her nerve endings would combust from the simultaneous pressure.

And that was only on the first thrust.

He pulled out, almost to the tip, and she thought she might die from the loss of him. Then he plunged in again.

"Fuck, Heather," he groaned and she was right there with him, lost in the amazingness of sensation.

He picked up his tempo, moving in and out with deep thrusts, their thighs slapping together as he rocked into her, the table jabbing into her legs with a surprisingly pleasing bite. And still she wanted him deeper. She lifted onto her tiptoes to meet his thrusts and that did the trick. Before she knew it, she was on the verge of a second orgasm. This one came on slower, but held as much strength. It rolled through her in big, wide waves, weakening her with pleasure.

As she seized with delight, Seth found his own release. He let out a near-feral grunt as he shoved into her, his fingers digging into her hips.

"Ah, Heather, that was...incredible. You were incredible." He bent over her and kissed the back of her head. Then he pulled out and she heard him dispose the condom, then zip up his jeans while she still lay limp and boneless across the table. Little by little, her vision cleared and her heartbeat settled and sense began to return. With its return came something else—a dark feeling that she couldn't name. Shame? Regret? Fear? It left her cold, despite the flush in her skin.

Standing, she kicked her panties off her ankles and pulled down her robe. Though she wouldn't look at him directly, she saw out of the corner of her eye that Seth had returned to leaning against the counter. She could hear his breathing as it calmed to a normal rate.

"Let me clean you up," he offered.

It was a nice gesture, but she was too cold for niceties. She just wanted to be alone so she could sort out her emotions. "No, that's okay. I'm taking a shower." Her tone was hard and guarded. Purposefully.

"Hey, Heather." Seth reached out, pulling her to him. "Are you okay?"

She shrugged out of his arms and moved out of his reach. "Of course I am."

"Are you sure?"

"I said I'm fine." She wasn't though. Not at all. Spankings and rough sex, and she'd liked them both. That was enough to confound her, but then add that it was with a guy that she'd never meant to get mixed up with. What did that make her? A whore? A hypocrite? Kink was fine and all, but with Seth... She couldn't even be seen with him. He was blue-collar. He was not the kind of guy she planned to be with. Above it all, her father's accusations ran through her head twisting and morphing until it was her own voice. *You're trash. Nothing but trash. All you'll ever be is trash.*

Heather could feel Seth's eyes on her as she gathered her panties and put them in her laundry basket. She wanted to know what he was thinking, but at the same time was glad she didn't.

"Ah," he said finally. "I see."

"What?" She spun to face him, her hands planted on her hips so he couldn't see them shaking. "What do you see? What? There is nothing to see so what could possibly make you say you see anything at all? Nothing. That's what. Nothing at all."

"Uh huh."

As if he understood. How could he possibly when she didn't? "What? Just say whatever it is you want to say." She folded her arms across her chest and waited.

"Just the minute you had enough blood in the brain to remember yourself, you put yourself back out of reach."

"Whatever." She was being a total bitch, but she didn't know how else to be right then. She just wanted the cold, dark feelings to end, and as much as she wondered if they'd stop if she let herself fall into Seth's arms, she was too scared to find out.

"See. Look at yourself. Even your body language says you're closed off. Which is insane because I gave you the chance to kick me out. You didn't. It would make sense if I had hurt you …" His face screwed up in concern. "Did I hurt you, Heather?"

"No." Well, the spanking had burned, but it also felt really good.

"Did it bother you that I spanked you?"

She hesitated. "No." It bothered her that she liked it. Bothered her a lot.

"Did you want me to stay?"

"Yes."

"But now you want me to go."

She swallowed then looked up to meet his eyes. She didn't want him to go, not really. But she was maddeningly stubborn. "Yes," she said. "I want you to go."

"Typical." He let out a brief laugh of frustration. "Fine. As you so command, princess." He bent his body in a mock bow, opened the trailer door and left.

With his departure, the cold, dark feeling grew worse. The tears that streamed down her cheeks felt like ice. Even after several long minutes under a hot shower, she shivered uncontrollably and wondered if she'd ever feel warmth again.

By the time Heather dragged herself out of her shower and wrapped a towel around her wet body, Lexie was waiting for her on the trailer's double bed, her feet curled underneath her as she played Angry Birds on her smartphone.

"I was beginning to think you'd never come out," Lexie said, closing her phone before she stashed it in her purse. "You must be all pruney by...hey!" She jumped up at the sight of Heather and put a hand on each of her upper arms. "What's wrong?"

"Nothing." Heather was not in the mood to talk about what happened with Seth. Or maybe she was, but she seriously suspected she'd overreacted, and talking about it sounded like a whole lot of embarrassing.

"Bullshit. You've been crying."

"I've been in the shower, how could you know that?" Her assistant had some sort of eerie sixth sense. With a sigh, Heather realized if she didn't fess up, Lexie would drag it out of her. "Yes, I've been crying."

Lexie rubbed Heather's arms, a comforting gesture. "Why?"

"Seth. The carpenter." Goose bumps formed on Heather's skin and she didn't know if it was from the chill after the hot shower or if it was from talking about Seth. Maybe she should throw some clothes on. She headed to the closet, saying over her shoulder, "We had sex."

"And you might be pregnant. I know."

Heather found the sweats and T-shirt she'd worn to the set that morning on hangers in her closet. A costume assistant must have hung them for her because she'd left them in a pile in the closet floor. It was amazing how nice people were to her. She certainly didn't deserve it.

Pulling her clothes off the hangers, she turned back toward Lexie. It had seemed like a lifetime ago that she'd been concerned about being pregnant, and Lexie still had no idea it was a false alarm. "No, actually, we didn't have sex at the hotel like I thought. So woo hoo! I'm not pregnant."

"Woo hoo!" Lexie raised her fist triumphantly.

Heather dropped her towel and, not bothering with panties, stepped into her sweats. "But he's working on the set. Weird, right?" She brushed past Lexie to the bathroom to find her discarded bra, saying as she did, "And we had sex today. With a condom, don't worry."

"Then why were you crying? Was he mean? Did he hurt you?"

Heather stood in the doorway, threading her arms through her bra straps then hooked the latch in the back. "He didn't hurt me. He...uh...he spanked me. But it was, you know..."

"Just part of the fun, I get it. Go on."

Heather had to work to keep her jaw from dropping. She'd expected Lexie to be shocked at the spanking bit, not excitedly clinging on to every word. "Um, well, after that we had sex." She waited to continue until after she pulled the T-shirt over her head. "And then I kind of got bitchy and told him to leave."

"Hmm." Lexie tapped her chin with her finger, staring at Heather with that expression that said she knew there was more to the story.

Heather hated that expression. She also hated what Lexie was going to say next without even knowing what it was. It would probably be something wise. Or something analytical.

Sure enough, after a few seconds Lexie asked, "Why do you think you did that?"

Heather groaned. This was the other reason she hadn't wanted to talk about it. Because there would be all this emotional dissection, digging to the heart of the matter crap. She spent enough time trying to understand the characters she played. Did she really have to figure out herself too?

She stepped past Lexie again and threw herself on the bed.

Lexie followed, stretching out beside her. "Talk to me. You'll feel better."

Twisting so she was facing Lexie, Heather propped her head up on her hand. "It was just weird. I don't know. The spanking and he was kind of bossy and stuff."

"So he's dominant. Did you not like it?"

"Actually, I really did." She stifled a giggle, her cheeks flushing with the admission.

"Heather!" Lexie's eyes widened with surprise. "Have you never gotten kinky before?"

The answer to that question was a definite no. The kinkiest she'd ever gotten was using a vibrator—with and without a boyfriend. Other than that, she was vanilla all the way. It wasn't because Heather had necessarily been opposed to kink. She'd just never had the opportunity. Despite how she'd been with Seth, she made most men work to get with her. Even after they worked, they usually didn't get the reward.

And the men that she did finally invite into her bed didn't handle her as Seth had. "Most guys I'm with treat me like I'm..." She searched for the word, cringing when she realized what it was. "Like I'm a princess. Delicately. Like I'm precious, or whatever."

"You've never played it rough?" When Heather shook her head, Lexie sat up and slammed her hand down on the bed. "Heather! You're thirty-three years old!"

"Twenty-nine."

"I know your real age, you bitch. Don't forget I fill out all your medical forms. I can't believe you're thirty-three years old and you've never had rough sex!"

"I haven't. Well, I hadn't." Was that really unusual? She thought back over her exploits, searching for any clue that any of them had wanted to go into the kink territory. The truth was that even if they had, she would never know. She was always the one calling the shots. "I guess I've always been particular. And kind of bossy. And maybe not very experimental."

"Then, honey, you've been missing out." Almost a full ten years younger than Heather, Lexie seemed to know what she was talking about. "Or maybe you haven't, if it wasn't your thing."

"That's just it." Heather sat up and wrapped her knees to her chest. "I think it was my thing. I think it *is* my thing. But I don't want it to be my thing. And I don't want Seth to be my guy." Damn, she sounded whiney. She'd just always thought she'd end up with a rich businessman or producer type. A guy like Patrick at Montblanc.

But maybe that wasn't really who she wanted to be with since Patrick, handsome as he was, didn't turn her on in the least. Still, she wasn't ready to say that Seth was the guy for her.

"Yeah, yeah, yeah. It reminds you too much of where you came from." Lexie sat back on her knees. "But why? Did you know a trailer park carpenter that rubbed you the wrong way? Did you walk in on your parents spanking each other and now you're forever traumatized?"

"God, no! I never saw my parents do...anything." She shivered with the grossness of the idea. "And spanking...it just seems so...trashy."

"What did you say?"

"Spanking seems trashy."

"Are you kidding me?" Lexie fixed her with a pissed-off glare. "Heather, I try to put up with your ridiculousness, not just because you're my employer, but you're my friend. But this..." She pointed abstractly to the air, as if the words Heather had said still hung there waiting to be exemplified. "This blatant show of ignorance on your part? That's what I call white-trash. Spanking, playing rough, kinky sex—none of it is bad. Or wrong. Or trashy. It's fun and sexy, even natural, if the participants are consensual. You'd be surprised the people who partake in it. People from all walks of life. Not just sweaty carpenters and people on a fixed-income. Believe me when I say this association you have with it is one hundred percent wrong."

Heather leaned back, startled by Lexie's outburst. "Whoa. I had no idea you'd take it so personal."

"I'm sorry if it hurts your feelers," Lexie said, not sounding the least bit sorry. "But I can't sit by and listen to you bullshit about something you seem to have very little insight on."

"Okay, okay." Heather put her hands up as if to surrender. "I don't know what I'm talking about. Obviously."

"Thank you for admitting it." Lexie's shoulders relaxed. "I can point you to some good websites if you're willing to educate yourself."

"Fine." Who knew Lexie was an expert in kink? It sort of made Heather uncomfortable, so she changed the subject. "And I don't have anything against carpenters. I just always planned on being with a guy who was...better than that. A guy who could take care of me. That I'd be proud to be seen with." Did she really just say that? She really did. She braced herself for another admonishment from Lexie.

But Lexie's expression held more bewilderment than irritation. As if she'd just grasped something she'd never thought could possibly be true. "For someone from the wrong side of the tracks," she said, "you're a real snob."

"I am. I hate that about myself."

Lexie sat forward so her head was leaning on Heather's knees. "Well, I love you no matter what. You know that, right?" Heather nodded. "But it sounds like you might be happier if you try to put the whole status thing behind you and try to enjoy being with a guy who gives you what you like."

"I hear what you're saying, and I want to. I do." She choked back a fresh sob. "But I've already fucked it up with Seth. Big time." Stupid tear slipped down her cheek anyway.

Lexie wiped at Heather's tear. "Really? You can't know that."

That was certainly true. Seth hadn't given her any indication that he was easy to scare off. In fact, she'd been nothing but a bitch to him since she met him and he kept on returning.

But there was still the issue of how he made her feel—all good and fucked up at the same time. "Even if he did give me another shot, I don't know if I'd handle it any differently."

"But you could try." Lexie and her unswerving faith. Why couldn't Heather believe in herself the way her friend did? She wasn't naïve enough to not realize it might have something to do with her being Lexie's employer. Still, Heather bet that even if she stopped paying her assistant, Lexie would continue to be on her side.

And friendship or not, paid assistant or not, maybe Lexie's words could still be true. Heather thought about not seeing Seth again, thought about leaving things as they were. She'd be fine like she always had been.

But then she thought about not keeping the status quo, thought about dumping her preconceived notions and her silly plans—plans that really only involved her being as far from where she grew up as possible. A plan she'd already more than achieved.

And did having Seth in her life change that fact? No. It did not. The only thing Seth threatened to do to her life was make it more exciting. More fulfilling. Both of which would be welcome characteristics.

She bit her bottom lip and nodded. "Yes. I could try," she said. She would try to work things out with Seth. He might be more forgiving than she realized.

But it was a good thing the shoot had just begun. Because apologizing to Seth? She might need a few days to get up her courage.

Chapter Nine

Seth read the text message one more time before putting his phone back in his pocket. *"Come to my trailer. H."* Well, at least she'd finally used his number. But after avoiding him for nearly ten days now, it seemed a like a whole lot of too little too late.

Of course, he wasn't exactly innocent himself. He hadn't been honest with her about who he was. He couldn't pretend he didn't feel just a little bit guilty. He had planned on telling her—almost did when he walked into her trailer. Then she'd been so worked up accusing him of stalking her and thinking she was pregnant and then they'd...well, he just didn't get the chance.

"Something important?" Natalia asked, her silky smooth voice drawing him from his thoughts.

"Nah. It can wait." For a moment, he'd forgotten what he'd been doing before he received Heather's text—namely, flirting with Natalia. He wasn't into her, but she seemed to be into him. It occupied his time on set, kept him from thinking about the actress he really wanted to be flirting with. So what was the harm?

"Then they'll just put the fake glass in here?"

"What? Yeah." But now his head was wrapped three ways around Heather and her message and he was stuck in the middle of showing Nat how he planned to attach the trick window that the stunt-double would crash through the next day. As if Nat cared about the process. She simply wanted to be near him—he wasn't a dummy. He just wasn't interested in sweet and nice and dyed blonde hair and fake, though attractive, breasts. He wanted the sassy authenticity that was all Heather.

Dammit.

Not that he was going to run off to Heather's trailer just because she summoned him. In fact, it was probably a good thing that Nat was there at the moment because otherwise he might very well be tempted to do just that. And he was too pissed about his last interaction with Heather and the empty days that had followed to go running to her so quickly.

Except it sure did pique his curiosity. What was Heather up to? Whatever it was that she wanted, thoughts of her trailer had him stiff in the pants with memories of his last visit. She'd been so wet for him, giving over to his commands with little hesitation, relenting to her own desires. She was so incredibly beautiful when she let herself go.

But he was beginning to doubt he'd ever see that again. That one time had proven too much for her. Good thing he still enjoyed building sets. He'd taken the job to be close to her, but except for that first day, the plan had backfired. It was a small cast and crew, but that woman knew how to stay out of sight when she wanted. When she wasn't filming, she made herself scarce, and he hadn't ventured to the actors' trailers. He wasn't going out of his way to find her again. Yeah, he could play stubborn too.

Seth lifted his drill—the same drill he'd lent to Heather for the plays—and screwed the last section of the false window frame into its place on the back of the set, angling himself so Nat wouldn't notice his semi. Wouldn't that just bite if she assumed it was for her?

"How do they put a new piece of glass in? If the first take doesn't work, I mean." She had moved closer behind him, pressing up against him in a way that would drive him mad if it were another woman. The day's shoot was over—didn't Nat have something else she could be doing?

"It just slides into the grooves. Like the glass on a picture frame."

"Oh wow. That's handy." Nat giggled.

A giggling girl. How did he get himself into this situation?

A throat cleared behind them and Nat jumped away. Seth took his time putting his drill into his tool belt, examining the secureness of his work. He needed those extra few seconds to wipe the gratitude for his reclaimed personal space off his face before he could look to see the source of the interruption.

But by then, Nat had already announced who it was. "Heather."

At the mention of her name, Seth turned toward the actress he'd been longing to see. He drank her in like a tall whisky—her eyes blazing with fury, arms crossed over her chest causing her boobs to perk nicely over the edge of her blue tank top. Her legs—it seemed almost unnatural for anyone to rock white skinny jeans like she did. Almost.

God, she was adorable like that—like a feisty little kitten. No wonder Nat's usually sweet tone had noted a hint of woman rivalry.

"You usually dart out of here after shoot," Nat said next, twirling her hair around a finger, a habit that Seth guessed was subconscious. "Pretty much everyone else is gone. Whatcha doin' around so late?"

The set was pretty deserted. He'd sent his own crew home twenty minutes ago, and the tech crew and other actors were long gone. Seth had stayed behind to make sure the set was ready for the next day. Nat, he assumed, had stayed to flirt with him. And Heather...had she also stayed for him?

His dick twitched at the idea.

Ignoring Nat, Heather kept her eyes fixed on Seth. "You were supposed to meet me."

Seth let out a laugh. "I wasn't supposed to do anything." It was hilarious and infuriating the way she thought he'd jump at the snap of her fingers. But the jealousy he thought he saw behind her fury—that was hot. Definitely hot.

"My text said—"

He mirrored her stance. "I know what your text said. That didn't mean I'd come running."

Several long seconds passed as they tried to stare each other down. Or communicate silently. Or undress each other with their eyes. He wasn't quite sure what the stand-off was supposed to accomplish, just that it felt good to finally be gazing at Heather again.

It would be better if they were alone.

Nat shuffled awkwardly next to him. There wasn't any doubt she was the third wheel in the scenario. "I, uh, guess that's all to the windows, isn't it, Seth?" Her eyes lifted as if she were waiting for an invitation to stay.

But Seth wanted her gone. Did that make him a major asshole? He didn't care if it did. All he cared about was the vixen in front of him.

"Maybe you can show me more, later?"

Another man would have thought it endearing that Nat kept trying. He wasn't that man. "Yeah. Maybe later." His eyes never left his target. Did Heather's lip curl at his dismissal of her costar? Perhaps he should have made her sweat it a little, flirt more. Though he probably would have failed miserably at that. Heather was too much of a blissful distraction.

"See ya tomorrow," Nat said on her way out.

"Uh huh." That was the only acknowledgment Heather gave Nat. Except she did wait until Nat's footsteps had faded into the distance before she lit into Seth. "You could have at least texted back that you were busy instead of leaving me waiting."

He turned back to his work, pretending to do more on his already completed project. "I don't respond to being summoned, princess."

"I didn't summon you."

He raised a brow and glanced back at her. "'*Come to my trailer.*' That doesn't sound like a summons to you?"

Heather's bravado faltered only slightly. "Texting is about abbreviated conversation. That was the shortest I could manage. The shoot was over for the day, I figured you'd be free. What else did you have to do?"

"Now you're assuming you know my schedule." He gathered up remnants of his project and tossed it into the scrap bucket at his side, not able to look at her any longer without wanting to jump her. Maybe he was playing hard to get.

"Well, I certainly didn't figure you'd be seducing the next available blonde."

"Jealous much?"

"No. Just..."

That vulnerability she hid so well peeked through. He couldn't help himself; he took a step toward her. "Just what?"

Insecurity bubbled up in the corners of her brown eyes. "How quickly you move on to another woman has an effect on my slut status."

Was that what her hesitations were? Was she worried about being too promiscuous? "Heather, you are not a slut. Not in the least."

"I don't know how you can say that when we end up in a sexual position every time we're together. Well, not now..."

"Not yet."

"What?" The blush on her face said she heard him.

He took another step toward her, cocking his head. "Why did you summon me?"

"Not for what you're thinking."

He moved closer and she didn't move away. "You sure about that?"

"Yes."

Seth leaned an arm on the back of the set, close enough now to touch her. "Why don't I believe you?"

"Because you're presumptuous."

"*I'm* presumptuous?"

Her hands fell to her sides as she let out a huff of air. "You're so damn infuriating. All you do is repeat what I say with a question at the end of it. I asked you to come to my trailer to apologize, you asshole."

His eyebrows shot up. "Wow. I wasn't expecting that." Wasn't expecting that at all. It was an interesting development.

Her bottom lip caught between her teeth, drawing his focus to her mouth. What he wouldn't give to have her lip between his teeth—or his lip between hers. He wasn't particular.

Apologies led to lip biting, right? "What exactly were you going to apologize about? There are so many things that come to mind that you might be sorry for."

"Touché." A small smile settled on her mouth. "For my behavior after...you know." She lowered her eyes and took a deep breath. When she raised her eyes again, her expression was soft. "I had a really nice time, but I didn't act like it. I'm sorry."

He nodded, watching as she wrung her hands together. She was nervous. Damn, but didn't that turn him on even more. It almost made him not want to let her off the hook so easily. But, today anyway, he'd be the nice guy. "Thank you. Your apology is appreciated."

"Thank you." She licked her lips. "I mean, you're welcome." Her cheeks heated to a delicious shade of pink.

"So." He grinned. It was killing him to not touch her, especially when she was so very near. But he held back, letting the tension pulse through his veins. "You had a nice time?"

"I did." She wanted to touch him too, he could tell. Her hands still fidgeted at her sides, her eyes flitted back and forth from his eyes to his lips.

He lowered his mouth, his breath mingling with hers. "A really nice time?"

Her breathing was heavy. He couldn't begin to explain what that did to him. "Yes, a really nice—"

Before she could finish talking, he'd covered her mouth with his. Their teeth clicked as his tongue slipped into claim her deeper, his hands circling around her waist to draw her closer. She responded by fisting his hair, pulling him to her with equal force, as though neither of them could get as close to each other as they desired. As though inside each other was the only acceptable place to be.

He'd missed this the last time—the kissing. He wasn't soft or precious about his sex, but he did enjoy kissing. He'd wanted to kiss Heather then, had planned on kissing her fiercely before he embarked on round two. But round two never occurred because she'd somehow gotten mixed up in her head.

And this time, though he wanted to cherish it and enjoy the feel of her tongue gliding across his gums, wanted to suck on her bottom lip until it was raw, he couldn't slow himself down. He needed the rest of her, needed to release the straining ache inside his jeans.

Either feeling the same need or sensing his urgency, Heather jumped on him, wrapping her legs around his hips. Surprised, he leaned back onto the set for support, shifting his hands to hold her ass. She tilted her hips up, stroking him with her crotch. Shit, it was so wonderful. So goddamned good.

She bucked again and this time he thrust up against her, reveling in the squeal she let out when he did. He thrust again, dry humping her as his mouth continued to explore hers. The way she rubbed against him in return—he wouldn't be surprised if he creamed himself before he even got his cock out of his pants.

"Yes, yes, right there," Heather said when he'd tried a new angle. "Right fucking th—"

117

"Everything okay?" A bright light shone in his face.

"What the fuck?" He brought one hand up to shield his eyes, letting Heather down in the process, and looked across the studio toward the source of the light.

Shit.

It was one of the security guards. Why he felt he had to shine his bright-ass flashlight in their faces was beyond Seth. It wasn't like they were doing anything wrong. The set was already lit.

Heather turned away from the guard right away. Realizing she wouldn't want to be caught in a compromising position—she did have fans that would run with the knowledge—Seth stepped in front of her, letting her hide behind him. "Hey, sorry," he said to the guard. "I had a few things to finish up on the set. My friend was keeping me company. We both have clearance to be here." He pulled his security clip off his belt and walked up to the guard to show him, hoping his badge would be enough to clear both of them.

The guard studied Seth's badge then handed it back without saying a word.

"See? Everything's fine." Seth clipped his badge back on his belt. "Thanks for checking us out."

The guard stared at him suspiciously, his eyes glancing down at Seth's telltale erection. Then he shone the light back in Heather's direction. "Ma'am? How about you? Everything okay?"

Was the guard concerned about a woman in distress or only that the woman might be a somebody? It had to be irritating to never know peoples' intentions. Right now, the idea that the guard might just be after a scoop had Seth clenching his fists at his side.

Fortunately, Heather was used to it. Keeping her head down, she lowered her voice. "All good here."

"Then may I suggest you keep it down in the future?" The guard turned off his flashlight and put it into its holster.

"We will. Thanks again." Seth stayed where he was, watching as the guard left the studio. When he was sure they were alone again, he turned back to Heather.

They burst into laughter.

Heather snorted, wiping tears from her eyes. "Oh my God. That was awful."

"Was it really?" Sure it had gotten his adrenaline pumping, but the encounter would certainly make the evening memorable. Not that he needed any help remembering anything where Heather was concerned.

"No, not really." Her laughter settled into a wide grin.

"Come on." Seth held out his hand for her. When she took it, he led her around the wall, farther behind the set. "We have more privacy here. In case he comes back."

"Or we could go to my trailer."

The thought of having to wait until they made it to her trailer made his balls throb. "We could," he said reluctantly.

"Let's not, though."

"I like that plan better." He tugged her back into his arms and started in on her neck with the same fervor they'd left off with, biting up to her earlobe.

Heather's hands pressed against his chest, tracing the outline of his muscles through his shirt until she reached his waistline. There they worked at the fastening of his jeans. Then her palm was on him, circling his cock with a firm grip.

"Jesus, that's so good." At least that was what he meant to say. It came out more of a moan than intelligible speech.

She slid her hand down. Then back up. Then down one more time before he remembered.

"Shit, Heather, stop." He pushed at her hands, trying— though not very hard—to extricate himself from her wonderful grasp. "I don't have a condom. We have to stop." He didn't generally keep his wallet stocked. The only reason he'd had protection before had been in hopeful anticipation of getting inside Heather's pants. Which had worked out better than he could have expected. Then when it hadn't ended so hot...well, he hadn't bothered to repack.

Now he was deeply regretting that.

Heather, however, didn't bat an eye. "Not a problem," she said. She placed a hot kiss on his chin, followed by another on his neck, then one at the skin just above his T-shirt. "I'll take care of you," she murmured, sinking to her knees.

Next thing he knew, her hands were replaced with her lips. Fuck, her warm mouth, sucking in his crown—he had to concentrate not to blow his load right there. She glided her hand up his stem as she took him in deeper, her hollowed cheeks touching him on all sides with each pass in and out, sending sparks of electricity through his body.

A part of him wanted to let her run the show. He had wondered if his controlling nature had been what had scared her off before. It gave him pause now—tempting him to hold back.

But that wasn't who he was, and he couldn't pretend that it was. He was already withholding so much of himself from her, not telling her why he was on her set, what he really did for a living. He didn't want to lie about this too.

Plus, the look in her eyes when she let go—he knew she experienced her best pleasure when someone else was taking care of her.

His decision made, he gripped her head tightly with both hands, and he took over the tempo, speeding up. She grasped his thigh with her free hand, probably trying to get her balance, but when she tried to take her other hand off his cock, he stopped her. "No. Keep it there." She replaced it, stroking up and down, meeting her mouth on each plunge. "Yeah, just like that."

He held her in place as he fucked her mouth with abandon, thrusting so deeply he hit the back of her throat. And the sounds she made as he moved inside her... So. Fucking. Hot.

His release snuck up on him, but not too fast that he couldn't warn her. "I'm about to come," he managed through gritted teeth. "You need to decide how you want to handle that." Not removing his hands from her head, he loosened his grip so that she could pull away if she didn't want him coming in her mouth.

She didn't move. Instead her eyes peered up at him and he knew then that she'd swallow. Not just that she'd swallow, but that she was looking forward to it. That was all it took to push him over the edge. With a final thrust, he pressed inside her, spilling his seed into her mouth with a groan.

She licked him clean, rocking with him until he was completely finished.

Man, but if she wasn't the most amazing woman he'd met in years.

After tucking himself back into his jeans, he held his hand out to help Heather to a standing position. He kissed her deeply, like he'd been longing to, showing her his gratitude, his appreciation. His amazement at discovering the woman he thought he had totally figured out was actually so much more.

Chapter Ten

"Your turn," Seth said against Heather's mouth, his fingers stroking the skin just above the top of her jeans.

She kissed him once more. Then pulled away, moving out of his arms. For half a second he wondered if she was freaking out again, but then she smiled. "Don't worry about it, tool boy."

"I'm not worried. I want to." And man, did he. Watching Heather come—there was nothing like it. "And tool boy? I assure you, I'm no boy."

"Oh, I know." He could hear the grin in her voice, even though she faced away. "But really, it's not necessary. It's good for me to do something unselfish every now and then."

"Well, that's certainly true."

She peered over her shoulder with narrowed eyes. "Ha ha."

"But trust me when I say that going down on you is not a chore."

Her cheeks colored. "Good to know."

He followed her to the set's living room, planting himself in a doorway as he watched her mosey around the space. She wandered to the back of the couch and trailed her hand along the back of the furniture piece. "You know," she said, glancing at him out of the corner of her eye, "another week and we won't need condoms. Assuming you're clean."

"I am." He missed her touch already, but what she was saying made up for its absence. He strode toward her, stopping at the end of the sofa. "So we're planning to have sex again?"

She shrugged. "I'm just saying that if we did then we'd be safe." She circled the other end of the couch to face him. "Of course, first I'm going to have my period, so we'd have to wait past that."

"I'm not afraid of blood."

"Why doesn't that surprise me?"

He hated having the couch between them, but even more than the physical barrier, he hated the unspoken circumstances of their last sexual encounter. It had to be cleared up before they could move on. Otherwise, he'd be walking on eggshells with her. And he was not a walking on eggshells type. "If we did end up fucking again, how can I be sure you aren't going to freak out?"

"How can I be sure you aren't going to jump in bed with Bobblehead?"

His brow furrowed. "Bobblehead?" She had to be talking about her costar. Bobblehead actually fit the eager-to-please woman. To be sure, he asked, "You mean Natalia?" There was that jealous blaze in Heather's features again. It warmed him to see it. Yet he couldn't stand that Heather thought the little wisp of an actress had anything on her. There was no one who compared to her. Certainly not for him. "Let me assure you, I have zero interest in Nat."

"Nat," she said under her breath like a curse word. "You were sure giving her your attention. And not just tonight."

She'd been watching him. Good. Yes, he'd spent time with Natalia the last several days, but it was always she who had sought him out. He didn't give her any reason not to, though. Maybe he'd been trying to stir Heather up.

He repeated his last words. "Zero interest in Nat." She scowled, not satisfied. "Would you be happier if I told that to her?"

"I would."

"Done." He was making a commitment to her with that agreement. Normally that would have his stomach churning. Instead, he felt oddly relaxed.

But he wasn't the only one who needed to give assurances. She hadn't yet answered his question. "Are you going to freak out on me again?"

She shifted from one foot to another. "I don't know." She turned away, this time going to examine the prop photos on the wall. "I'm not sure myself, really. I don't think I will. Did you always want to be a carpenter?" Her voice lilted up with the abrupt subject change. "Or work on movies?"

"Not exactly. And yes." He didn't want to talk about that. First of all, it reminded him he was lying to her. Second, the topic she was avoiding was the one that interested him. "Maybe it would help if you told me what set you off. When you freaked out, I mean."

"Maybe." But she jumped right back to the lighter conversation. Lighter for her, anyway. "Then if not a carpenter, what would you want to do?"

"Design." He tried not to flinch as he said it, barreling into his next question for her. "Was it the sex itself?" He hoped not. Just remembering her bent over her dining table as he pounded into her made him hard again.

"No, it wasn't the sex. Design? Like set design?"

"Production Design." This was his opportunity. He could tell her the truth—that he already worked in design, that he was good at it. It was understandable why he hadn't said anything before. He'd tell her he hadn't wanted the cast of the plays to know. Then it just never came up. He could say he took the job on her film simply as a favor to a friend. He could even tell her that part of the appeal was that she'd be there.

But even though they'd jumped some hurdles in their relationship, or whatever it was they had, he remembered why he lied in the first place. Because he wanted her to want him even if he was the person that she thought he was—a set carpenter. Because that was who he used to be. That was where he came from. He was proud of that. If she couldn't accept him as that guy, then there was no future between them, just like there had been no future with him and Erica.

Huh. That was weird. He hadn't been thinking about Heather in terms of long lasting, but now that he had, it didn't sound half-bad.

So he let the opportunity pass, and turned the truth time back on her. "Did it bother you that we barely know each other?"

"Not that." She shook her head to emphasize her answer. "Production Design's pretty ambi—"

"Then the spanking," he interrupted, focused on getting to the bottom of her freak-out. Focused on not discussing what he did for a living.

She took a deep breath in and then let it out.

Bingo. It was the spanking that had bothered her. "You liked it though—your body did anyway." He took a step toward her and stopped when she took a step away. "But not your head. What's up with your head, Heather?"

"It's just..." She lowered her eyes. "I can't. Seriously, I can't talk about this."

He wanted to push her. Partly because he thought he understood, but also because he was pretty certain she'd feel better if she talked about it.

But after all the progress they'd made, he wasn't about ready to scare her off. Instead he asked, "So if I were to spank you again..."

She turned toward him, a shy smile spreading across her face. "I would like it." Then her smile faded. "Are you planning to spank me now?"

"No." He laughed. Now that she'd mentioned it, he was sorely tempted. "You probably deserve it. For being a bitch last time and not talking to me about what was really going on."

"I suppose I have that coming." She met his eyes, holding his gaze with such steadiness he wondered what she saw when looking at him. A guy who worked with his hands. Who didn't measure up. Who didn't fit the mold of her perfect fairytale life.

Or maybe she saw what he hoped she could see. A like soul. Someone who made her face her bullshit, but didn't leave her alone to do it. A guy who could take care of her but never make her feel weak while doing it.

Or could she see the guy who was keeping secrets from her while demanding she be open about hers?

Without any warning, she ran to him, burying her head into his shoulder. "I'm sorry, Seth. This is hard for me."

He wrapped his arms around her, running his fingers through her tresses. Any doubts he had about keeping his secrets vanished in that instant. She was opening up to him in a way he suspected she wouldn't have if his supposed status hadn't forced her to. Though he wasn't an advocate for lying, he felt justified.

Well, mostly justified.

Maybe his doubts hadn't completely vanished after all.

He couldn't think about that, couldn't dwell on his guilt. He had to stay centered on her, help her through her issues. "I'm sorry it's so hard for you. I think I can understand."

"You can?" Her voice was muffled in the fabric of his T-shirt. How much of a girl would he be if he said this was his new favorite shirt?

"Yeah, I understand." He spoke carefully, voicing his suspicions. "The spanking makes you feel...dirty."

Her head nodded into his chest.

"And slutty?"

"Yeah," she said, her voice choked.

He kissed her temple. "Especially because you like it."

"Yeah."

Gripping her gently by the upper arms, he pushed her away just enough that he could bend to look at her directly. Her eyes were brimming with tears. He'd hit the nail on the head. Even though he'd suspected, it wrenched his gut to see her so uncomfortable with herself. With who she was. Why was it always the women who exuded the most confidence were the most fragile inside? "But it doesn't make you either of those things, you know."

When she lowered her head, he squeezed her arms. "Heather? You know that, right?"

This time she met his gaze. "I know. Well, I'm starting to know."

"Keep going in that direction." He cupped her chin with his hand and ran his thumb over her cheek. "And if you feel uncomfortable, talk to me."

"But we don't really talk about anything. We fight. And make out." Her teeth grazed her lower lip. "Not that I'm complaining."

"We're talking now."

"So we are." She dabbed at the corner of her eye. "It's kind of nice."

"It's a whole lot nice."

She stepped out of his arms, refusing to meet his eyes, and he could sense she felt awkward about the emotions she'd displayed. "Can I ask you something? While we're talking and all." Or maybe she felt awkward about what she had to say next.

"Shoot."

"The, uh, spanking and stuff." She crossed behind the armchair before turning to face him, leaning on the chair back as if she needed the support. "Are you, like, a Dominant?"

So she'd been doing some research. Interesting. "I like to dominate. But I'm not a Dominant." Not that he'd ever tried it, but it seemed like too much work and planning. He was more impulsive. "I don't go to sex clubs or any of that crap either."

127

"Then you aren't expecting me to, um, you know, wear a collar and kneel in front of you and let you tie me up while you whip me and stuff?"

"Well, you've already knelt in front of me of your own accord." He loved that he could make her blush so easily. "And tying you up sounds like a whole helluva lot of fun. But no, I'm not into the collars or whips or chains or any of that Mistress/Sir shit. I like to be in charge. And I like it rough." He gave her a sly smile. "I'm willing to try new things if that's what you're into though."

"No!" She nearly jumped with her emphatic denial. Her color deepened, and when she spoke again, she was calmer. "No, that's okay. I just wanted to know what I was in for. If we had sex again, I mean."

"Oh, we will." He didn't think she could blush any further but apparently she could. Damn, she looked good all pink. He needed to touch her. Crossing to her, he held out his hand. She took it, surprisingly, and he led her to the couch where he sat before pulling her next to him.

With his arm around her, she leaned into him. It was instantly comfortable and easy. He played with her hair, wrapping it around his fingers and releasing it again. "What about you? How do you like your sex?"

"I'm not really sure anymore. I've never been a prude. I mean, I've always liked sex. But I was raised to believe..." She paused and he could hear her swallow. "My father acted like kissing guys made me a whore. It put a damper on a lot of my sexual experiences because there's always this guilt thing hanging over me."

No wonder the spanking had bothered her. "That's tough."

"Yeah. It is. The sex itself hasn't always been as fulfilling as it could have been. I've never experimented though, because of the guilt. Always stuck to the basics."

He wondered briefly what basic meant. Like, missionary only? But she'd moved on before he could ask.

"And the guys I've been with have been…" He grimaced at the thought of her with other men. "I don't know…gentle. Overly gentle. As if I needed to be served or adored or whatever."

"They treated you like a princess?" He chuckled.

"Don't even…" She sighed. "Yes." Lifting her head to look at him, she said, "Now you're going to say it's because I act like a princess so what do I expect, right?"

"Not at all. It's because you act like a princess that I think you need to be a little bit manhandled."

"I think you're right." She pivoted her body and draped her legs across his lap. This was nice, they could face each other more easily now.

"So then, with me. I know it was only the one time, but was it missing anything?"

"It was. It was missing a proper ending. I shouldn't have freaked."

"We're past that. No worries." He rubbed his hand up and down her leg, delighting in the goose bumps that rose on her arms. "But before the ending…"

"It was good, Seth. Really good."

"Fulfilling?"

"Yeah." She lowered her eyes. "Though there could have been kissing." Her eyes lifted again to meet his. "I like kissing."

"I do too." They held the gaze for several seconds. Then talking about it wasn't enough. He had to kiss her. He leaned in toward her and she, understanding, brought her face in to meet his.

Just before their lips met, they heard a sound behind them suggested the security guard was returning for his next round. It broke the mood.

She shifted out of his arms and stood. "I need to be getting home," she said. "I have lines to work on. And I should really get in a workout before bed."

He stood too, stuffing his hands into his pockets so he wouldn't be tempted to reach out for her. He could give her a workout, and he almost said as much, suspecting she might even want an invitation to not complete her to-do list. But even though they'd been talking about sex, the current conversation seemed quite different from their usual naughty flirtation.

He had another idea now. Rocking back and forth from the balls of his feet to his heels, he wondered if he should just say goodnight or run with the wild hair he'd gotten up his ass.

The wild hair won. "Would you want to do this again sometime? The talking without belittling each other?"

Heather tilted her head. "Like a date?"

"Yeah. I suppose that's what it's called."

Big brown chocolate eyes branded him. The way she stared at him—stared *into* him—it was like getting a tattoo with all the same burn but also a whole lot of euphoria. He couldn't remember the last time a woman had that effect on him. Was that why he was so crazy over her? Taking a job several steps below his skill level, lying and hiding the truth. Practically stalking. He didn't deserve to have anything with her, let alone what they'd shared, but he couldn't stop himself from wanting more.

Heather took a deep breath. "Can I think about it?"

Well, he shouldn't have expected anything else. She needed time to deal with her conflicting emotions. It had taken her ten days to seek him out after they'd had sex in her trailer, after all. He could give her time. "I hate that you have to. But I suppose you can."

His eyes didn't leave her. He couldn't stop staring—she grew more beautiful the longer he looked. He couldn't have designed a more enchanting specimen if he spent his life trying.

She blushed under his gaze. "What?"

There was only one thing he wanted at that moment. "Can I kiss you?"

"That seems so weird for you to ask after...everything."

"Well, it seems we're on new ground. I'm not sure what the rules are here." He felt like a teenager. Awkward and horny.

"Me neither." She lifted her head up. "But yes, you can kiss me."

He leaned in slowly, taking his time. When his lips met hers, they moved together without destination, without need to get off. It was like a first kiss. Tender. Deep. Sweet.

"Goodnight, princess." He'd started her nickname as a way to mock her snootiness. This time when he said it, he meant it as a term of endearment.

He watched her as she walked off the set toward the parking lot, his chest aching with each step she took.

Chest aching? Term of endearment? Was he falling for Heather Wainwright?

Aw, shit.

He'd asked her on a date. Seriously? Heather didn't date. Dates were too difficult—paparazzi and fans fawning over her. They wouldn't have any privacy. All the media outlets would purport them as an item. Was she ready for that? To be paired with Seth in front of the whole world?

No, she wasn't.

But she wanted to get to know Seth better. Wasn't that what dating was supposed to be about? Figuring out if you wanted to be with someone. Getting to know them before you had to make those decisions. It wasn't fair that her life didn't allow her that simple cultural norm.

She chewed her bottom lip as she climbed into her trailer. After shooting a text to Lexie, telling her she was ready to be picked up, she curled up on her couch with her script to work on her lines.

But she couldn't focus, her mind still on Seth. She could have stayed with him while she waited for Lexie. He might have even offered her a ride. More than one kind of ride. The thought sent a shiver down her spine. She was already so needy and turned on. Maybe she should have let him get her off after all.

Except she needed to take this slow. Well, slower.

As she'd told Lexie she would, she'd researched about sex and spanking, learning a lot of information that had opened her eyes. Wide. She wasn't so ignorant to not know about the whole Dominant/submissive world and the punishments that went with it, but that had never interested her. Still didn't. Beyond that, she'd thought spanking was abuse. That the men who spanked their women during sex were the same assholes who got 911'd for beating on their wives. She'd seen a lot of that in the trailers—poverty could turn people to their worst selves. Some it drove to drink like her mom. Some it drove to drugs like her dad. Some it drove to be just plain mean like half the people in her park.

But when she'd read the websites Lexie had given her, and then Googled sex and spanking and found hundreds of articles about regular, everyday couples having rough sex all the time, she had to swallow her pride and admit she was uniformed with a capital U. She'd always been into hair-pulling and nail-clawing, but she'd never dared to push that further. Apparently, the men she'd been with didn't either. Seemed that her always being in control had some serious downfalls. Like never getting to learn new things. New things that could possibly be enjoyable.

So now she was intrigued. She wanted to explore this recent discovery. She wanted to explore it with Seth. But she was still timid about it, and that was why she'd let her evening with him end. Besides, she'd liked the note they'd ended on.

With him asking for a date.

She lay back with a sigh, her script open against her chest. A date wasn't impossible. It would take careful planning to ensure they kept under-the-radar. They'd have to meet somewhere. Somewhere discreet. She wouldn't want to don a disguise. Somehow disguises always seemed to attract more attention. If she put enough energy into it, she could think of a place that wouldn't require that level of hiding. A simple excursion. Maybe a picnic at a park. Or hiking.

Or she could just let Seth handle the planning. That was how dates usually went, after all. The one who did the asking made the arrangements. Could she trust him to manage the details needed to maintain discretion?

If she couldn't, then there was no point pursuing a relationship with him.

A relationship with Seth.

My, but she liked the sound of that.

Chapter Eleven

The next day, Heather didn't lose sight of Seth. Over the week and a half that she'd avoided him, he'd been everywhere, but she hadn't given herself permission to notice. Now she did. Damn, was it an improvement.

Her acting also improved. She would have imagined that being focused on him would be a distraction, but it wasn't in the least. Instead, she felt more relaxed—more comfortable with herself than she had in ages. Her lines flowed, her scenes were perfection. She was "on".

And her mood was decidedly brighter. She didn't dread off-camera time like she often had before, spending it bantering with the crew and her costars instead of hiding in her phone. Even Bobblehead—um, Natalia—seemed less annoying. Her excessive cheerfulness was somehow easier to stomach when Heather was happy herself. Knowing that Seth wasn't into the younger actress might have helped a bit. Helped a lot.

She didn't actually get to speak to Seth until lunch. She'd planned on seeking him out—strategically, of course, so as not to draw attention—to let him know she'd go out with him. But first, she stopped at the catering table knowing, the selection would be slim if she didn't get in early. As she searched for a lunch that fit into her daily calorie limit, she felt his presence behind her. She knew it was him without turning around, her body tensing with pleasure, her arm hairs standing on end as if to announce his presence.

"Is there something I can help you with?" he asked as he reached over her, his voice making her thighs clench.

"What do you mean?" She selected a Chef Salad and pretended to decide between yogurt flavors. Normally, there was no deciding. Strawberry was her choice, hands-down. Right now she didn't give a flying fig about yogurt. Unless she was licking it off Seth.

He moved beside her, grabbing two bottled waters. "I thought that maybe what you wanted to eat wasn't on this table." Damn, could he read her mind? "Since you've been staring at me hungrily all morning."

Her cheeks heated. Hopefully he'd been the only one to notice. "You're not cocky at all, are you? Wait, don't answer that." He'd have some sexy comment about his cock. And she really didn't need to be thinking about his cock right then. They were alone at the table, but not so alone that she could jump him.

Alone enough to talk though. Or flirt. Whatever it was they did. "All right, I might have been staring. I was just thinking that I haven't had the opportunity to see you with your shirt off." *And that a date might be a way to fix that.*

He grinned at her, his blue eyes gleaming. "Is that something you'd like to see?"

"Very much so." Her inner voice screamed something about taking it slow, but Heather wasn't listening. Once she'd made up her mind that Seth was who she wanted to be with, she wanted him as soon as possible. To hell with taking it slow.

"I can think of ways to remedy that." He leaned in closer and quieted his voice to a raspy whisper. "For example, if we were the only ones here, I'd strip you down and have you grab onto that pipe right there." He pointed to a lighting track that had been lowered to allow the crew to adjust the lights. "While I fucked you senseless."

So much for not thinking about Seth's cock.

"Sounds...awesome." She was breathless just thinking about it. "But how does that remedy me seeing you without your shirt on?"

"I could agree to be naked too." God, he was adorable. "I, uh, I talked to Natalia, by the way."

His quick change of subject almost threw her for a loop. "To Bobblehead?" Since she'd been watching him all morning she already knew. She'd also seen how Nat's energy had been a bit down in her scene after that. How much of a bitch was she that Nat's broken heart made her happy?

"Yes, to Bobblehead. She didn't seem much of a bobblehead after I talked to her though. Had to tell her that I was sorry if I'd given her the wrong impression, but that I sorta have a thing with someone else."

Heather swallowed her glee. "Sort of have a thing?"

"It's undefined."

"Hmm. Interesting." More than interesting. He'd followed through on what he'd said he'd do. He didn't have to do that. It wasn't like he'd promised. He really didn't owe her anything. But he'd done it anyway, and wow, did it feel good.

"Thank you, Seth." She met his eyes. "I'll have to think of some way to repay you."

Seth reached across her again, picking a box marked as a roast beef sandwich. "I have condoms."

For half a second she got excited. Until she remembered. "I have tampons." Her period had started that morning. What timing.

"I told you, blood doesn't bother me." Abso-fuckin-lutely adorable.

"You did say that." She'd dated other guys who didn't care. She was usually the one who called period time Off Limits. She could do the same now, make him wait. Renew her decision to take it slow.

She *could* do that.

Or she could bring up the date he'd asked her on.

Instead, she found herself saying, "My scene after lunch requires a total make-up and hair redo. I'll need a shower first." She paused only long enough to know for sure that she really wanted to say what she said next. "Join me?"

He gave her the sexiest smile she'd ever seen. "You know all you have to do is ask."

"That's right. How could I forget?" If she stayed this happy, she'd for sure have to get Botox to rid her of smile lines.

Out of the corner of her eye, Heather caught movement— someone walking near them. She turned back to the catering table, hoping it looked like her conversation with Seth had been casual. Yeah, she wanted to be with him, but privately. In her life, privacy was not something she took for granted.

The person walking by stopped. "Seth Rafferty?" Heather inconspicuously looked toward the man who owned the voice. "Wow, good to see you. It's been ages."

Seth seemed surprised, maybe even worried, to see the man who was a stranger to Heather. She gave the new guy a quick once over. He was dressed business casual, expensive watch and wedding ring. The sunglasses propped on his stiff head of hair were designer. Not part of the crew, but maybe someone on the producer level. She placed him in his late thirties, which could easily mean late forties with a good plastic surgeon.

"Brandon." Seth's voice, though friendly, seemed unnatural. He shifted his bag and bottles of water to the crook of his arm so he could offer his hand to Brandon. "God, it *has* been forever."

"Since *Time of Night*. Yeah."

Heather recognized the movie title, a suspense film that had come out several years before. Seth must have been on the crew. She could look it up on IMDb later. Maybe if she found out what this Brandon guy did on that film, she could figure out the strange tension that had begun when he showed up. Or she could just ask Seth later.

"So what brings you here?" Seth asked, redistributing his food to both arms.

"Our company is producing *Girl Fight*. It was my turn to stop by and check things out." Brandon's eyes raked up and down Heather's body. "And things look good from where I'm standing."

Did he think she didn't know he was looking at her? She was two steps away and not stupid. One of the cons of her job—people thought she was an object instead of a real person. It really sucked sometimes.

If Seth hadn't been tense before, he certainly was now. Despite the unease in the air, Seth's reaction to Brandon's wandering eyes gave her tummy flutters.

With gritted teeth, he said, "Brandon, isn't your wife a fan of Heather's? You know each other, I'm sure."

Heather turned toward Brandon, having been invited into the conversation.

"We haven't met officially." Brandon took Heather's hand. "Brandon Drake. My wife can't wait for the premiere. She's dying to meet you." He continued to flirt with her while talking about his wife. How smarmy. Maybe that was why Seth was acting all weird—because Brandon Drake was a perv.

Whatever Seth's beef with him, Brandon was also a producer of her movie. Her boss, in other words. So she had to play nice. "Aw, thanks." She sweetened her tone to a ridiculous level that bordered on sappy. "Always nice to hear I have a fan."

"I'm a fan too." He winked at her, still holding her hand.

Until Seth cleared his voice, at which point Brandon dropped it promptly. "So what are you doing here? Did you take over as P.D.?"

Heather's brow furrowed. "P.D.?" It wasn't unusual for producers to not know their crews, but why would Brandon assume Seth was the Production Designer?

Seth ignored her question. "No, Joe Piedman is. Of course." Despite the air-conditioned studio, Seth had a fresh layer of sweat on his brow. "You know he lost his crew on short notice." And he was talking weird. "And we've been friends for a quite a while." In short bursts. "So he called me." As if making his speech up as he went. "I had a hole in my schedule. So I offered to come on board."

"As lead carpenter?" Now it was Brandon who looked confused.

"Yep." Seth's jaw twitched.

Brandon's brows rose. "Man, you must be really good friends."

"Something like that," Seth said under his breath.

"What was that?" Brandon asked.

Seth covered quickly. "So your team got nominated for the Globes last year. That must have felt good."

Heather cringed at Seth's attempt at acknowledgement. Everyone in the biz knew the Golden Globes were a crock of shit. The Foreign Press who gave the awards ran nothing but a giant popularity contest. Maybe the tech level wasn't aware. Or was Seth trying to change the subject?

"Yeah, it was awesome." Brandon's teeth were gritted but he kept his smile. "And I heard that you might be up for—"

Seth cut him off. "I'd totally be up for getting some drinks sometime." Though Heather didn't think that's where Brandon had been going with his statement. Yes. Totally weird interaction.

But before Brandon could react, his attention was caught by the movie's director passing by. "Oh, hey, I gotta talk to Don. Catch up later?"

"Sure thing." The tension visibly rolled off Seth the minute Brandon walked away.

"What the eff was that?"

"What do you mean?" Seth asked, turning back to the buffet table as though there might be something he still wanted.

"Do you not get along with him or something? Because the energy between you two was way wacko."

"Between me and Brandon?" Seth shuffled through bags of sandwiches. "We get along. I just was surprised to see him, that's all."

"Uh huh." Except that wasn't all it was. Heather was sure. The conversation had just been...off. "Why would he think you'd be the Production Designer?"

He shrugged. "I have no idea. Maybe he remembered I'd been interested in that area. Or something. He must have assumed I'd moved up. Since we haven't seen each other in a while."

Now Seth was using that weird talk with her. She narrowed her eyes. "But how did he even know you if you were on crew?"

"I was good at networking."

She wasn't convinced, and she was pretty sure her face told him that.

"Look," he said. "The Art Director on the movie we worked on was a drinking buddy of mine. He introduced me to Brandon at a cast party. The party got kind of wild, if you know what I mean. We haven't seen each other since."

Well, didn't that open a whole slew of questions? Like what had happened between Brandon and Seth? And was it something she would've wanted to be part of?

But she'd done some crazy things at cast parties that she'd die about if brought out in the light of day, so she simply said, "Gotcha." Still, even if the two guys had gotten mad drunk and made out, there was something else weird about their conversation. "It seemed like he was really surprised that you were working as a carpenter. Wasn't that odd?"

Seth took a step closer to Heather and leaned in. So close she could smell his carpentry man smell that she loved so much. "What's odd," he said in a rumbly voice that clothed her in goose bumps, "is that we're still here talking when we could be somewhere else completely not talking."

Damn. She bit her lip as her lady parts were coated in a fresh pool of moisture. "Give me twenty. Don't worry about knocking. Just come in." She paused, wondering if it would be impolite to ask her next question, but decided—rude or not—it had to be asked. "You'll be discreet?"

He grinned. "You mean not announce to the whole set that I'm about to meet you for wild monkey sex?"

She rolled her eyes. "I meant when you come to my trailer could you, like, make sure no one sees you when you walk in?"

"Yes, princess." He performed a mock bow. "Wouldn't want the royalty seen with the hired help."

"That's not—"

He cut her off. "I know. I'm giving you a hard time." Had he emphasized the word hard or was her mind in the gutter? "I'll be discreet."

"Thank you." She had to take a deep breath before taking off for her trailer. *Wild monkey sex.* She was already wet with excitement.

Seth pinched the bridge of his nose.

That was close. *Too* close.

He'd told Joe when he took the job on *Girl Fight* that he didn't want anyone to know he was anything but a carpenter so Seth hadn't expected to encounter anyone who knew differently. But Brandon Drake...the movie they'd worked on together had been one of the first that Seth had designed. Brandon would never have expected Seth to be building a set. He'd have to try and catch Brandon and tell him to keep it on the D.L.

Actually, what he should do is come clean with Heather.

He almost groaned at the thought of Heather. At the wonderful thought of showering with her. At the horrible thought of telling her the truth.

He couldn't do it.

Not just because he was still intent on finding out if she could truly like him no matter what he did for a living, but because now he'd let it go too long. Now there was no way she could think of it as anything but a betrayal. And wasn't that exactly what it was? A betrayal of her trust? A betrayal of her emotions?

Shit, he was screwed.

But even though it was tearing him up inside, he had to protect his lie. Either that, or lose Heather, and he wasn't ready for that. He looked at his watch. He had almost twenty minutes before he was supposed to meet her. Hopefully he could catch Brandon before then.

Tamping down thoughts of the lusty afternoon that lay just ahead, he headed for the director's trailer, figuring that was where he'd find Brandon. The door was shut when he got there, but even without pressing his ear against the door, he could hear Brandon's voice inside.

He'd have to wait.

Seth leaned against the side of the trailer and checked his watch again. Fifteen minutes. Might as well get lunch in while he waited.

He'd finished his sandwich, a bag of chips and one whole bottle of water before the door opened. Thankfully, Brandon walked out by himself, putting on his sunglasses as he did. Seth glanced at his watch once more. T minus three minutes. He'd have to make this conversation quick.

"Brandon," he called out, brushing his chip-greased hands on his jeans. "I hoped I'd find you again."

Brandon pushed his sunglasses back on his head and crinkled his brow. "You were looking for me?"

"Yeah." He hesitated. Why hadn't he thought up a good lead in while he was waiting for the guy? Now he was winging it. "Well, like I said, I'd love to catch up sometime. But I don't think I have your number anymore."

Brandon cracked a grin. "Good thinking. I'm sure I don't have yours either." He pulled out his wallet and leafed through it until he found what he was looking for. "Here's my card."

"Awesome. Thanks." Seth didn't even look at Brandon's business card before stuffing it in the back pocket of his jeans. "Oh, one more thing." He lowered his voice. "You know, I'm doing this gig as a favor to Joe, and just so there wouldn't be any awkwardness with the crew, I'm keeping my resume hush-hush."

Brandon snapped his fingers. "That explains it! Man, I couldn't understand why you weren't the P.D. I was about to ask around."

"Please, don't do that." Definitely a good thing he talked to Brandon.

"Oh no. Not now that you said something. But you are still in the P.D. biz? Because you're too good at it not to be. Your talents are wasted in this shit position."

Seemed Heather wasn't the only one on the set with a narrow-minded view of the hard-working crew. But he knew that. It wasn't his first time around the block. The moneybags were almost always pompous. Why was that?

"Yes, I'm still a P.D.," he said with gritted teeth. "But it's been really nice to get my hands back on the set. Keeps me in touch with the job and the people who work for me."

Brandon's face soured. "Whatever's your thing, man. In my opinion, that's a real nice favor you're doing for Joe." It was

143

Brandon's turn to lower his voice. "Hey, um, maybe you could do me a favor as well."

A favor for Brandon? He wasn't sure he wanted to know. "Shoot."

"Heather Wainwright..."

Fucking slimy asswipe. He fought the urge to punch the guy in the face. "Come on, Brandon, you're married."

Brandon shrugged. "We have an understanding."

He should just let it go. Seth knew Heather wasn't about to hook up with a type like Brandon. Yet he still felt compelled to let Brandon know as well. "Heather isn't your girl. She's not into anything that might bring bad press. And she'd never go for a married man, whatever your understanding is. She's kind of a princess."

"That's too bad. That chick has one heck of a smoking body." He sighed and again Seth wanted to punch him for the dirty thoughts Brandon was surely having about Heather.

Then, Brandon's face lit up in understanding. "Wait, are you into her?"

"Uh..." Seth hadn't been prepared for Brandon to be insightful.

"You are!" Brandon clapped him on the back. "That's all you had to say, man. I'll keep my hands off. Tell ya what, maybe you could give me a holler when you're through with her."

"Yeah, that's exactly what I'll do." The statement dripped of so much sarcasm he wouldn't be surprised if Brandon noticed. Frankly, Seth didn't give a fuck. He'd done what he came for and now—he looked at his watch—now he was late for Heather. "Sorry to cut this short, Brandon, but I have an appointment."

Seth didn't wait for a proper goodbye, taking off as soon as he'd finished speaking. But he didn't miss Brandon's shout after him. "Great seeing you again, Seth. Good luck with that fine slice of pussy."

Seth cringed. *Such a crass mother fucker.*

Not that Heather didn't have a fine slice of pussy. She did. She also had so much more.

Of course, as he walked into Heather's trailer, the sounds of a shower already going in the other room, it wasn't the *so much more* that was at the forefront of his mind.

Chapter Twelve

Heather's stomach twisted. Seth was late. Seven minutes late. Maybe he got caught up on the set. Or lost track of time. Or wanted to give her a few extra minutes to finish her meal.

Or maybe he wasn't coming.

Since she'd barely been able to get food down, anxious as she was for her shower with Seth, she'd thrown away her half-eaten salad ten whole minutes before she expected him to arrive. Then she'd brushed her teeth and removed her eye make-up. And washed under her arms. Yeah, she was taking a shower, but she'd been sweaty after a day under hot set lights and she preferred not to subject Seth to her less than ladylike smell.

Then she waited. And waited. And waited.

At five minutes past the time Seth was supposed to arrive, she considered curling up on the bed to mope. But she had to shower before her next scene, even if it was alone. She'd already stripped from her costume before she'd eaten. Now she untied her robe, letting it fall in a heap on the linoleum floor and leaned into the shower to turn on the water.

The temperature had just begun to warm up when she heard the bathroom door open behind her.

"Now that's a beautiful sight. Would be even more beautiful if your backside was red from my hand, but beautiful nonetheless."

She bit back her smile, hiding the relief she felt. *He'd come.* Thank goodness she'd already removed her tampon. Taking it out now would have been awkward.

"You're late," she said, shaking the water off her hand. She meant to scold him further, but when she turned to face him the sight of him took her breath away. He'd already stripped out of his clothing—presumably at lightning speed since she hadn't been in the bathroom that long—and damn did he look fine. The hard planes of his pecs and trim waist were smattered with a fine mist of hair. His arms were pure muscle. His abs, which she'd always suspected would be well-defined, were absolutely killer. They looked professionally sculpted. As if the reason he'd been late was because he'd stopped in the make-up trailer and had shadows and ripples applied. Generally the men she knew that looked like that only looked that way because of lighting and cosmetics. Or Photoshop. Men didn't look like that in real life. Yet there was Seth, naked in her bathroom, looking *exactly* like that in real life.

A hefty shiver ran through her body. "I had no idea," she whispered. She couldn't stop staring at him, his arms spread across the doorframe in an open posture that showcased everything. Including his thick, hard shaft. She could barely believe that amazing organ was connected to an even more amazing body. His thighs and hips—all of him—strong and defined.

"No idea about what?" Even with his brows furrowed, he was hot as hell.

"How built you were." She was amazed she even had a voice. "You're incredible."

His face broke into a wickedly sexy smile. "I'm glad you approve." His eyes blackened with desire. "But what's incredible is what I'm looking at."

Her body flushed red, and not only because the room had heated from the running shower. "I can't imagine how what you see compares to what I'm seeing."

"You know, instead of just looking we could be touching."

Her heart thumped in her chest. "Now that sounds incredible."

He crossed the small bathroom in one stride. His hands wrapped around her face, tilting it toward him. Then he was kissing her, kissing her, kissing her. He kissed all down the sides of her face and neck and when he returned to her mouth, he tasted of make-up and sweat and roast beef and plain old yummy male goodness. She could kiss him like that, *be kissed* like that for a very long time.

Before she could get her thoughts together and remember she needed to get clean, Seth was pulling back the shower door for them to step in. He guided her backward until she was pressed up against the stall wall. Then he shut the door behind him and crushed her body with his.

Just as she had reveled in this first time that she'd gotten to see him in all his glory, she reveled in this first feel of their naked bodies touching, the warm pressure, the tingling sensation everywhere their skin touched.

And their skin touched everywhere.

It was a small space, which made it easy to maintain contact, but not so tight that they didn't both fit with ample room to touch and massage and explore. Their hands wandered and caressed as their lips kissed and tasted, their tongues licking water droplets off each other's skin.

Again, it was Seth who had enough sense to think about the necessities. He untangled himself from her, and reached for her body wash on the built-in shower shelf. He poured a dollop on his palm and then applied it generously to her skin, massaging and kneading her muscles as he traveled his hands up and down her limbs.

He spent extra time on her breasts, squeezing the mounds as he washed her. He teased her nipples, whispering past the points with his finger, never giving them quite what she desired.

He made up for his taunting when he reached her ass. His strong hands rubbed into her fleshy skin and down past the curve of her buttocks with such deliberation, she found her throat choking back an unexpected sob. The release of tension from her knotted muscles combined with the care he demonstrated toward her—it was overwhelming, yet welcomed. Each second he spent worshipping her skin, her core grew needier, desperate for contact.

When he'd soaped every inch of her body, she expected him to move there, to the place she most ached for his touch. But he surprised her, setting down the body wash and reaching for her shampoo.

A thrill of anticipation ran down her spine. She absolutely loved having her hair washed and even though she had it done frequently, she never grew tired of it. And the idea of Seth washing it? Even better.

On the other hand, he'd skipped washing her pussy and it throbbed from the lack of attention. She was conflicted between trusting him and addressing her need. Her need won out. "Aren't you missing a spot?"

Seth turned her back toward his front, but she could hear the smile in his voice. "I don't see the point of washing down south. You're just going to get dirty again."

"I am?" She looked over her shoulder, blinking her eyelashes in feigned innocence.

The smell of her strawberry shampoo filled the air as he began working it through her tresses. "You are and you know it. Now hush. We don't have enough time together to waste any."

She melted at his words and the feel of his hands massaging into her scalp. Her head was alight, tingling with the electricity that passed through Seth's fingers to the nerve endings buried at the roots of her hair. The sensation was so intense that she barely had any thought function left. Yet curiosity—or rather—a need for an explanation tugged at her. "We'd have had more time if you hadn't been late."

He pulled the suds through her hair in long strokes. Was it her imagination or had his movements grown tense? She didn't mind. If felt wonderful. So much so that she lost herself in the pleasure of it, barely caring that he'd yet to respond to her comment on his tardiness.

Seth positioned her under the showerhead and tangled his fingers through her hair as he rinsed the suds in the steaming hot water with the same attention he'd given to washing it. After several pleasurable minutes, he put his arm around her and tugged her toward him, out of the stream of water. Keeping one hand at her back, he dabbed her eyes with a washcloth from the towel rack.

When her eyes were clear of soap and water, she opened them and met his intense gaze.

Washcloth still in hand, he moved to cup her cheek. "I would have been here early if I could have been, princess."

Her breath caught. This thing with Seth was just sex, wasn't it? An examination of her sexual desires. A chance to try something new.

But the way he was looking at her, the way he was touching her—it made her chest tighten and her tummy feel all fluttery. She leaned up and brushed her lips against his. "What kept you, then?"

He closed his lids then opened them. "Stupidity," he said softly. He broke her gaze, and nodded toward the shampoo shelf. "Conditioner?"

"No. My hair is too fine. It makes styling more difficult." The moment from before lingered and she knew she could forget words altogether and concentrate only on Seth. Except, his answer had left her intrigued. "Stupidity, huh? Are you going to explain?"

He pulled her to him firmly and she felt his erection pressed against her belly. "Is that really what you want me to be doing with my lips right now?"

That was all he had to say and the time for talking was over. She lifted her mouth toward his and ran her tongue along his bottom lip. With lightning speed, he captured her tongue with his mouth, sucking at it fiercely as his teeth raked along the bottom. It was the moment of his unleashing—the moment she realized the extent of the self-control he'd demonstrated as he'd scrubbed her clean.

While one hand held her at the nape, the other hand found her clit without detour. Splaying his fingers across her lower belly, he circled his thumb and stroked her into a frenzy. She was wet and more than ready when a few short minutes later, he urged her thighs apart with his knee and rammed his stiff cock inside her.

Heather gasped at the initial shock of his entry. He was rough and didn't wait for her to adjust to fit him before pulling out and ramming in again. It was brutal and delicious and unlike any sex she'd had before. It fulfilled so much of what she craved that she felt near orgasm before he'd plowed into her a third time.

The hand that had held her neck moved to lift her thigh around him, his fingers digging into her skin.

"Are you ever gentle when you fuck?" she asked as he plunged in again, deeper this time with the new angle.

"No, I'm not." He picked up his rhythm as if emphasizing his point. "Is that a problem?"

"No. It's not." It wasn't a lie. His savagery, the way he pulled at her hair, manhandled her body...it was a huge turn on mentally. And physically, he did the job in a way that no one ever had. Seth's blunt jabs hit a spot at the very end of her—a spot that rippled with pure electricity every time his tip slammed against it.

151

It was short moments before she was clamping down around him, her orgasm moving through her in a brutal burst. She fell limply against Seth's chest. When he had completely rubbed out her climax, he pressed her tighter against the wall. "Grab the towel rack," he commanded. His hands gripped her hips and angled her upward.

Fuck. She was spent, completely spent. But in this position he reached even deeper, rubbing against the upper wall of her vagina in such a way that she knew another orgasm would soon follow. It did, building through her with an aching slowness, like an impending sneeze or a gathering storm. Then it released in a similar fashion—rolling over her with such intense longevity. Even her hands lost feeling, her hold on the rack slipping. If it weren't for being trapped between Seth and the wall, she would have fallen to the shower floor in a heap.

Just as her second climax began to cease, Seth's rhythm picked up and three strokes later he joined her release, groaning as he did.

It felt like decades passed before their breathing returned to a somewhat normal pace, before Heather had feeling in her lower limbs.

"Seth?" she said when she could speak. Not because she had anything to say or ask. She just needed to say his name, needed to know he'd been as affected as she'd been.

And somehow he understood. "I know," he said. "Me too."

When she could stand by herself, he pulled away enough to reach for the body wash. She laughed as he soaped her inner thighs and private parts. "There. Now you're clean."

Except now, she sort of felt dirty. But for once, it didn't bother her. It was an amazing kind of dirty. Freeing and naughty and exactly okay.

Seth turned off the shower and stepped out of the stall. He grabbed a towel from the linen shelf and held it open for her. "Your towel, my princess."

She swat at him. "Stop it." Her protest was halfhearted. She liked his nickname for her. It made her feel special—singled out in his universe. Assuming she was the only one he called that, anyway.

"Never." He wrapped the white fluffy towel around her and pulled her in for another kiss. This one was slow and languid— their tongues dancing to an unheard adagio. In its warmth, any last fragment of doubt she had about Seth melted away. He wasn't her past. What he could be, though, was her future.

When the kiss ended, he spoke first. "About that date—"

"Yes. I want to go out on a date with you." A fresh wave of heat filled her cheeks. She'd cut him off—maybe he'd changed his mind. "That is if you're still offering."

He laughed. "I just fucked you mindlessly. In your shower. In the middle of a working day. You think I'm not going to offer? Hell yeah, I want to take you out. Repeatedly, if you'll let me. Even if only half of our dates end in sex."

It was a mystery how her skin could spot with goose bumps when she felt so warm. "Why would only half of our dates end in sex?"

He laughed again as he secured a towel around his waist. Heather frowned to see his beautiful body covered up. "I'm not suggesting that only half would."

He picked up Heather's discarded robe from the floor and held it open for her. She turned her back to him to slide her arms in.

He leaned in, his breath caressing her neck. "I was only pointing out that I want to be with you, Heather. Even when your clothes are on and you're lashing at me with words instead of with that sweet tongue of yours."

God, he had a hold on her. She didn't even know him. And he didn't know her. He might not want another date once he experienced what it meant to be part of her world. "Let's start with one date," she said, dropping her towel and tying her robe in its place. She turned to face him, rubbing her hands against the sinewy muscles along his shoulders. "But I must warn you, I'm not an easy person to date."

"I've already figured that out." He reached for another towel and bunched it around her hair, squeezing the excess water into the material.

"Not because of my personality, you ass. Because it's hard to get privacy." She took the towel from him and gathered it like a turban on her head.

Seth grabbed the towel she'd discarded on the floor and used it to dry his hair before tossing it in the laundry basket. "And privacy is important to you."

"It is important to me." Heather opened the bathroom door and stepped into the trailer's bedroom. She smiled at Seth's clothes piled on the bed then turned back to see him still standing in the bathroom, watching her with a furrowed brow. "Not because I'm embarrassed to be seen with you, if that's what you're thinking."

He followed her into the bedroom. "Thank you for clarifying. I get it. It's the fans."

"Yes." Stupid fans. She hated to be the type of person who complained about them. She recognized they were the ones who kept her in a job. But couldn't they love and admire her without encroaching on her personal space? Sometimes she couldn't even pee without being bothered.

Seth picked up his jeans and dropped his towel. Heather's heart picked up at the semi he still sported. What she wouldn't give to spend the rest of the day naked with him in her trailer instead of filming.

Pulling his jeans on sans underwear, Seth said, "Well, personally, I'd prefer my dates to be with you. Not your entourage. So trust me when I say I will plan accordingly."

"Seth?" A man into wild monkey sex and conscientious of her groupies? What more could she ask for? "You're awesome."

"You can't possibly mean that." He paused while he put his T-shirt on. "I mean, I am awesome, but you don't know that. Yet."

God, if he didn't stop grinning at her like that, she'd never be on time for make-up. "I think I—" The sound of a door opening stopped her. She put her finger up to her mouth to gesture to Seth to be quiet. "Did you hear that?" she whispered.

"Yeah," he whispered back. "You expecting anybody?"

A chill ran through her. People didn't just walk into the actors' trailers. It was cause for termination and everyone on set knew it. Also, the lot was secured. No one that shouldn't be there could have gotten access. She shrugged off her anxiety. "It's probably my assistant. She's the only person I know who would walk in without knocking." But what if it wasn't? It would be obvious to anyone that she and Seth had just showered together, both of their hair still wet. "Shit. I should have had you lock the door. I'll, um, do you mind staying put while I check it out?"

"Yeah, yeah." Seth sat on the bed to put on his socks. "Tell me when the coast is clear or give me some sort of sign." He winked at her.

"Thanks."

Heather took a deep breath and pulled back the partition enough to step through, then shut it behind her. She saw him immediately, sitting on her sofa, his feet propped up on the table while he played absentmindedly with his lighter.

At the sight of her, one side of his mouth curled up in greeting. "Well, hello, baby doll."

Heather closed her eyes, hoping the sight in front of her was a figment of her imagination—some cruel waking nightmare. Why here? Why now?

But when she opened her eyes, he was still there, lounging in her trailer as if he belonged.

Her heart sank at the reality. "Hi, Daddy."

Chapter Thirteen

Heather pulled her robe tighter, unable to lose the chill that had overcome her. It had been almost two years since she'd last seen her father. That time he'd shown up at a movie premiere and threatened to cause a scene if she didn't talk to him. She'd given him money to go away, as she always did when she saw him. Why else did he ever show up?

She braced against the counter for support, her legs suddenly feeling wobbly. "How did you get in here?" He would have had to pass a security guard to get on the lot. Dean Hutchins was a crafty man though. Security rarely deterred him.

Dean pocketed the lighter he'd been playing with and held his hands out to his sides. "Now, is that any way to greet your old man?"

She glanced up at the clock on the microwave. She was due in wardrobe at exactly that moment. She didn't have time for this.

And Seth!

He was still in the room behind her, a flimsy partition the only barrier between this part of the trailer and that. He'd hear everything, no matter how she hushed her voice.

She swallowed her sob of humiliation—she couldn't worry about Seth now—and repeated her question. "How did you get in here, Daddy?"

Dean took one booted foot off the table and put it on the floor. "I opened the door. Didn't even have to pick the lock this time."

That had been nearly five years ago. When she'd done a six-week run in *Cat on a Hot Tin Roof* at the Ahmanson Theatre. He'd picked the lock to her dressing room, was waiting after a show. "I told you if you ever did that again I'd have you arrested."

"But you didn't mean it, baby doll."

"I did mean it." Though she wasn't sure about that. Pressing charges against Dean would bring him into the limelight. Everyone would know about him and, subsequently, everyone would know about her. What her stock was. That she was, at heart, nothing but trash.

She always took precautions now. Lexie knew about her father, extra security was written into all her contracts. *The lot was secured!* "Who let you on the lot? You have to have clearance to get through security."

Dean waggled his brows. "Guess I had clearance."

"Tell me!"

He sighed. "Turns out the security guard is a Heather Hutchins fan—oops, I mean Wainwright. Or at least a fan of her sixteen-year-old body in a skimpy bikini."

She knew that picture. There were few from her childhood; they hadn't owned a camera and her mother was generally too drunk to care about preserving memories. Heather had bought a disposable camera to take candid pics with a friend. A handful happened to be taken in their swimsuits while they were tanning. If she hadn't run far and fast from her home when her father had kicked her out, she'd have gathered all those personal items. Besides her name, she'd left a lot behind—things that Dean had sold off over the years. Wasn't that what parents' did when their children became famous?

What was more surprising was the security guard. "He let you on the lot in exchange for a picture of me?" No wonder she had a general distrust of, well, everyone. "Hope it was worth it. He's not going to have a job here after today."

157

"Now, Heather. You don't need to be a bitch." Dean plopped his other foot on the floor and leaned forward, his hands on his knees. "You've always had it out for the working man."

Her father hadn't been a working man since she'd first hit it big. He lived off the money she threw to him—money she gave him in hopes that he'd finally leave her alone and let her put her past behind her. "What do you want?"

Dean stood and walked to her, spreading his arms open in an inviting hug. "Can't I just come by to see my baby doll?"

"Yeah, I'm not buying that." She ducked out of his embrace. "Look, I'm at work here and I need to be in make-up. So let's skip all the usual bullshit and cut to the chase. What do you want?"

"Work?" Dean scanned the trailer. Heather knew what he saw—the forty-two inch flat screen TV, the granite countertops, the stainless steel appliances. He was probably adding up their worth. "Sure as shit doesn't look like work to me. Deluxe trailer with all the fancy? Nah, this is what I call a vacation."

Her patience had reached its limit. "What. The fuck. Do you want?"

"Okay, okay." Dean lifted his hands in surrender. Then he put on his serious face, his voice growing somber. "It's not for me. It's your mother." She'd definitely gotten her acting skills from her dad. "She needs to go to rehab."

"Again? That was your excuse last time." Why did he even bother with reasons? She'd give him the money anyway in the end, whatever he said. "How much is it going to cost?"

"Two hundred."

Her eyes popped. "Two hundred thousand?"

"It's a six-month program. She needs the intensity. Seems the thirty-day bullshit doesn't work for her."

She doubted her mother had ever been to rehab for two days much less thirty. The money she gave to her father paid for booze and coke. She wouldn't be surprised if Dean was coked up now.

It made her sick to think about it. Made her pissed. "You know what? I can't do this anymore. I told you that the last time you came begging for money. Frankly, you're not authorized to be here. I could call security." She picked up the cell phone she'd left on the counter earlier and held it up, threatening.

"You could. But you won't want to cause a scene." His lips tugged up into a smile that bared his drug-yellowed teeth. "See, baby doll? I know you."

"You don't know me at all." And yet he did. He knew she was embarrassed by him, knew that she wanted to sweep him under a rug. Her threats were empty.

"I do know you." He patted her on the arm. "And I know you wouldn't turn your back on your family."

Even though she'd shrugged away from his touch, it was just enough contact to stir her emotions. She folded her arms across her chest as a tear slipped down her cheek. "You mean, like you turned your back on me?"

"Now, Heather. You're the one who ran away."

"You kicked me out!"

"We had a spat. That's all."

He probably really saw it that way. Thought that her whole reason for taking off boiled down to one argument on one night of her young life. But it hadn't. She'd wanted to leave for years—since she was old enough to think about running away. She hadn't because she thought for some crazy reason that she might be needed. Loved, even.

Except, every day of her teenage life proved differently. She was treated like she was a burden, told she was worth nothing, yelled at and screamed at and belittled. So when her father kicked her out, it was the permission she needed to leave. To let go.

159

Yet, she hadn't ever been able to do that last part. Well, she was doing it now. Once and for all. "Okay, I'm done. Please, leave."

"Not 'til I get what I came for." He took another step toward her. "What I deserve."

She couldn't back farther, trapped between her father and the counter. She tried not to shrink away, to stand up to the man. "You don't fucking deserve anything from me. Get out!"

"Don't you talk to me like I'm some stranger, Heather." Dean grabbed her arm, pinching her skin between his fingers. "I'm your father. Your flesh and blood."

"Let me go." She wasn't afraid of him—he'd smacked her around before, but never really hurt her. It was her pride wounded now. She was pretty certain there'd be a bruise from his grip and she sure as hell didn't want to explain that to makeup.

"Not until you show me some respect." His grip tightened.

"Let me go!" She yanked her arm away, but it wasn't her own action that released her from her father's hold.

It was Seth.

"The lady said to let her go." In a blur of movement, Seth had Dean's face slammed against the refrigerator, his arm pinned behind his back.

"Don't you worry yourself about this," Dean said, his high-pitched tone the only sign he was bothered by his predicament. "I'm her father. We're fine."

Seth pulled Dean's arm higher. "I don't care if you're the goddamn pope. She says to let her go, you let her go."

Heather's stomach lurched with conflicting emotions. On the one hand, Seth's hero act was very touching. She'd dated guys that protected her from fans and overzealous paparazzi. But this...this felt different. Sweet, to say the least.

On the other hand, Dean was her father. The father she hid from the world. If she wanted him to stay hidden, he'd have to go quietly. Seth's approach promised a whole lot of noise.

She bit down on her lip until she tasted blood. "Seth, it's fine."

"Heather..." His voice trailed off, his expression speaking volumes. *You don't have to go through this,* it said. *You don't have to take this from him. Not anymore.*

It was nothing she hadn't said to herself time after time after time. But the words remained stuck in her head and shining in Seth's eyes. She couldn't act on them, no matter how convincing the argument. "I appreciate this, Seth, I do. But you can let him go."

With a heavy sigh, Seth released his grip on her father.

"See?" Dean smirked with his victory.

"Daddy, you need to leave." She wished she had more conviction. She so wanted to be in control of the situation.

And Dean fed off that. Fed off her doubts and inferiority complex. "I'm not going anywhere 'til we get what we discussed." He said it with honey in his voice, but there was no mistaking the threat.

Seth shifted as though he wanted to take Dean down, his hands flexing at his sides. Through gritted teeth he said, "Heather, I'm calling security."

"No!" She did not want security there. "No, just...let me take care of it my way. I have it under control." As if saying it could make it true.

"Yeah, it certainly looks that way."

"Who is this asshole anyway?" Dean's *be sweet* tactic was gone, replaced with *be a dickhead.* "Your bodyguard? Why doesn't it surprise me that you're fuckin' around at *work*? You sure did live up to be the trashy slut you promised to be."

Seth took a step toward Dean. "What the fuck did you say to her?"

161

"She heard me."

Dean had to be coked up. Or stupid. Or both. Because he showed not an ounce of anxiety about the fighting gleam in Seth's eyes and Seth could take the scrawny Dean out in one blow.

There was no denying that part of her would love to see that. Would love to see Dean lying on the floor in misery, a payback for all the misery he'd put her through.

But violence would bring an even bigger scandal. The scene was already embarrassing—her drugged out father, she and Seth still wet from a shower. Gossip columns would go crazy.

She stepped between Seth and Dean, Seth's warm rage radiating on her back. "Daddy, I'm not a slut. And I'm not trash. I moved out of the parks and got where I am by myself."

Dean rolled his eyes. "Real hard work, wasn't it? You're paid to let men all over the world fuck you with their eyes. What an accomplishment."

Seth stepped around her. "It's time you left."

"You gonna make me?"

"I'm sure as hell happy to—"

Heather slammed her hand down on the counter. "Shut up! Both of you!" She bent down and opened a low cupboard that hid the small safe where she stowed her purse. After entering the code, she fished around for her checkbook and a pen. She filled in the blanks, adding another hundred thousand to the amount Dean had requested, and scribbled her name before standing again.

"Here," she said, handing the check to her father who snatched it away with a greedy swipe. "Take this. Leave. Forever. I don't want to see you again." Another tear rolled down her cheek. "I mean it this time, Daddy. Next time I'll press charges."

"Heather." From behind her, Seth's hands settled on her arms, his breath tickling at her neck. "You don't have to give him anything."

"Stay out of this, pretty boy." Dean folded the check and stuffed it in his back pocket. "Thank you, baby doll. Your mama will be right proud."

Dean leaned down to kiss her cheek, but Heather ducked away. "Just leave."

"I'm going, I'm going."

Just like when Heather left the trailer all those years ago, Dean didn't look back. The trailer door bounced behind him, not latching. If only he could stay as gone as he was right at that moment.

"Heather..." Seth rubbed his hands up and down her arms. He was strength, a pillar she longed to cling to, a warmth she wanted to bury herself in until the chill was gone from her bones.

But before she could fall into him, she'd have to explain. And she wouldn't do that. She couldn't.

She wiped the moisture from her cheeks and shrugged out of his hands. Seth's presence was like a too hot electric blanket. She wanted it, wanted him, but he was too warm to endure. "I don't want to talk about this."

"I know, princess." He reached for her hand and massaged her palm with his thumb. The pressure and heat of it felt so good, so inviting that she almost abandoned her shield.

Seth prodded on, his tone gentle. "Why did you let him bully you like that? He's not bigger than you, you know."

Dean was bigger than her. Black hole size big. How could she expect Seth to understand? She didn't. That was why she wasn't going into it with him. Not now. Not ever.

"I said I don't want to talk about this." She pulled her hand out of his, immediately missing the sliver of comfort it had given her. Hiding behind her wall of shame wasn't her first choice. It was her only choice.

She wrapped her arms tightly around herself, wondering if she'd ever be able to let anyone in, fearing the answer was no.

Just like that, she'd closed him off.

Less than twenty minutes before, Seth had been in the shower with Heather, had been inside her. She'd conceded to a date. They'd made progress—she finally seemed to have placed some faith in him.

Then, in an instant, it was gone.

Seth shook his head, not sure what his next move should be. As it was, they were at a standoff, eyes fixed on each other, miles of distance between them. He wavered between leaving and crushing her to him. But what did she want? He decided to ask. "Do you want me to go?"

She opened her mouth, her chest shaking as she took a ragged breath to speak.

Before she could say anything, the trailer door banged open. A young woman with short curly brunette hair, blood red nails, and a nose ring appeared with fire in her eyes. "Heather, what the fuck? You're late for wardrobe."

The woman—not much more than a girl, really—scanned the trailer. Seth felt her assess the situation, saw her features mold in concern when she spotted the actress with tear-stained cheeks. "What's wrong?" She glanced at Seth, then back at Heather.

Sensing the accusation in the quick flit of her eyes, he put his hands up. "Hey, it wasn't me."

Heather took a breath. "My father..."

The girl's eyes doubled in size. "Dean? He's here?" She peered past Seth into the bedroom, her spine straight, ready to fight.

"You just missed him," Seth volunteered when Heather seemed unable to answer.

"Oh, shit. Hold on." The girl pulled out her phone from her pocket and dialed. After a few seconds she said, "Hey, it's Lexie. Heather's got a migraine."

"I just need a few minutes," Heather whispered.

The girl—Lexie—nodded as she continued her conversation. "No, she's taken something for it, but we need a few more minutes for it to get working. I'll get her there as soon as I can."

Seth watched Heather as Lexie finished her call. He was intrigued by how the young girl came in and took care of business without waiting for permission. Even more intriguing was how Heather let her. He suspected there were few people Heather let take charge, how hard it must have been for her to trust him. His chest swelled with the sudden clarity.

As well as Lexie seemed to handle the situation, there was still something else that needed to be done. "We should call security."

"No," both women said at same time.

"But, Lexie," Heather went on, "the guard does need to get canned. He let Dean on the lot. Can you contact whoever it is in charge of that?"

"I'll take care of it."

Seth flexed and relaxed his hands, needing something to occupy himself, needing something to do. She hadn't asked him to leave. Yet. She hadn't asked him to stay either. Well, he might be signing his walking papers, but he had to know. "How can I help, Heather?"

To her credit, she paused before she answered. "Nothing. You can't help this."

Like hell there was nothing he could do to help. He could help her in so many ways if she let him. He got this. He understood drug addicts and desperation and being ashamed of his parent.

But it would take a fight to try and convince Heather. This wasn't the time for that. "Okay. I better get back to work, then."

He wanted her to ask him to stay. She didn't.

"You must be the carpenter." Lexie held out her hand to him. Strangely, it felt like she was postponing his departure.

"You must be the assistant." He shook her hand.

"Very nice, Heather." She clicked her tongue appreciatively. "Very nice."

"Not now. Please." Heather rubbed her temples. "I need to freshen up." She turned toward the bedroom then stopped, remembering something. "Lexie..."

Her assistant could read her mind. "I'll get your valium."

"Perfect. Thanks." Heather disappeared into the bedroom, shutting the partition behind her.

Since Lexie hadn't moved, Seth took the opportunity to get some answers. "Hey, what's the deal with all that?"

"Look, she can hear me so I can't talk to you."

Right. Of course not.

He turned to leave, but Lexie put a hand on him to stop him. Loudly, she said, "I'd love to help, but, you know. My job and all." Seth watched as Lexie dug in a drawer and found a notepad and pen. She continued talking while she scrawled something. "My loyalty is with Heather," she said as she ripped off the paper and handed it to Seth. "Clearly."

"Yeah, yeah. I understand."

Though he didn't understand. Not until he read the paper. It had Lexie's number and a message, *Call me and I'll clear things up.*

"So you better leave now."

Seth looked up at Lexie and found her smiling. "Thank you."

Her reply was a whisper. "Anytime."

Chapter Fourteen

Heather glanced at the dashboard clock before leaning forward to look in the passenger mirror as she applied makeup to her right eye. Out and about at nine o'clock in the morning on her one day off from set was not what she called a good time. Why Lexie thought she'd be cool with it made her seriously question her assistant's judgment.

Though Heather had already spent the morning bitching about it, she wasn't done. "Day off doesn't mean day to do PR shit. It means day off."

"We've been over this," Lexie said, glancing over her shoulder as she flipped on the turn signal. "It's for Urban Arts. You never tell them no."

"I rarely turn them down. Not never. There's a difference." She certainly wouldn't have booked herself for an Urban Arts gig during a film run. Days on set were long. Twelve to fifteen hours long. Days away were treasured. She needed them to catch up on her sleep, to get in a good workout. To schedule a much needed waxing.

Though there hadn't been any need to keep trimmed in the lower regions since Dean had shown up five days before. She'd had zero intimate time, only seeing Seth in passing on set and acknowledging his texts with brief responses. It wasn't like she'd been avoiding him exactly. Just kinda sorta.

"At least I didn't book you for the Jenna Markham interview."

Heather rolled her eyes. She heard Jenna Markham's name so much from Lexie, she was beginning to wonder if her assistant was trying to keep her riled up. "Whatever. You bring her up every time you're mad at me."

"Her people call every day, Heather. I turn them down constantly. What if I accidentally said yes one of those times?"

"Is that your lame attempt at a threat?"

The car lurched as Lexie slammed on the brakes causing Heather to smear her mascara. "Dammit, Lex, what the fuck?"

Lexie threw up her middle finger toward the car in front of them then fixed a glare on her boss. "Heather, you've been a crab-ass for days. Stop. Now. I mean it, I can't take any more."

Heather bit back the nasty comments she wanted to return and licked her finger before rubbing at the smudged black makeup under her eye. She didn't want to piss off her only friend, and Lexie's patience seemed to be wearing thin.

Way thin, since Lexie's lecture wasn't over. "Now, I'm sorry you had to get up on your one day off, but it will do you good to do something for someone else for a change instead of wallowing in that pity party you've got going on. It's getting old, Heather. And it's unattractive."

Heather flipped the mirror shut and tossed her makeup into her purse. She didn't have it in her to argue. She'd been wallowing a whole lot since Dean. Truthfully, she didn't know how to get herself out of her funk. Maybe Lexie was right about doing something for others. It wouldn't hurt to try.

The blinker sounded again, and this time Lexie turned into a school parking lot. Heather took a deep breath and tried to ignore the surroundings. The elementary school looked freakishly similar to the one she'd gone to—the building old and worn down, the blacktop lot crumbling, the playground appearing on the verge of collapse. The neighborhood that bordered the school was obviously low-income. The houses were falling apart and in need of new paint. The yards were dead and cluttered with junk. The scene hit home. Hard.

The car pulled up to the front of the building and headed toward the guest parking. As they got near, Heather could see an empty spot next to a brick red pick-up truck. A man stood at the back of the vehicle, leaning against the tailgate. She squinted. She knew that man. Knew him quite intimately, in fact.

Seth.

Lexie parked the car and turned to Heather. "Besides, this isn't really a PR gig."

Heather's mouth suddenly felt dry, and her skin tingled. Seth was there. And Lexie was saying something about the PR gig not really being a PR gig. "What do you mean?"

"It's a date in disguise."

Heather froze, her hand still on the seatbelt release. "What do you mean a date?"

"Well, he called me. And you did tell him you'd go out with him. And I arrange your calendar." Lexie put the car in park, her entire demeanor one of nonchalance. As if what she was saying wasn't absolutely huge. Arranging a date with Seth behind her back? Yes, absolutely huge.

Lexie looked over and noticed Heather's stunned expression. "Don't look at me like that. I saw the way you lit up just now. You want to be with him, and don't you dare deny it."

Heather wanted to deny it but she couldn't. She did want to be with him. More than anything.

Apparently, Heather's face confirmed Lexie's accusation.

"Yeah, I knew it," she said. "For some reason he wants to be with you too. Even though you've been nothing but a major bitch."

"Because I am a major bitch."

"That's not a badge of honor."

"I know." It was her shield, her safety net. It kept her hidden. But it was useless to try to hide things from Lexie. Utterly useless. "Fine, I do want to see him."

"Then why have you been avoiding him? Does it still bother you that he's a carpenter?"

"No. I don't know. I'm not sure." Heather peered over her shoulder to look at the man in question. Seth was still standing at the tailgate, waiting for her to get out of the car.

He was waiting. For her. Why?

Her doubts were overwhelming, keeping her from understanding the way she would have liked. "Why does he want to be with me? After what he saw. It's humiliating." Her coked up dad, her past on display. So humiliating.

"What the fuck ever. Get over yourself." Lexie had her How-Can-You-Be-So-Stupid look on her face mixed with a dose of annoyance. "Do you really think he cares? He cares about who you are now. And if it took where you came from to make you this person, then don't you think he respects that?"

"If he does, he's a better person than me." Afraid Lexie would agree if she gave her the chance, Heather changed the subject. "So is there even a PR gig?"

"Yes. You guys are talking to the kids in the Arts Program here. Seth set it up. He set it up so he could spend some time with you. You hear me?"

Heather nodded as guilt washed through her like an ice shower.

But outside her door stood warmth. All she had to do was get out of the car. She tugged her fingers through her hair. "Do I look okay?"

"You look goddamn gorgeous. As always."

"Are you sticking around?"

"Nope. I'm turning you over to the carpenter for the day. You'll have to do a paparazzi dump so they don't notice you leaving together, but I'm pretty sure Seth has something worked out."

Heather fought the urge to panic. There was so much about her life he didn't get, that he couldn't possibly understand. Like how invasive cameras could be. Could she be certain that he took the correct precautions? That no one would catch them together on film?

She wasn't sure. But she wanted to trust him, so she let herself do just that. "Okay then. Here goes nothing." Heather took another deep breath before opening the door and stepping out onto the blacktop. She crossed to Seth in three short strides.

Damn, he looked good. Better than the last time she thought he looked damn good. Was that possible? He wore jeans again, light blue this time with a dark-blue button down opened to reveal a maroon T-shirt. Memories of the sculpted body he hid under his clothes flooded her in a rush, igniting a fire in her lower belly. God, he turned her on. Turned her on and upside down and man, was it wonderful.

She gave him a weak smile, not sure how he'd receive her. "Hey."

He returned it with a sexy grin. "Hey, princess."

Her chest prickled with a mixture of warmth and guilt. She'd barely said two words to him in several days, and yet Seth looked at her with as much desire and faith as he had when they'd showered together. She didn't deserve it.

But if he was offering to continue where they left off, she wasn't willing to dissuade him. Not in the least. "Thank you." *For being here, for giving me another chance. For wanting me.* "For arranging all this."

He winked as if he understood her unspoken words. "I had help. Speaking of Lexie..." He put his hand out protectively, ushering Heather closer as Lexie pulled the car out from the parking space.

Heather shivered at Seth's hand at the small of her back as she looked after Lexie driving away. "I don't know if I should fire her or give her a raise."

Laurelin Paige

Seth rubbed a small circle on her back before he withdrew his hand. "You definitely shouldn't fire her. She's on my side."

"Then that's exactly why I should fire her." She relaxed in the easiness of their conversation. "Except you're wrong. Lexie's on my side. She helped you because she's on my side." Because Lexie knew what Heather really needed—Seth.

"I had a feeling that might be the case."

They locked eyes for a few seconds, and Heather could feel the sparkle in his baby blue's all the way down to her core. She blushed and had to look away.

Seth gestured toward a group of people Heather hadn't noticed standing by the half-broken bike rack in front of the school. "I really couldn't have done any of this without Urban Arts. They loved my idea of doing a school visit and they jumped on my suggestion to arrange for some of the stars to come."

Heather held her hands over her eyes to block out the sun and spotted a few board members she recognized from Urban Arts in the group, as well as Matt Shone.

"I only cared about getting one star in particular here," Seth said behind her, "but I didn't want it to turn into media fodder. That's why Matt and some of the UA board are here too."

Her heart buoyed, disappointed that she'd have to share her day with Seth, but grateful for his thoughtfulness at the same time. "Smart thinking."

They walked together, not outright touching but close enough that their hands brushed as they climbed the few steps toward the others waiting at the school entrance.

"Interesting choice for a first date," she said as they walked. "Tool boy."

"Oh, this is only the beginning of the date. There's some things I think you'll learn here that might make the rest of the date easier."

172

She halted. "Because the kids are poor? I get poor, Seth. You haven't figured that out yet?" Her words weren't harsh, but they weren't gentle either. She trusted him more than she trusted most people, but if he had some grand plan to make her accept her past, he needed to understand it wasn't happening.

"No, I've figured that out. What you haven't figured out is that *I* get poor."

She wanted to remark on his statement, but Janice, one of the Urban Arts Directors chose that moment to step toward them.

"Heather! Seth!" Janice shook their hands. "I'm delighted you could both be here. They're expecting us inside so if you don't mind, let's get going."

The next hour passed quickly and with little chance for Heather to interact with Seth. She tried to stay as close to him as possible as the principal gave them a tour of the school's art, music and theater rooms, pointing out how their programs had been benefitted by donations and support of Urban Arts and the 24-Hour Plays. The school certainly had more equipment and resources than the one Heather had attended. The evidence that the principal presented—statistics that showed that the arts program had increased the likelihood of students matriculating and moving on to high school—those were stats Heather was thrilled to hear. Her chest warmed at the knowledge that she'd been a small part of giving these needy children access to the arts.

The highlight of the tour came when the principal led the group to the small auditorium where the art students had gathered to hear from the celebrities. Before Heather, Seth and the others took their turns talking, a few select students performed pieces they'd prepared. Seth took a seat next to Heather who tried to display as much indifference as she could muster, secretly delighted to be able to casually knock her leg against his.

First, a trio sang for them, followed by a painter who showed off some of his best work. Finally, a spunky Latino girl named Clara delivered a monologue that she had written herself. It was funny and spirited and completely amazing.

"What did you think?" Seth whispered as the crowd applauded Clara's finish.

"She's adorable."

"I doubt she'd like being called adorable. She's eleven."

"Awesome then," Heather corrected herself. "Brilliant, amazing. Bound to go places."

"Definitely." Seth's eyes clouded as if he had a difficult point to make. "She's also from a very bad neighborhood. A bad school too. Does that mean she can never rise above?"

For half a second, Heather considered getting irritated at Seth's obvious comparison of Clara's life to her own. Then she recognized he was only trying to connect with her. It was sweet, actually.

"I get what you're doing," she said. "But, it's...it's not that simple, Seth." The honest answer was that she didn't know if Clara could rise above. Clara might never get all the places she wanted to simply because of where she came from. And if she did, she might never be able to put her past behind her. It was a sad truth. That was why Heather invested so much in the Urban Arts. So that maybe, *maybe* it would be different for girls like Clara than it had been for her.

Seth tilted his head. "I'm not saying that it's easy. I'm not even trying to prove a point or change your mind. I just wanted to know what you thought."

"I don't know what I think." She considered for a moment how tied she still was to the person she'd been half a lifetime ago. "Actually, I think it's crap. A whole bunch of crap."

One of the things Heather admired most about Urban Art's celebrity days, such as this one, was the format. Instead of forcing the actors to stand on the stage, lights shining in their eyes as they talked with the audience, Janice invited the kids to join the actors on stage in a large circle. It allowed them to talk face-to-face and heart-to-heart.

Heather, being the old pro, began the discussion. She gave her basic spiel, encouraging kids to go after their dreams, telling them that dedication and hard work were what got her where she was today. As she always did, she felt a pang of regret that she wouldn't allow herself to share all of it—that she wouldn't tell them about the poverty she came from. She knew it could inspire them. And there wasn't any media in the room with them. She could share her story without fear of it spreading.

But to speak the words aloud, to claim Dean and that life...she just couldn't do it.

Matt followed her with a similar speech. Seth was the last to talk. He surprised everyone right away by getting off his chair and sitting on the hard stage with the kids.

Heather sat forward, not knowing what to expect from her date.

"When I was growing up," Seth began. "I went to a school very much like this one. Except we had trailers outside for a lot of our classes. They had no heat in the winter and no cooler in the warm months. It's funny how the cold seems so much worse when you go to school hungry. And I went to school hungry a lot. Because my family didn't always have money for food. I bet some of you know what that's like."

A chorus of "yeah's" and "uh huh's" followed, the kids completely engaged with this big man who was comfortable enough to get down to their level.

"Being poor sucked shit." The kid's shocked ooo's alerted Seth to his mistake. "Whoops, sorry," he said looking at the principal apologetically. "I meant to say it wasn't fun. When I got to middle school and high school, things got even worse. That's when my dad went to jail and my mother had to take a second job. Without them around, I got myself into some trouble too."

A lump lodged in Heather's throat. She had suspected Seth had had it rough, had associated him with her own less-than-joyful past. But she had no idea—no idea at all that he'd experienced that kind of pain. He'd said he got it. He did.

"What did you get in trouble for?" a kid asked.

"Lots of things." Heather could sense he was trying to be evasive as well as honest. Not an easy task. "Joy riding. Messing with people's stuff."

She imagined messing with stuff was a way to say vandalism. She'd known kids like that growing up. Kids who were so enraged about their own lack of material possessions that they found solace in destroying what belonged to others. She took a deep breath, allowing her new understanding of Seth to settle through the very fiber of her being.

"What did your dad go to jail for?" This from another kid.

"Um." Seth paused, seeming to search for a way to explain to young kids. "He took things that didn't belong to him."

"He stole things," the kid said. "That musta made you sad."

"Yeah, it did. It made me very sad. But there were two things that made my days brighter: design and carpentry. We didn't have a cool Arts Program at my school like you do though. We did have a great shop. I spent all my free time there, making up new designs of things to build. Wait—there was one more thing that made me happy. Going to the movies. I couldn't afford to pay for a ticket, but there was a local theater that was easy to sneak in to."

The principal cleared her throat.

Seth caught her disapproving eye. "Which is a totally bad thing to do. Don't do that." He exchanged a guilty smile with Heather. "Anyway, I spent as much time as I could in that theater. I saw everything that came out. Sometimes I saw the same movie over and over. I started to fantasize that I could have something to do in the movies. But I had no experience acting. And I didn't know sh—I mean, I didn't know anything about directing or writing. What I did know was building. Working with my hands."

Seth met Heather's eyes briefly. She wanted to keep his gaze, but he moved his focus back to the crowd. "So the day after I graduated from high school—and let me stress the importance of graduating—stick it out, even if it's the most miserable thing you ever do. It gets better, I promise, but only if you put in the work."

Heather caught the principal's satisfied gleam.

"So the day after I graduated," Seth continued, "I hitched a ride." The principal's gleam was replaced with a cringe. "Which is another thing you should never do. Very dangerous. Anyway, I came to L.A. and I knocked on doors until I found a set design company that was willing to hire me."

"And the rest is history," Heather said softly.

"And the rest is history," he repeated. "Any questions? You in the blue."

"How long have you been working on movies?" the kid in blue asked.

"I've been here for twenty-one years now."

"You must be old." This comment came from a young girl causing all the adults to laugh, including Seth.

"Yes, I am old," he said. "And guess how many movies I've worked on?" He paused, letting the kids shout out numbers that ranged from twenty to a hundred. "Not quite that many," he said to a particularly high guess. "But over fifty. I spend almost every day on a movie set. I get to work with famous directors and actors—like Matt and Heather. My life now is nothing, *nothing* like the life I grew up with. Even though I'm not proud of where I came from, I'm proud that it didn't keep me from getting where I wanted to be."

His eyes caught Heather's, and in them she saw his desire. Not just physical desire, but desire to connect. Desire for her to understand that he really did get it. The realization stole her breath away.

"So now you build sets for movies?"

Heather didn't see where the question came from.

"Yep."

"Do you design them too?" Now she saw it was an older boy sitting in the back, the boy who had shared his artwork earlier.

"Well, um, not exactly. I started out at the bottom of the set crew. Those are the guys who do all the crap jobs like carrying the heavy stuff and putting up drywall. I kept working and I worked my way to lead carpenter—that's the boss of all the set builders. Some people can go from there to designing sets. Even, uh, even to higher jobs sometimes. Like designing the whole look of the movie from the set to the makeup to the costumes. Those people are called Art Directors or Production Designers."

Seth struggled with his speech now and Heather wondered if he was embarrassed that he hadn't achieved that level of success. Would he be less embarrassed if she wasn't there? She'd been such a snob about his career, never giving him credit that he had built it entirely out of nothing. Just like she had.

She couldn't fight the tug to validate him now. "Lead carpenters are very important on set, though. They have to be there every day, sometimes making adjustments on the fly. Like, if the director says, 'I wish there was a door here,' then the lead carpenter takes care of it. Just like that." She snapped her fingers to demonstrate.

She met his eyes again. "They're very important," she repeated, this time directed at Seth. "If you get a sliver as far in your career, you should be proud. No matter where you started from."

She recognized the words she spoke could easily be turned back on herself, and for the first time ever, she could see herself from the outside. Like she'd stepped into Dickens's *A Christmas Carol* and had been taken away by the Ghost of Christmas Present, she saw what other's saw, what Seth saw—that she'd come far, that she should be proud, that she wasn't that sixteen year-old girl from the trailer parks anymore.

It wasn't a complete transformation, but she recognized the moment for what it was—the beginning of release.

Chapter Fifteen

As the session ended and the celebrities said their goodbyes to the children, Heather felt a growing anxiousness to be alone with Seth. The principal walked the group to just inside the doors before excusing herself and Janice to discuss scholarship details. The other board members took off immediately, but Matt stood around with Heather and Seth for what seemed like a lifetime before declaring it was time for him to get going.

Finally, it was just the two of them. Seth opened his mouth to say something, but she cut in, needing to speak first. "I'm sorry I've been distant."

"You needed space." He shrugged his hands stuffed in his pockets, but the twitch in his jaw said he didn't feel that nonchalant about it.

"Maybe." She placed her hand on his arm, aware they were still in a public space, but no longer able to keep from touching him. "Maybe what I really needed was you. I missed you." Her throat tightened. "A lot."

Seth's voice was equally strained as he said, "You have no idea how much I want to crush you to me right here and show you how much I've missed you back."

She snuck a peek at the stiffening bulge in his pants. "I can guess how much."

"Yes, it's pretty evident." He grinned.

God, his grin was so sexy. Her inner thighs stiffened at the sight of it. "There's more to this date though, right?" Did she sound as eager as she felt?

"You'll get your chance to maul me later, if that's what you're asking."

Yep. She sounded eager. "The way I remember it, it will be you who mauls me."

"Oh yeah. That *is* how it goes." His eyes moved down to where her hand still rested on his arm, and she sensed he was soaking in the warmth of their subtle contact, just as she was.

With great strength, she removed her hand and stepped toward the glass doors, peering into the parking lot. "So what's your plan for getting us out of here unseen?" Cameras had been allowed in for their tour, but had been kicked out for the discussion. She expected they'd be outside now, waiting for the stars to emerge. Now that Matt had left, she was the lone star they'd be waiting for.

"Oh yeah. It's simple." He joined her looking out. "There's a hidden area over behind the school, a little over a half mile away. You can drive to it by following that road over there." Seth pointed to the road that went around the back of the grounds. "I'll jog down there and you can drive my truck over and pick me up. No one will see. Especially since there's hardly any press out there."

Heather's spine went rigid. "I can't do that."

"Why not?"

"I can't drive your truck."

"Sure you can." He pulled the keys out of his pocket and dangled them in front of her. "It's an automatic. Easy to drive."

"No, it's not that. It's just..." God, this was embarrassing. She licked her lips, hoping to add moisture to her suddenly dry mouth. "Seth, I can't drive."

"Like, at all?"

Seriously embarrassing. "Nope."

Seth laughed, incredulity lighting his features. "How do you not know how to drive?"

She crossed her arms over her chest. "It's not as strange as you're making it out. I was kicked out of my home before I got my license. Not that we had a car I could have driven anyway. Then I never had the opportunity or the money. When I could afford it, I just hired an assistant to drive me."

"Wow." He'd stopped laughing now. "Well, this sucks."

"I'm sorry."

"No, I'm sorry. I should have asked Lexie."

But really, why would he have asked? Didn't everyone know how to drive? It wasn't his fault. She was the one ruining their date. "I'm a real loser, aren't I?"

Seth's eyes turned dark. "Don't ever say that, Heather. You're perfect just the way you are."

Her gut reaction was to roll her eyes and disagree profusely, but his seriousness and her recent awareness of herself caused her to pause first. "Thank you," she said after a few seconds. His brow shot up in surprise. "I'm trying to see myself the way you do. It's a new thing. We'll see how it goes."

"I like that. I bet it goes well." He stuck his keys back in his pocket. "I feel bad, though, because I don't have another plan."

Heather squinted down the road. "Look, I can walk down there and you can drive over to meet me."

"No way. You can't walk out there by yourself. If anyone's watching, it will be easy to follow you."

"There's barely anyone here." Though she could make out a TV crew in the parking lot. She couldn't see any independent photographers, at least. They could be hidden in one of the parked vans, but charity events usually only had the big media players.

Seth peered out the glass doors, his eyes resting on the TV van. "I can't let you do that. I said we'd be discreet. We'll make it happen." He pinched the bridge of his nose and Heather could tell he was trying to come up with another solution.

Out of the corner of her eye, she saw Janice leaving the principal's office. "Let's ask Janice to help us," Heather said to Seth as she waved the director over.

Heather explained their situation to Janice, leaving out the bit that she and Seth were on a date. Having worked long enough with celebrities in the Urban Arts program, Janice understood and agreed to help.

The three of them walked out together. As Seth got in the truck and pulled away, Heather stopped to answer a few questions for the cameras, hoping if she gave a little now they'd leave her alone as she and Janice drove away.

"Will they follow us?" Janice asked as they climbed into her Copper Prius.

"Not usually if it's the local news, like these trucks seem to be. It's the unmarked paparazzi that get crazy. They're the ones selling the story to the highest bidder so they try to make the story as good as possible." Heather looked over her shoulder as she put on her belt, surmising the interest of the media. The TV crew was already loading the camera in the back of the truck and the other photographers were chatting with no sign of rushing off. "I think we'll be safe."

Janice drove out of the parking lot and turned the opposite direction Seth had, making a wide circle before turning back to the road Seth had pointed out as the meeting place. They were in luck—no one followed.

It seemed like hours passed before they were parked and Heather was out of the car and stepping into the truck, waving goodbye to the Urban Arts Director.

And then she was exactly where she wanted to be. Alone with Seth.

Thank Christ that his truck had tinted windows, because the Prius wasn't even out of sight and Seth couldn't stop himself from pulling Heather across the bench and into his arms. He had to have his hands on her, couldn't spend another minute without touching her. The morning had been long and good-for-the soul but it had also been hard-on-the-dick, his desire for her a pleasant ache that never eased.

Her mouth opened in a soft gasp as he moved in on her, and he took it as an invitation for his tongue, sliding it into the moist warmth between her lips. His hand twisted in her hair as their tongues tangled around each other, teasing and tasting, stroking and sucking. His other hand palmed her breast, each squeeze eliciting a breathy moan from Heather's throat that he gladly swallowed with his kiss. Damn she was sexy. So sexy he could barely see straight. So sexy that she overwhelmed him entirely.

With unimaginable determination, he pulled away, and gazed down on her. Her face was flushed and her chest rose and fell in quick short breaths.

"Don't stop," she murmured, her eyes still pinned on his lips.

"There is nothing more that I want to do than keep kissing you, princess." His thumb traced her jawline. "But I will not be able to stop with kisses. And though fucking you in my truck sounds incredible, it's not on the agenda."

"Screw agendas."

He leaned forward to whisper in her ear. "There is screwing on the agenda." He let his teeth bite down on her sensitive lobe, his cock twitching at her sexy moan. Then he reached over her, pulled her seatbelt across her, and latched it before scooting to his place behind the wheel. "Just not here. Not yet."

She groaned. "Oh my God, I've already waited a lifetime."

Seth put the truck in drive and pulled out onto the road, glancing furtively for any stray media. "I would have come to you anytime last week. All you had to—"

"—do is ask," she finished with him. "I know, I know. I was being stupid."

He scowled at her self-admonishment.

"I'm not being hard on myself, Seth. I'm being honest. I didn't think you could handle my baggage."

"I can."

"I see that now. I'm sorry you had to go through the things you did, but I'm sort of glad too. Because I know you get it, even though I didn't give you credit. It wasn't personal. I don't ever think anyone can handle my baggage."

She turned in her seat so she could face him head on. "Which is really what I meant when I said it feels like I've waited a lifetime. I didn't just mean this week or this morning—I meant I've literally spent my whole life waiting for someone to call me out and pull me in all at the same time. Does that make any sense?"

"It does." While he relished the serious timbre of their conversation, Seth wanted their date to be fun. Heather had enough serious in her existence. "And I'm more than happy to pull out and push in whenever you need it."

She laughed a whole-hearted belly laugh that made him wish the crotch of his pants had more stretch. "That's not what I said, you perv."

"Hmm. Guess I wasn't listening close enough." He swept a look along the sides of the highway, half intent on finding a place to pull over and put sex earlier on the agenda. But he could be patient. She was worth the wait, every time. "We have a little over an hour before we get to our destination. You can pick a station if you want. Or we can talk."

"And if I ask where we're going?"

"I won't tell you."

She stuck out her lower lip in a sexy pout that brought naughty images to his mind caused him to adjust himself for the millionth time that day. *Think of puppies,* he told himself. *And nuns. Nuns with puppies.*

"And if I insist?"

"I'm pretty sure any method of persuasion you might use would be considered dangerous when I'm driving a moving vehicle."

"Then I'll just have to accept that I'm going to be surprised."

It startled him that she gave in so easily, but more than that, it pleased him that she would, again, give her trust over to him. His chest tightened at all that it implied. Even thoughts of nuns with puppies couldn't stop the warmth from spreading from his center to his outer limbs. It felt like sitting in the sun, like finishing a good workout. Like falling in love.

At the edges of the warmth, darkness threatened to cloud his spirits with a reality he didn't want to face. The truth that he had lied to her—*was lying* to her about what he did for a living. That he'd gone to great lengths to keep the truth hidden from her. It was a darkness that could end them and whatever they had together.

"I need to go over my lines for tomorrow in my head. Do you mind if I zone out over here for a bit?"

She drew him out of his momentary spiral of emotion, distracting him from the guilt of his deceit. But the sweet heated feeling remained. It was in his bones now, becoming a constant. Because of her. He needed to put the brakes on. It was too fast—he was falling too fast.

He swallowed, grateful that she couldn't read his thoughts. "Zone away." The quiet might do him good as well, might help him get hold of his feelings.

Zone out turned into softly snores within ten minutes. Seth glanced at her curled up against the door, her face pressed against the passenger window. Even in an entirely unattractive position with a bead of drool resting at the corner of her mouth, she looked beautiful. Stunning, in fact. As it happened every time he looked at her, Seth was surprised at how struck with Heather he was. Completely and entirely struck.

There wasn't any use trying to slow it down—he'd already fallen.

Which was why he had to come clean. Today. He'd tell her today, on the car ride. After she woke up.

But Heather slept the entire drive, not even waking when Seth pulled the truck into the campground he'd set up earlier that day. He couldn't tell her now. That would ruin the whole afternoon. Later, then. He'd tell her before the date was over.

Leaning over her, he kissed her forehead. "Wake up, Sleeping Beauty. We're here."

"Another princess reference?" Heather stretched and rubbed at her eyes before looking out the window. Her brows creased. "Where are we?"

Seth hadn't been sure how Heather would react to his chosen date spot, but he suspected she might be less than crazy about it. "Indylwood Camp in the San Gabriel Mountains," he said, watching her closely. "We're just below Mount Wilson."

"I'm sorry, but that means pretty much nothing to me."

"Not a camper? Why doesn't this surprise me?" He opened the door and climbed out of the truck, then walked around to Heather's door to help her down.

"Holy shit, Seth!" she exclaimed as she surveyed the campsite. He hadn't really done much—he'd pitched a tent, set up a hammock, put out camp furniture, and brought a large grill, which he'd left chained to a tree.

Her smile told him the work was worth it. "And I was complaining about being up early on our day off. What time did you have to get up to do all this?"

Seth shrugged. "Early."

"I have to say, tool boy, you give good paparazzi-free date." Her eyes scanned the tent again. "I, uh, can't sleep here. I have to be on set by seven a.m."

If he wasn't mistaken, there was disappointment in her voice. Hell if he didn't feel that way too. What sort of heaven would that be—spending all night in the outdoors with the woman that he...with Heather? It would be paradise.

But all night wasn't in the plans, not this time. "The tent isn't for sleeping."

Her mouth curled up into a sly grin. "Then what's it for?"

"What do you think?"

She blushed and he thought he might have to forgo grilling the chicken he'd brought and devour her instead. Her cheeks, her lips, so luscious and pink. She looked delicious.

He tore his eyes from her and unloaded the cooler from the back of the truck. "Are you hungry?"

"Starving."

"Good. Come. Sit." He led her to a reclining camp chair that had a footrest. It was a little cushy for his version of camping, but he'd bought it for her. Hopefully it would have more than a one-time use.

After she was comfortable, the sun to her back and a wine cooler in her hand, he started up the grill. He could feel her eyes on him as he worked. Her eyes were on *him* when around them Mother Nature displayed awe-inspiring beauty in a mixture of dark and light green foliage and a vibrant blue sky.

Maybe she didn't appreciate the outdoors like he did, but she wasn't bitching. And could he really complain if she was more interested in watching him? Wasn't he more interested in gazing at her?

"You cook?" She sounded impressed.

"I grill." From the cooler, he pulled out the chicken breast he'd marinated overnight. "That's about the extent of my cooking skills."

"Well, nobody's perfect."

"Except you."

Her grin was intoxicating. "Right. Except me."

They spent the next forty minutes in easy conversation as Seth grilled chicken and vegetables and sliced strawberries. The site didn't have a picnic table—the weather worn wood seats sucked shit as far as comfort anyway—so they sat at his camp table and enjoyed the meal.

"It's good to see you eat."

"I eat," Heather exclaimed around a mouthful of food.

"Whatever. You're skin and bones. And breasts." Beautiful full round breasts that pressed tightly against her low-cut tank top. He was having those for dessert.

"Glad you noticed." As if anyone couldn't.

She dabbed at her mouth with a napkin and sat back in her chair, her hands on her belly.

Now, he told himself. *Tell her now.* It was the perfect opportunity—the conversation had lulled, they'd been fed, they were comfortable.

But she broke the silence before he did. "So why here?"

"The mountains? I love the mountains. It's home away from home."

"I can see why. It's peaceful. That's hard to find these days." He watched as she took in her surroundings, delighted that he was the cause of her relaxed features. "And why this campground? Indylwood Trail, was it? Is it special?"

He took a swallow of his beer and stretched a leg out to tangle with hers. "That it is. First, it's not used much for camping. We'll see some hikers go by, but this camp spot is far enough away that I figured we'd get the privacy we were looking for." And they had gotten privacy, not seeing anyone since they'd arrived.

"And why else?"

He raised a questioning brow.

"You said 'first' which implies there are other reasons."

"There is. One other reason, anyway." He reached over and grabbed her hand, then pulled her into his lap. With his face pressed next to hers and his arms wrapped around her, he pointed in the distance. "See that tree line over there? It borders private land—some of the only private land you can find up here since the National Forest owns most of it. I'd love to buy a piece of it someday, build a cabin that overlooks the river."

"Why don't you do it?" He felt her wince after she said it, probably realizing that a lead carpenter didn't make that kind of money.

But I'm not really a carpenter, I'm a Production Designer. He imagined himself saying it, telling her at that moment, the words on the tip of his tongue. He'd tell her that money wasn't the issue.

Except when he opened his mouth, nothing came out.

He chickened out and instead focused on her question—why didn't he buy the land? He'd dreamed and planned building on Mount Wilson for years. More than once, he'd gathered the money and the papers he needed to make the purchase, but he always stopped before going through with the deal. It wasn't that he doubted the decision, though owning a cabin in the San Gabriel Mountains was a definite risk. Fires spread easily through the area and finding someone willing to insure any buildings was near impossible.

That wasn't what made Seth hesitate. If his cabin burned down, he'd just rebuild it. It would be awful, but not devastating. No, the thing that halted him every time was the dream was missing a crucial element—a companion. That was why the closest he'd ever come to buying the land was when he was with Erica. Then, after she left... He didn't want to build a cabin only to spend time alone in the beautiful mountains. What was the point? He wanted someone who would want to stay there with him, who would have input on his design, where the bathrooms should go and how big the closets needed to be. He wanted to sit on his own back porch with a woman he loved and look out over the grounds while their children played hide and seek in the forest brush. Without the woman, the dream was meaningless.

But right at that moment, his usual reluctance was absent. Perhaps it was because he realized he was getting older. Time was slipping by and if he wanted to have a cabin built while he was still young enough to have kids, he should get working on it.

Or perhaps it was because for the first time since Erica left, he actually thought he might have found the type of woman he wanted to build a cabin with. Not the type of woman, but *the* woman.

"I will do it," Seth said. "Someday." Maybe someday soon.

"I bet you will." She settled into him, and he breathed in her orange scent mixed with the piney fragrance of the outdoors. "I can imagine it—a haven just outside the city. No fans, no cameras. I don't know why I never thought of spending time up here."

"Because there's also no running hot water."

She jabbed her elbow playfully into his ribs. "Whatever."

He grabbed her hands, holding them so she couldn't jab him again. She struggled, giggling, trying to free herself. But she was no match for his strength. She gave up, relaxing her head back onto his shoulder and sighed.

He kissed along her neck, and she rolled her head to open up for him as if she wanted his mouth on her as much as he did.

"Your cabin will have hot water though. I hope I still know you when you build it. I'd love to visit."

An unexpected weight dropped into his stomach at the thought of her not being around. It was that weight, that

191

heaviness that prevented him from telling her his secret. Because he wasn't ready to lose her and his truth might alienate her completely.

He knew then that he wouldn't tell her. Not that day, anyway. He needed more time. He needed to be sure she felt the same way about him as he did about her. Then he could tell her.

Brushing his nose against her jaw, he said, "You better still know me when I build that cabin. I'm getting awfully attached."

She twisted her head to face him. "Are you really?"

"I am. Really."

She turned more into him and he released her so she could cup his face. "I've gotten attached to you too." It was a whisper, barely a spark of confidence behind it, but it only took a spark to start a fire. He'd take it. If that was all she ever had to offer, he'd take it.

He leaned in to claim her mouth, the plump lips that had teased him all afternoon. Just before his mouth met hers, she said, "Even though you made me rough it today."

"Oh, princess, you haven't seen rough yet."

Then he showed her rough, crushing her to him and burrowing his tongue into her mouth. He loved the feel of her tongue gliding against his. He captured it, sucking before he bit into the tender skin. She mewled and the sexy sound fueled his desire. Taking her face in his hands, he kissed her with the intensity he planned to use when he buried his cock inside her later. Soon. Real soon at the rate that he was thickening and hardening below.

Heather twisted in his lap to straddle him and ground her pelvis into his crotch, pressing her tits into his chest. She was not helping the situation. He needed more of her. Now.

Moving his arms to cradle her ass, he stood. Without missing a beat, she wrapped her legs around him. Jesus, she fit him perfectly, lining up with him just so. He could fuck her like this, moving up against a tree or his truck when his legs weakened.

But it was midday and she was a celebrity and even though they'd seen no one so far, that could change at any moment. He carried her instead toward the tent, not breaking their kiss until they reached the opening. With reluctance, he set her down and held open the flap for her.

"Get in." His voice was strained—almost as strained as his pants.

She bent over to crawl in and he couldn't resist swatting her lovely behind as she did. She let out a shriek, and his cock leapt. Then he was inside with her, flattening her into the sleeping bags he'd rolled out for comfort—minimal comfort that it was on the lumpy ground.

Heather didn't seem to mind, rolling around as she wrestled with him to remove his shirt. It was a battle since his hands were intent on staying where they were—one pulling through her hair, the other clasping her breast. After a few minutes of struggle, he pulled away with a frustrated groan.

"Get naked," he commanded.

He loved how she obeyed him, stripping without any delay. He removed his clothes faster than she, so he watched her, stroking his length while he did. It wasn't that he needed to fluff—he was already hard as stone—but seeing her undress was such a big fucking turn-on, he couldn't keep his hands off himself. Especially when her eyes clouded with lust as he moved his grasp up and down, up and down.

But it wasn't enough. He needed her. Needed inside her. Needed to taste her.

"Kneel," he commanded next. She did, and he lay on his back in front of her, his head facing up at her gorgeous round tits. In a fluid movement, he pulled her over him until her head hovered over his pelvis, and spread her thighs with his hands so that her opening was at his mouth. He circled her clit with his nose and inhaled. Fuck, she smelled delicious—musky and sexy and wet for him.

With one long swipe of his tongue, he covered her slit from one end to the other. She moaned and he did it again. Reaching his hands up to grab her ass, he stroked her and laved her with his tongue. He clutched his fingers into her skin to hold her in place as she twitched above him, continuing his assault with fierce tenacity.

But then her lips were on him—on his cock—and his rhythm faltered as she assumed her own movement sucking up and down his length, her breasts bouncing against his abdomen. Holy shit, her mouth felt like stepping into a hot tub, so good and too much all at once. He couldn't remember the last time he'd sixty-nine'd with someone. Why didn't he do this more often? It was so...so...amazing.

It was also so hard to keep focused. And each pass of her tongue brought him closer to climax which he was determined to do inside her, and not inside her mouth.

Summoning to mind nuns and puppies, he renewed his attack. He brought a hand down to finger-fuck her as he licked and swirled his tongue around her bud. With his other hand, he swatted her ass, not able to get quite the smack he'd like at that angle, but certain he marked her just the same.

She cried and twitched and he could feel her tightening around his fingers. Another smack and she was there, shuddering over him, spilling over his hand, crying out as she came and came and came.

Now it would be his turn.

He flipped her over, her body still quaking, and aligned his form with hers. Grabbing her ankles, he bent her legs up, spreading her open as he did. Then he drove in, impaling her deeply. Without pause, he pulled out and rocked into her again, his thrusts assuming a vigorous tempo. His muscles began to tense, and his vision darkened when he felt her clenching around him, signaling she was coming a second time.

He joined her, spots of white light sparking before his eyes as his climax ripped through him. When he could think again, he realized he still had a vise-grip on her ankles. He released her, rubbing the indentations he'd left on her skin. "Jesus, did I hurt you?"

"Nope. Not in the least," she purred. She tugged at his arm, urging him to the ground next to her. He lay down beside her and she curled into him.

It felt good. Damn good, lying with her pressed against his chest, her sweat mixed with his, their labored breathing the only sound. He stroked her hair, taking it all in—every scent, every sensation, absorbing it into every fiber of his being, letting it hold him in a state of dreamlike peace.

"I was such a bitch."

He waded back into consciousness, his brow furrowing as he struggled to pinpoint what Heather was talking about. "When?"

"Always. Since you met me."

He chuckled. "I haven't been that nice myself."

"But I was..." She drew her fingers randomly along his chest as if searching for her words. "I was truly horrible. The way I treated you...why did you put up with me?"

Seth thought a minute, remembering the beautiful flash of vulnerability he'd seen in her, how he wanted to see more of it, how he sensed it was something to be treasured. And damn, had he been right. But how could he ever explain how he knew that back then?

He circled his nose in her hair. "Have you ever heard sculptor's talk about the art that was hiding in the block of clay?"

She nodded against his chest.

"It's the same with wood. When the pieces are lying there spread apart, I can see what they can become—something completely different yet totally the same. The thing they want to be. Don't ask me how, but just like that, I could see it for you. I could see what you wanted to be."

"What was that?"

"Loved."

Chapter Sixteen

Heather pressed on the gas pedal, heading the truck toward the rear of the empty parking lot. Though she'd never had a real interest in learning to drive, she'd adored the three weeks of lessons Seth had given her, and not just because it meant spending time with him—sneaking off together almost every day to a nearby church lot after shoot. The rush of picking up speed, of having utter control of a vehicle was incredible.

She'd also discovered driving was a good way to blow off steam when she'd had a long day or when she needed to relax, like tonight when she was anxious about her Jenna Markham interview the next day. If she did drugs, she'd guess she'd been high when she agreed to do the damn thing. It wasn't drugs—it was Seth.

"Now, ease on the brakes." He sat next to her, his knee bouncing with obvious anxiety.

She threw her foot on the brake pedal, her head lashing forward from the sudden stop.

"Ease! I said ease!" He shot his hand out to brace himself on the dash. "You'd think you'd have that down by now."

"Come on, my way is more fun." The best part of their lessons was messing with Seth, who seemed to find her preferred method of driving quite stressful.

"It's more like a roller coaster ride, yes, but that doesn't necessarily make it more fun."

"Are you sure? Let's find out. Hold on!" With a saucy grin, she turned the truck toward the center of the empty lot. Gaining speed, she did her best attempt at a donut. "Woo hoo!"

Seth curled his fingers into her thigh, his other hand still gripping the dashboard. "What are you...? Heather! Oh, my God, you're going to kill us. Heather, stop!"

She slammed her foot on the brake again, not because she didn't know how to slow down, but because she enjoyed seeing Seth's pained expression.

"Okay, I can't take this anymore. We're done for the day. Trade me places."

"Killjoy." Heather put the truck in park, turned off the car, and scooted out from under the wheel. She inched her dress up so she could move over Seth, who sat in the middle of the bench. Instead of continuing over him, she twisted to straddle him and stayed.

"Whatcha doin?" he asked, his hands already finding their way to her ass.

"It seems my teacher's a little stressed." She ran her hands down his arms, thrilling in the feel of the tight muscles poking out underneath the sleeves of his T-shirt. "Maybe I can help him relax."

"Hmm, hard to say since you're the reason he needs to relax." He ran his fingers up and down her back in delicious random strokes. "I'm surprised you aren't stressed, what with your big interview tomorrow and all."

Heather was definitely nervous about the Jenna Markham interview. She'd turned down the request so many times that when Lexie finally told them yes on Heather's behalf, Jenna's people had to call back and make sure it was legit. It had been a pretty big change of heart. Before she'd met Seth, Heather would never have considered spilling her guts to Jenna on national television. Now, she was okay with the whole idea. More than okay—she was actually looking forward to it.

"The Jenna Markham thing? Piece of cake."

"Well, then, if you're stress-free, maybe you can help me join you."

She smiled then leaned in to claim his mouth, letting her smile disappear into his. She started the kiss soft and sweet, gently grazing his lips before she let her tongue tango with his, building into a fire that spread through her chest right down to her center.

God, she loved kissing him.

Loved.

That word. Seth had said she wanted to be loved. She hadn't stopped thinking about it in the three weeks that had followed their camp date. The three *glorious* weeks that had followed. They had spent every free moment together on set, and though no one said anything, their affair wasn't a secret from the cast and crew. Good thing everyone had non-disclosure contracts, otherwise Seth and Heather would be plastered all over the gossip mags by now.

They were careful off set, always leaving separately, meeting up in private locations. The lot where they practiced driving was always empty. Seth hadn't been to her house and she hadn't been to his, still spending their nights apart for fear of a paparazzi bust. Instead, her trailer had become their love nest. There were as many of his possessions there as hers, his clothes littered the bedroom floor, his body wash hung in the bathroom caddy. She would live there with him if she could. Holed up with all she ever needed—a kitchen, a bed, and Seth. As it was, they were always the last to leave the lot at night.

It wasn't lost on her that she'd spent her entire adult life running from the trailer she grew up in and now the trailer was her favorite place to be. Ironic and absolutely fine.

And through all their time together—through every shared shower and lunchtime delight—Seth's word had clung to her. *Loved.* She wanted to be *loved.*

It wasn't untrue—in fact, it was maybe the truest thing anyone had ever said about her.

But there was so much that was left unsaid, questions that Seth's comment had sparked. Was he saying he loved her? Or that he could love her? Or that he wanted to do the action of loving, which didn't necessarily mean the feeling of loving? Or did he simply mean he knew she wanted to be loved?

He hadn't brought it up again, and she didn't try to either. Mostly because before she could address it, she'd have to figure out what she wanted him to mean. More than that, she'd have to figure out how she felt about him.

And that was a mystery she hadn't yet solved. Not entirely.

She felt things for him, things that weren't just sexual. She'd gotten past his lack of status and he no longer reminded her of her own history. And the rough sex—she was getting used to that too. Craved it, in fact. Couldn't wait to be manhandled and played with, even when they'd just gone at it.

But there was still something that held her back from saying the "L" word. She suspected that something had to do with how she felt about herself. How could she love another person when she couldn't love herself? It was a familiar notion, trite even, but that didn't keep it from holding weight. Before she could move on with Seth, she'd have to let go. The surprising thing—the amazing, wonderful, magical thing—was that for the first time ever, Seth made her feel like she could let go. Truly and completely.

She was ready.

And her next-day interview with Jenna was the perfect opportunity to both let go and move on. It was time.

But first, she had to get her brave on and ask Seth the question she'd been avoiding.

After one last sweet sweep of his lips with her tongue, Heather put her hands on his shoulders and pushed back. She took a moment to gaze at him, struck not for the first time by how good-looking he was. She reached for his face and rubbed her thumb across his jaw, scruffy from the long day.

He covered her hand with his. "What's going on in that pretty head? I can hear the wheels turning."

She brushed her teeth across her lip. "I was just trying to figure out what we're doing."

"Well, you were learning to drive, and I was teaching you. Which wasn't going so hot. Now we're making out. And that's going real hot."

"That's not what I meant." She laughed. "I meant, what are we doing?" Her voice lost its volume, not of her own accord. "You and me. Together."

"Oh. Yeah. I wondered when this conversation would come up." His eyes remained on hers, which was both reassuring and unnerving.

She grabbed a handful of his shirt in each fist, needing a place to channel her nervousness. "It might have come up sooner, but usually another thing comes up and talking gets postponed."

"That other thing is threatening to come up now too."

Heather followed his eyes down to his crotch, where she already felt movement.

"Down boy, down," he said.

"Soon, I promise." Though she was tempted to forget the talking this time too. Seth's dick was quite a distraction.

Peeling her eyes and her mind away from his growing erection, Heather returned her stare to his face. "So? Thoughts?"

Seth sank into the seat and moved his hands to run them up and down her bare thighs. When he spoke, it was slowly and with caution. "I think we're more than just sex. Don't you?"

In contrast, her response was quick. "Yep. Definitely." Her eyes flicked back to his stiffy. "Though the sex is really, really awesome."

"Yes. It is."

"But there is more to us." She bit her lip again. "Right?"

"I let you drive my truck. Nobody drives my truck. No matter how good they are in bed."

"That does imply a certain level of fondness for me." His hands on her thighs...they were doing crazy things to her. She had to regroup or the conversation would be lost in physical connection. "So then what are we?"

His hands paused. "Are you asking if I'm your boyfriend?"

"Actually, I was asking if I'm your girlfriend."

He cocked his head. "I'd like to think you are." He cleared his throat. "I do think you are. I have for a while. But I know that you're wary about these things. I don't take what you've already given me for granted."

I do think you are. It was hard to concentrate on everything he'd said after that; she was so giddy by his simple declaration. What had he said? Something about taking it slow for her? "I appreciate that. That you've put up with my need to go slow." *Wary*, he'd said. "And I am wary. Because of what the media will turn it in to. What they'll say about us. But lately, I don't really give a shit. They could say whatever they want about me and you—it doesn't matter. And I...enjoy you so much, I want to tell everyone." The words tumbled out. She couldn't have stopped them if she'd wanted to, and she didn't want to.

His brows rose, and if she wasn't mistaken, he'd stiffened. "You want to go public about us?"

He wasn't ready. She'd thought he would be just because she was, but maybe she'd misjudged. "I was thinking maybe. Yeah. In my interview with Jenna Markham tomorrow. Maybe that's stupid? I'm sorry, I guess I assumed that you would want that, but I don't want to—"

He cut her off with a finger to her lips. "Heather. Stop it. I didn't say no."

"So what do you think?"

His hand trailed down her throat, caressing her skin. "I could think of worse things than being paired with a beautiful and talented movie star."

She let out the breath she'd been holding, elated by his response, yet still mindful of what she was asking. "You can't take this lightly. This would be huge."

"I know."

"The press can be really uncool. They seriously encroach upon your life."

"I get it. I've thought about it already."

"You have?"

"I have. How could I not? I'm with you all the time. I see it from the sidelines. It's brutal, I can tell. I hate that you go through it alone. I'd be honored to share that spotlight with you." He stretched forward to rub his nose against hers. "But mostly, just because I want to be everywhere with you. And if that means I have to put up with a bunch of dickwads with cameras and gossip mouths, then so be it."

"That's really nice of you."

"Yeah, you're supposed to do nice things like that for your girlfriend."

"Girlfriend." A lovely thrill ran through her veins at the word.

Seth leaned back. "Are we too old to be saying girlfriend/boyfriend? Because I am thirty-eight, you know."

"I'm still twenty-nine, so we're good." Wait, she should probably tell her boyfriend her real age. Though she'd never told Collin her real age. Then again, she and Collin were never that serious, and Seth...Seth was different.

"Damn, I'm robbing the cradle," he said.

Covering her face with her hand, she said more to herself than to him, "It's not a good idea to start an official relationship with a lie."

Seth tensed. "What did you say?"

She couldn't believe she was doing this. She never told anyone her real age. "I'm not really twenty-nine. I'm thirty-three."

"What?"

"Twenty-nine is what's on my resume. Thirty-three, according to my birth certificate."

He relaxed and laughed a wonderful sexy laugh that made her thighs tickle. "My girlfriend lies about her age? That's great."

"Girlfriend." Was it possible she'd never tire of that word? Just hearing Seth say it made her girl parts squeeze with need. "I really like the sound of that."

"Me too."

"I mean, really, really." In the small cab of the truck, she could smell her desire. "Like, I have to have you. Like now." She sat forward and began kissing up his neck and underneath his jaw. And could she help it if her pelvis was suddenly twitchy, causing her to wriggle on his lap?

"I can't argue with that." She felt him grow harder underneath her, but he didn't kiss her back. And he was still talking. "But, Heather, before you go public about us, I have to...we have to talk."

"Um hmm."

He grabbed her face between his hands and waited until she looked up from under her heavy lids. "I mean it. We have some things that need to be said."

"Fine. Whatever." She was sure she knew what he wanted to talk about—the details of how their relationship would work in front of the media. It wouldn't be easy, and talking about it more was a good idea. "But not now. Now I want you."

He considered for a moment. "Okay." He sounded resigned. "Get off me so I can drive us someplace."

"No." She dug her nails through his shirt, into his chest. "I want you here. Now."

"Are you sure?"

Heather saw the desire in his eyes. She knew his hesitation was about her. "Right here, right now."

"It's not quite dark yet. Someone could—"

"I don't care. Fuck me."

"Well, damn. I can't argue with that proposition." He took her then—fiercely—stealing her breath as he licked into her mouth and sucked at her lips.

Heather closed her eyes, happy to let Seth take over, his body telling her what to do and how to feel. It never ceased to amaze her how freeing it was to become a slave to him, to give in completely, to surrender to his love. Perfection.

His hands reached to the straps of her dress and tugged them down her arms. They broke their embrace just long enough for her to slip free, the material at her torso falling below her breasts.

"Lean back," he told her now. "Put your elbows on the dashboard."

She did as he told, shaking with anticipation as she rested against the dash.

"Good girl." He pulled the cups of her bra down underneath her breasts, exposing her already alert nipples. He licked his lips and she longed for him to put his mouth on her to tug and bite as he liked to. But he didn't, not yet.

He sat back and made a sound of approval. "You're so goddamn gorgeous like that. Your tits on display just for me. One day I'm going to put you in handcuffs so I can spend all the time I want on those tits and you won't be able to do a damn thing about it except moan and come."

Fuck, when he talked dirty to her she was a goner. And handcuffed? She'd sign up for that in a heartbeat. "I own a pair."

Laurelin Paige

"You do?" His hands crept under her dress, his eyes locked on hers.

"They're fur-lined." She twitched as his touch reached the thin crotch of her thong. "They were supposed to be my prop at the plays. I left them in the car that night." His fingers slipped under the material, finding her tender skin. "Ah! Hence why I needed your drill." Her speech was breathy and likely incoherent. She had no idea why she was even attempting conversation.

"Oh, yeah, I remember now. We'll put them to use." His thumb settled into rubbing a circular pattern on her clit. Without removing his hand, he leaned forward and took a breast into his mouth, tugging with his teeth. "And what about now?" he asked, briefly releasing her nipple. "Do you still need my drill?" He resumed his play, moving his free hand up to squeeze her other breast as he sucked and bit the one already in his mouth.

A fleeting thought of being really impressed by his extraordinary hand and mouth coordination was buried by the more urgent need to have him between her legs. "If you mean do I need your cock, then yes, I do." And oh, did she. Was there a word that meant needier than need? Because whatever that word was, that was how much she needed him.

"Ask for it."

And now he wanted her to talk more? "Seth, I need you." She shifted her weight to lift a hand to his hair, an awkward move with her body still braced against the dash and her pussy going crazy from his ministrations. "I need your cock," she panted. "I need your mouth. I need you."

"Ask." He increased the pressure on her clit and relaxed the sucking, a combination that threatened to throw her over the edge.

"Please, Seth. Please. God, I'm about to come."

"Wait." Seth released her abruptly and sank into the back of the bench, leaving a cold emptiness in the places he'd been touching her. "I want to come with you." His hands fumbled with his jeans. Then he wriggled them down enough to release his cock. It sprang out of his denim prison, hard and long. She could see it throb as he put a hand around her to pull her closer, his other hand returning to her crotch to move the fabric away from her opening.

He tucked the tip of himself inside her and brought her upper body toward him so their mouths were only separated by a few centimeters. "Come with me," he said.

She nodded weakly and he plunged in. In, in, so far in. Sitting on top of him, straddling him like she was, she could feel him so entirely, feel him so deeply as he moved inside her. She moaned, already close to orgasm. She could go now, before he even pulled back out.

But he'd asked her to come with him and though she could probably come now *and* again with him, she accepted the challenge to wait. For all the time he'd spent waiting for her to get her shit together, she could wait for him this once.

Seth controlled the activity, even with Heather on top. He placed a strong hand on each side of her hips and brought her body up and down on his cock. She helped as much as she could, as much as he'd let her—pushing up with her thigh muscles which were already quivering from the effort it took to keep from releasing before he was ready.

He'd be there soon, she was certain. His tempo was at once brisk, his pelvis pumping into her at rapid fire, his expression strained with intense focus. It was hot and so erotic to be face to face with him, to watch him work so hard for this thing he desired—this thing that was her, this thing that would be shared just between them. The connection between them at that moment, it was nearly too much.

She was done for.

Her orgasm overtook her slowly, starting with the clenching of her thighs and ass, then spread down her legs like a gathering storm until it reached her feet. Then her toes were curling and she was screaming, screaming his name, falling limply into his arms.

And while she did, while her skin and bones disintegrated into a blaze of heat and combustion, Seth came with her. His moans became a poetic harmony to her screams, his taut muscles a perfect brace for her languid body, his touch a salve for her burning skin.

She recovered slowly, her head buried in his chest where the thud of his heartbeat and the rhythm of his breathing synchronized with her own. She felt unspoken words between them—things they both needed to say but seemed trite after the poignancy of what had already been said with their lips, their bodies.

I love you.

Those were her unspoken words. They were on the tip of her tongue, itching to be voiced, the only urge left in the wake of her post-orgasm. It wasn't time yet, though. One more thing she had to do first—the interview. Then. Then she could move on. Then there would be time for all the *I love yous*.

Maybe even a lifetime of them.

Chapter Seventeen

He had to tell her. Today. Had to tell her that he wasn't just a carpenter, that he'd reached the top of his career ladder. That he was a Production Designer, that he'd lied and tricked her. God, he was such an asshole.

He should have told her last night, had tried to, but then gave in to her passion. Could anyone really blame him? Sex in his truck was hot.

Then after their tryst, he couldn't find the words. He'd spent himself in her and he didn't want to destroy the afterglow with his confession. He was filled with excuses, he heard them in his head and recognized them for what they were. No more of them. He'd tell her. As soon as he saw her again. Tell first, sex later. If there'd be sex after he told her remained to be seen.

No, he couldn't think like that. She had to forgive him...right? He wished he could be sure.

He tossed and turned through the night, trying to decide what he'd say, how he'd explain his deceit. When the sun came up the next day, he still had nothing except bleary eyes from lack of sleep. Well, bleary eyes and a semi because he always had at least a semi when he thought about Heather.

He rolled out of bed early for a run, hoping it would focus his thoughts before he got ready to meet up with Heather. They had the day off from filming, but she had invited him to her house for her big Jenna Markham interview. Just thinking about the interview made his heart pound. She planned to tell Jenna about Seth—about her and Seth. Which was awesome and terrifying all at once. It was a lot—going to Heather's house for the first time, announcing that they were an item, and on top of that, planning to drop the bomb that he'd lied to her for weeks. Not good timing. He should have told her earlier.

But he hadn't.

Now he couldn't wait. Once his name was out in the world, someone would discover his resume. That would definitely not be the best way for Heather to find out.

He had to be the one to tell her. Before the interview.

After a quick shower, he dressed in khaki slacks and a dark blue button down shirt, then downed two cups of coffee in succession before shooting Heather a text asking if he could come over early.

"*Come now,*" was her reply.

He dismissed the automatic "*That's what she said,*" response, which he would have given if there wasn't so much weighing on his mind, and sent, "*On my way,*" instead.

It wasn't hard to find her house. He'd known where she lived for a while, even though he'd never been there. The drive was at least thirty minutes from his place in Hollywood Hills if he could manage to avoid traffic. Which he didn't.

Almost an hour and a half later, Seth pulled into the drive outside her home. The house was ridiculous, especially for a woman living alone, though compared to the nearby Bel Air houses, Heather's seemed fairly modest.

It took a lengthy self-pep-talk before Seth could get out of the truck. What the fuck was he pussying out about anyway? He'd done something shitty and now he needed to come clean. *Take your lumps like a man,* he said to himself. He'd do it as soon as he saw her. Do it quick like ripping off a band-aid.

After working through his hesitation, he headed up the front pathway and rang the bell. When the door opened, he expected to see Heather, or at the very least Lexie. Instead, he was greeted by a bald guy wearing a headset.

"Is Heather...around?" Seth knew he had the right house. He had to have a code to get past the front gate and the one she had given him had worked.

The bald guy creased his brows. "Yeah, is she expecting you?"

Fuck, he didn't want to explain himself to some strange dude—a muscular Seal look-alike who'd answered his girlfriend's door, no less.

But Seth decided not to let himself get all prickly. He obviously had no idea what the situation was.

Teeth gritted, he forced a smile and held out his hand in greeting. "She is expecting me. Seth Rafferty."

Seal ignored Seth's outstretched hand and pushed a button on his headset. "Seth Rafferty's at the door." He paused. "Yep." He turned back to Seth. "You're cool."

"I know I am. And who are you?" But the dude was already heading deeper into the house.

Seth shut the front door and followed suit, his eyes widening at the marble entryway and grand staircase as he passed by them. The place seemed much more pretentious than the Heather he'd known and grown to, well, care for, but she'd also changed a lot in the several weeks since they'd met. This house was a hundred miles from the world she came from, the same world he'd come from. Like her, he'd also crawled out of the ditch, but he'd never felt the need to run as far as she did, to put so much distance between himself and his roots. Her ostentatious crib reminded him how full of self-loathing Heather had been. Had he been the sole reason for the change? He hoped what he had to tell her didn't affect how much she'd grown.

He followed after the Seal wannabe through a great room and to an outdoor patio where a whole lot of hustle and bustle was occurring. Seal began helping a group place bright lights around the area, a boom operator appeared to be setting mic levels, a cameraman was cleaning his lenses—it was as if he'd walked onto a film set.

It took him a minute to find Heather in the midst of the hubbub. She sat in a director's style chair, her eyes closed and her chin tilted up as a makeup artist powdered her face.

Damn. This was the interview crew. He hadn't gotten there early enough.

Seth looked at his watch. It wasn't even ten yet and he'd been under the impression the crew was arriving at eleven. There went his chance of talking to her before she went on-film. *Damn, damn, damn.*

Heather spotted him the minute she opened her eyes, as if she were drawn to him like a magnet. Her face brightened with a gorgeous smile. "Seth!"

He made his way to her. "I didn't realize they'd be here already."

"They got here early. Right after you texted. Which is fine. I was a mess waiting for them anyway. I did want to spend time with you beforehand. And we never got a chance to talk. I know you wanted to last night and now it's crazy here."

From her babble he could tell she was nervous. Or excited. Or both. It was adorable. His gut twisted again with the guilt of his lie.

She took his hand in hers. "Do you want to slip away for a few minutes?"

He paused. He needed to talk to her, but this was an important moment. He couldn't upset her right before she went on film. "You can't do that."

"Actually, I can. They can't do anything without me. Part of the perks of being the star."

"I imagine that is." He cherished that even though she'd become more grounded since they'd met, she still had a good amount of diva inside. He wouldn't have it any other way—that was who she was, and a part of him longed to take her up on her offer to escape, not to tell her the truth, but to fool around before she had to be onscreen.

Probably not a good idea.

"No, don't worry about me. We can talk later. You need to focus."

Seth turned to find a much-too-skinny middle-aged brunette standing next to them and holding a clipboard, apparently waiting for their conversation to wrap up.

"Hi, I'm Myrna, Jenna's assistant," the skinny woman said. "Sorry to interrupt, but I need to prep Ms. Wainwright." Her expression said that she was anything but sorry.

"I'll join you for this." Lexie appeared out of nowhere at his other side.

Seth looked to Heather, who nodded reassuringly. "I'm fine."

"Then I'll just be over there." He pointed vaguely to the area behind them. "Out of the way. Call me if you need me."

Finding an out of the way place proved harder than he'd thought. Everywhere Seth tried to stand, he was in the pathway of someone trying to hang a light or run an electrical cord. Eventually, he secured a spot on a garden wall that was close enough to watch what was going on yet far enough away to not be a hindrance.

On the sidelines, time seemed to drag. Myrna "prepped" Heather for ages with Lexie at her side. It drove him crazy. His leg wouldn't stop twitching and if he had long fingernails, he was certain he'd have chewed them all off by now, no matter how much it made him look like a little girl.

Man, what was his problem? He'd been on a thousand sets—this was no different.

Except that his job was always off camera, and even though his face wouldn't be on camera this time either, his name would be. Then he'd be on cameras all the time, everywhere he went with Heather, whenever a fan held up his iPhone or a photographer wanted a "Day in the Life" pic.

The idea of instant stardom didn't bother him that much. It would be different, definitely would take some getting used to. But no big deal. What bothered him was what he knew the media would find out about him. Thank God he didn't have a bunch of secrets he was hiding. Just the one, but it was a big one. He was ready to spill it as soon as he was alone with Heather, which wouldn't be until this whole circus was over. So if the prep time could hurry up and finish and the stupid interview could just start, then the sooner the whole thing would be over with and he and Heather could move on once and for all.

Funny how he'd lost Erica because of lying, and now he was worried about losing Heather for lying again. Somewhere, there should have been a lesson in that.

After about a lifetime, Myrna finally appeared satisfied with Heather and her answers. Then the makeup artist returned to freshen up the star. Then Lexie returned to lean over Heather, and from the looks of it, prep her in an entirely different way than Myrna had. Unable to make out what they were saying, Seth crept closer.

"I can still tell her it's an off-limit subject," he heard Lexie saying when he was near enough.

Heather shook her head. "She wouldn't go for it. Jenna demands full access. Besides, I want to talk about it."

He guessed they were talking about him, about coming out about their relationship. It made sense that Lexie would want to make sure Heather was okay with it. Hearing about Jenna's full access demands, though, made him worry Heather had been pressured. Was she announcing he was her boyfriend simply because this snooty reporter expected it?

Lexie didn't seem to think so—or if she did, it didn't bother her. "I don't know what you did with Heather Wainwright, but I'm starting to like this imposter."

"Oh, don't patronize me."

"That's my job." Lexie adjusted Heather's hair to fall gracefully on her shoulder. "Now, sit up straight. Don't chew on your finger. Or say 'um' too much. And an occasional smile wouldn't hurt."

"Oh my God. This isn't my first interview." Seth could feel Heather's eye roll, even though Lexie hid her face from his view.

"It's your first Jenna Markham interview. She's brutal. She makes everyone cry."

"She's not going to make me cry."

Lexie took a step back and crossed her arms. "Are you sure about that?"

"No." Heather bit her lip. "But I'll be okay if I do."

Crying? What kind of an interview was this supposed to be? Each second of this prep conversation was making him uneasy, and this wasn't even the real deal.

He took a step toward them, coming into Heather's view, needing to assure for himself that Heather was going to be okay.

"Seth!"

"Hey, princess." He took her hand, pulling her to stand near him. "Are you good? Do you need me to do something?"

"No, I'm good. I really am. You look a little lost though. Are you all right with all of this?"

"Yeah, yeah, I'm good." Her hand was sweating within his. Or his was sweating. Hell, he was sweating everywhere. "I'm kind of nervous," he admitted, though she had to see it already. "How do you do this over and over again? It's insane!"

She took his other hand in hers and squeezed both of them. "You get used to it after a while." She laughed. "What am

I saying? I'm totally nervous too. Like, so nervous. It isn't usually like this at all. This is more preparation for an interview than I've ever had. It's crazy!"

For half a second he wondered if she was just saying that to make him feel better, but one look in her eyes and he knew what she said was true. "Well, be reassured that I'm right there with you."

She smiled. A stupid, silly grin that made his groin pull. "I'm going to mention you when she asks me about the 24-Hour Plays. I'll tell her we met then." She let out a deep breath. "Are you okay with this? I could back out. I mean, I don't have to mention you at all. Unless you want me to."

He pulled her close enough to lean his forehead on hers. "I want you to. You know that." Then he remembered her conversation with Lexie. "Are you sure *you* want to? You aren't just doing this because you think you have to, are you?"

"No!" She pulled away so she could wrap her hands around his neck and meet his eyes. "I'm doing this interview because I want to talk. About you. About me. I'm excited about it. *And* I'm a mess of nerves."

There was something else he was worried about, and didn't know quite how to say it. It wouldn't have been an issue if he'd gotten to talk to her alone before the interview, but he hadn't so he had to find the words. "Heather, would you mind not...would you mind not mentioning what I do?"

"Oh, baby, are you embarrassed?"

He wanted to laugh. He wasn't at all embarrassed. He was worried she'd look like a fool when she wrongly declared that Seth Rafferty was a carpenter on national television.

"I'm not. But I don't want it to turn into that—that I'm using you for your money, all that. The media will find out soon enough. It won't bother me when they do. But we don't have to make their job any easier."

"Good point. It doesn't matter to me anyway. What you do. Not anymore. Since it doesn't matter, there's no need to mention it."

Damn, he wanted to take her away from this insane scenario and make love to her for hours. He'd wanted so much to hear those words from her, and now she'd said them at a time when he could do little to cherish them.

He was still soaking it in when Heather was called to her place. She pulled her phone out of her bra where she'd been keeping it and handed it to him. "Can you keep this for me? You are staying to watch, right?" she asked.

He took her phone from her hand and stuck it in his pocket. "That's why I'm here, remember?"

"Good. Thank you. I know it probably seems weird, but it means a lot to me that you're here. I wouldn't be able to do this without you."

"It means a lot to me that you would say that." His eyes skimmed down to her lips. "Will I mess up your makeup if I kiss you?"

"Who the hell cares?"

She initiated the kiss, placing her lips gently on his. Despite her blasé attitude, the kiss was chaste, but the sweetness of it tugged at his heart.

He pulled her into a hug. "You'll be amazing, Heather," he said into her ear. "Have I told you I believe in you? Because I do."

"No, you haven't. But I know." She kissed his neck before pulling out of his arms. "I think you're crazy, but I know."

"Crazy about you."

"Aww." It was half appreciation, half groan. Maybe more than half groan.

"Too cheesy?"

"Pretty much." She put her thumbs up. "But it's good. I like it. Bring on the cheese."

217

An assistant led Heather to her seat, but it was another twenty minutes before they were ready to shoot. Only then did Jenna Markham make her first appearance since Seth had arrived, having spent all the prep time in Heather's guesthouse. If Seth had to guess, he'd say Jenna was in her late fifties. She wore a cream skirt and jacket, a nice contrast to her perfectly coifed brunette hair. She looked good next to Heather, sitting in one of the armchairs the crew had brought out to the deck. Heather's light blue dress with cream trim seemed to match the older woman's. With as much fuss and detail as had gone into the event, it wouldn't surprise him if they had been coordinated.

Seth bit back a laugh. He knew that Heather was known as the diva of Hollywood and that Jenna would most likely highlight that in her interview. But within seconds, it was obvious that the diva on set was Jenna. Not only had her grip of assistants done her job while she sat back in an out-of-the-way location for the entirety of the morning, but once she'd appeared, it seemed the crew forgot all about Heather and focused every bit of energy on Jenna.

Appropriate, he supposed, seeing how Jenna was their boss. Still, it made him tense, feeling as though his girlfriend had been left to the wolf in pretty clothing.

It only took an hour for Seth to be able to attempt looking relaxed. After ninety minutes, he actually began to feel relaxed. So far, the questions had been fairly routine. Jenna had asked about Heather's career, starting from her earliest jobs to her more significant works. Perhaps her preparation offset was more essential than Seth first thought. She was laid back with her approach, often stopping between questions to talk to Heather candidly before going back into interviewer mode. With so many breaks, no wonder it took several hours of footage to get a decent fifteen-minute piece.

After two hours, a catering crew arrived to serve lunch. Jenna again disappeared into the guesthouse so Seth and

Heather joined Lexie at a table near the pool. Even though everything seemed to be going well, Seth could hardly eat. Jenna hadn't asked about him yet, and he knew that she was planning to. He noticed Heather barely touched her meal as well.

It was after lunch that the interview really took off. Jenna's questions became more pointed and direct, less the standard variety. Each new word out of her mouth made his chest tighten and his body go more rigid as she asked Heather about her diva reputation, her ex-boyfriend Collin, and about rumors of other affairs.

Then the conversation turned to Heather's charity involvements, and Seth stopped breathing altogether.

"You've done a lot of work with the Urban Arts Foundation," Jenna said.

Half of her questions weren't even really questions, but statements that elicited a response from Heather. It was quite crafty.

"Mostly the 24-Hour Play Events," Heather said. "But I've done a lot of school visits as well."

"Why this group? What is it about Urban Arts that you're attracted to?"

Seth leaned forward in the director's chair that he'd commandeered once filming began. He sat where Heather could look over at him if she needed to, though she'd kept her eyes off him most of the interview. Now her eyes flicked to him and he suddenly realized that Jenna's question could lead to Heather's past as easily as it could lead to him.

"Well." Heather's eyes returned to her host. "They're a fantastic organization. Their goal is to keep arts in schools and bring arts to schools that can't afford it. The people who are involved are the most generous, giving, dedicated people I've ever met."

Seth had to cover his mouth to suppress his sigh. Heather had successfully escaped having to talk about her life growing up. Lexie surely must have given Jenna guidelines about what was and wasn't off-limits. Not that he'd mind if Heather did talk about her past, but he didn't think she was ready for that. Not quite.

"Sounds like there might be someone special in the bunch?"

Here it was—the moment when she'd mention him. God, he was almost giddy.

"There is someone special. Seth Rafferty." She smiled and he melted.

Melted? Dude, what was going on with him?

Whatever it was, it was pretty fuckin' perfect.

"Is Seth your..."

"Boyfriend," Heather finished for her. "We've been seeing each other, um, well, since the plays in L.A." She paused. Then with a deep breath, she sat up straight. "But he's not the reason I've been so dedicated to the foundation."

The hairs on his arms stood up as he suddenly understood what Heather had planned, why she'd agreed to this interview. It wasn't for him.

"What is that reason then, Heather?"

It wasn't for him and that made him damn ecstatic.

"Because those kids—those kids who only survive their poverty because they've got something good to look forward to. I get those kids."

Seth closed his eyes so he could hear her next words without any visual distractions. So he could savor them with her.

"I was one of them."

Chapter Eighteen

There it was. She'd said it. It was out there for the world to know now.

And it totally felt good.

They'd planned it, of course. Jenna Markham wouldn't allow an interview without hitting all the hard topics, and Heather knew that going in. But she'd wanted to talk about her past. Was finally *ready*.

"Your father," Jenna said now in that compassionate tone she put on for deep subjects. Man, the way she played the emotions, she could have been an actress herself. "He was a recovering coke addict."

Heather let out a *pfft*—half sigh, half laugh. "He was never recovering. Recovering implies he was trying to get better. He never tried to get better. Anytime he was clean, it was just because he hadn't landed the next score yet."

"And your mother?"

She shrugged. "Drunk usually. Daddy was more functional than her. I don't know what was worse. At least I knew what to expect from Mama. I didn't know what version of my father I'd get from one minute until the next."

Heather hadn't prepared any of her answers—she'd tried, but thinking about it beforehand made her edgy. Instead, she'd decided to go with the flow. She was surprised at how easily her words came. That wasn't to say that talking about her family was a picnic. It was more like throwing up—it felt terrible while you were retching, but afterward, you felt kind of good.

"Did he hit you?"

Memories of slaps and shoves ran through her mind in a flash. "Not...um, sometimes. Not on a regular basis. Not like I feel like I was an abused child." Most of her father's hits had been when he was jonesing, when he hadn't had a hit in days. When he was desperate. She just happened to be in the way.

"You didn't feel abused," Jenna said, her words slow and drawn out. "Weren't you, though? Abused and neglected by the people who were supposed to care for you?"

Damn it. Jenna *was* going to make her cry. "Yes, I guess I was."

"And now? Are you close to your parents now?"

Hell no. "I'm not."

"Do you wish you were?"

Hell no times ten. "No." She paused, deciding how honest she wanted to be. What was that they said about no guts, no glory? Well, she'd already had a lot of glory. Maybe it was time for the guts. "I wish they weren't around at all. I wish they didn't know how to find me. I wish they were dead." She choked on the last word, but didn't regret it. It was honest. It was real.

"Why is that?"

Heather shook her head, unable to speak.

"Why have you kept your family hidden from the media?"

Tears burned at the corners of her eyes. "Because I was ashamed." Then the tears were streaming down her cheeks. "I'm ashamed of them. I'm ashamed of me."

The next several questions were a blur. Heather knew Jenna asked stuff and that she'd said stuff, but the specifics weren't clear. It didn't really matter anymore. The point was that her biggest secret was out and she was fine. Better than fine. She no longer had to fear the press finding out. Her father couldn't swindle money out of her. His threats wouldn't hold water anymore.

She was finally free.

It was evening before the catering had been cleared and the crew had packed up and left. Then another good part of an hour before Lexie said her goodnights, leaving Seth and Heather alone at last.

Heather stood at the front door after Lexie left for several seconds, her back to Seth. She suddenly felt oddly nervous and needed a moment to gather herself. Actually, she felt like she needed several moments, but with the weight of his eyes on her back she had to take what she could get.

With a deep breath, she spun around, a smile on her face. "What an insane day. I can't believe it's finally over." Why were her hands so sweaty? The interview was done. She should be calm now.

"Thank God." Seth seemed apprehensive too. He stood several feet away, his hands in his pockets as he rocked back and forth on his heels.

"I guess it's not really over though, is it? This is just the beginning. I mean, the interview doesn't air for almost two weeks. That means no one will even know about any of that stuff until then. Not about my past or my dad. Or us. Unless it gets leaked or they use certain promo clips." She knew she was babbling. She did that when she got nervous. It was easier than focusing on whatever it was that she was anxious about.

"Heather?"

"Or if someone that was here today talks. I don't care, really. I just want to be prepared. And if you and I are already hanging out, the press will start talking about us because they'll see us together."

"Heather?"

Oh shit, maybe he wanted to wait. "Unless you want to stay on the down-low until the interview releases. I don't know which is better. What do you think? Because I don't want to hide anymore, do you?"

"No." His voice had finality to it. "I don't want to hide anymore."

"Then we just go out and about and let it happen then. And my dad—well, I can't worry about that. But, shit, he's going to be mad when he sees it."

"Heather?"

She met his eyes. "What?"

"You were amazing."

With those three simple words, she understood why she'd been fretting. She hadn't known what Seth thought about her interview. She hadn't even asked his opinion about spilling her life beforehand, she just did it. Now she wanted—*needed*—his validation. "Was I really okay?"

"You were. You planned that?"

She nodded weakly, her voice too tight to respond.

"I'm..." He took a step toward her and she could see his Adam's apple bobble as he swallowed. "Is it patronizing to say I'm proud?"

"No."

He smiled. "I'm very proud then."

Goose bumps skidded along her arms. She was naked now, she realized. Not literally, but more naked than she'd ever been before. Without the wall built up around her, he could see right into her. "I did it for you," she whispered.

"I...I never asked for that."

"That's not what I meant." So much for feeling like he could read her now. Apparently, explanations were still needed. That was fine because she wanted to tell him how she felt. "I meant you gave me the strength to do it and...and the desire to do it. For the first time ever, I wanted to move on. So I could move on with you."

"Oh, princess." He took another step toward her then stopped, his face hardening. "We...I need to say something."

"Okay." He opened his mouth but she spoke again before he could. "I love you."

"I...what?"

"I love you." She couldn't stop herself. The words ran out of her mouth as though they'd been let out of a cage. The last unspoken phrase between them. "I wanted to tell you before, but I had to let go of everything from the past before I could say anything. I needed to know nothing was holding me back because I want my *I love you* to mean something. I want it to mean we have a chance at something real—maybe the first real thing I've ever had. A chance at a future. That's what my *I love you* means. I love you."

"Heather..." Seth blinked. "I..."

Even his stammering didn't bother her. He might not feel the same, but she didn't regret saying it. "I'm sorry I interrupted. I know you had something else to say and I don't mean to highjack this conversation or pressure you. You don't have to say it back. You've just been so transparent with me from the beginning and I've been anything but. Now I can be as honest as you. And I honestly love you."

She wiped at the tears that had appeared out of nowhere. Crying again? She was such a baby. Well, she could either let this be awkward or she could move things along. "Now, what were you going to say?"

"I...." His eyes were pinned on hers, searching. Then his features softened. "I was just going to say, I love you too."

She was in his arms so fast she wasn't sure who moved to whom. Their mouths found each other instantly, like they were tuned into each other, and their kiss was at once deep and urgent. Though she loved being lip-locked with him, this kiss was meant as a gateway to more fulfilling passions—desires that already pulsed in her lower regions with heavy need.

She moved closer, trying to ease her ache by grinding against the bulge in Seth's pants. Desperate for him, her mind started plotting a location. The bedroom was too far, the stairs would be uncomfortable. There was a marble column to the side of them—could they fuck there, standing up?

Seth's passion matched hers. His hands unzipped the back of her dress, then traveled down to her ass where he fondled her thong-bare cheeks. "I need to be inside you." His voice was husky against her lips, eliciting a pool of want at her core.

She set her eye on the column and tried to press him in that direction. Then without warning, he lifted her and tossed her like a sack of potatoes over his shoulder.

"Seth!" she shrieked. "Put me down!"

"No way." He began up the staircase. "Bedroom?" It was more of a grunt than a question.

"Turn left." Then, when he started to turn right, she said, "Your other left!"

She was a thin woman, but still his ability to carry her, up a staircase no less, hit all her hot buttons. Of course, she was already turned on to no end. Being carried was just extra fuel to her already stoked fire.

Swinging her torso to try to see around Seth, she directed him toward her room. "The double doors." Deftly, he opened a door with one hand and made his way through the spacious room to the king size bed.

Instead of simply setting her on the ground, he threw her into the middle of the bed. A fit of giggles threatened to overtake her, but then she looked up at Seth, who had already toed off his shoes and was now pulling the belt from his pants. His eyes showed no humor at all. They were completely glazed with lust and something else—love. Yes, that was what was different. His whole face, eager with raw desire, also glowed with an affection she hadn't seen before. Maybe she just hadn't been looking hard enough. It was definitely there, and she imagined it mirrored her own expression.

"Take off the dress." His low tone vibrated through her thighs as he unfastened his pants.

God, what his commands did to her. Besides increasing her arousal to astronomic heights, it pleased her to obey. She scrambled to her knees and slipped the dress over her head before tossing it to the ground.

Seth took in her near-naked body with a hungry stare. He stepped toward her and with one hand, unhooked the front clasp of her bra, letting out a pleased groan as her breasts spilled from captivity. He bent to nibble at one, taking her nipple into his mouth and sucking it to attention. He repeated his ardor on the other breast, her soft moans seeming to stir him on.

Too soon, he pulled away. His eyes still fixed on her, he lifted his shirt over his head and stepped out of his pants, leaving both in a heap on her floor.

Heather's mouth watered at the sight of his erection straining against his boxer briefs, the tip peeking out above the band. She watched, enraptured, as he rubbed his hand up and down his bulge before removing his underwear. Then there was his naked cock. Her eyes widened with eagerness.

But she didn't have long to gaze at his bounty before he was directing her again. "On your hands and knees."

She complied, sticking her fanny up in the air. Maybe he didn't have it in mind to spank her but she wanted to give him the signal that she did.

He chuckled. "Such a tease."

She peered back at him over her shoulder and fluttered her eyelashes. "It's not a tease if I plan to let you have it."

"If you let me have it? Don't you mean, if I let *you* have it?"

"Whichever." She circled her butt in front of him, eager for his touch. "Just have at it already!"

The weight of the bed depressed as he climbed up to his knees behind her, pulled down her thong, and threw it aside.

227

Then he placed his hands on her rump, sending electric sparks directly to her pussy. Warmth spread through her body as he kneaded his fingers deeply into her tight muscles—who knew that an ass could get so tense? She relaxed under his touch, moaning as he continued his massage.

His first strike came without warning followed by another round of massage. The sting of pain followed by the intense pleasure drove her mad. She was so wet she wouldn't be surprised if she were dripping.

The next hit was on the other cheek. She gasped as he struck her, and he echoed her with a groan. This time, his massage took him past the curve of her ass to the place she wanted him most. She bucked into his hand as he slid several fingers into her hole at once. There, there. That was what she needed. More, though. Much more.

She rocked back and forth, trying to manipulate his stroke to ease her need—a need that could only be fulfilled with his cock. So focused on his attention to her pussy, she wasn't prepared when his other hand struck her rear again. The combination of two erotic zones being pleasured/pained at once was almost too much to handle. She felt herself climbing that wall, nearing the top where she'd fall over into cataclysmic orgasm.

Then he stretched his thumb up to rub at her clit. He struck her rear again, and over she went. White light streaked across her vision as her entire body exploded, her arms and legs shaking with the force of her release. No longer able to hold her weight, she collapsed on the bed.

Her vision hadn't returned before Seth flipped her over and settled between her spread thighs. Anchoring his fingers in her hair, he entered her with a solid thrust.

Still numb, Heather felt the gathering tightness in her belly. God, she couldn't come again. Not yet. But he nudged her thighs back, angling her so that he touched a spot—*the* spot—that drove her crazy. Soon the tightness was spreading and

Seth's strokes deepened and his hands pulled tighter in her hair and everywhere her nerves were alight.

He captured her lips for a probing kiss, then pulled back. "Look at me."

She opened her eyes and met his.

"I love you, Heather Wainwright." His words were strained and spaced between thrusts. "No matter what happens. Everything I've done since I've met you has been for you."

She blinked, her eyes growing heavy with her orgasm just at bay. Though she couldn't fully comprehend his meaning, she could feel the intensity. Could feel the importance.

"Did you hear me?" he grunted, and she could tell he was close to release.

"Yes," she managed.

"Good." His tempo increased and it was only a handful of thrusts before she was clenching around him and he followed with his own release.

Seth rolled off her and gathered her into his arms. He showered kisses on her face as their breathing returned to normal. It was sweet—the kind of adoration she had realized was not really her style. But in his embrace, it felt wonderful. Maybe she had just needed to find the right guy. And that was Seth—the right guy in every way.

She lifted her face to meet his eyes. So many things she could say to him, so many ways she could say them. She wouldn't mind if she spent forever trying to say it all.

For now, she turned her body into his and said the words that seemed most appropriate for the moment. "Again, please."

Seth lost count of how many orgasms passed between the two of them before they finally settled, worn out, in each other's arms. It was the first time that their fucking had been something deeper. It had been making love. He winced at the

229

term. She'd turned him into such a big ass pussy. And he didn't even care.

The night would have been perfect if there still wasn't that one last brick in the wall between them—*his* brick. His lie. He'd wanted to tell her, again had tried. But she'd confessed her love and he was lost. Lost in his own love for her.

He pulled her tighter to him, clutching to her.

She snuggled into his body. "What time are you on set tomorrow?" Heather's voice was weary, her eyes already closed.

He stroked his hand through her hair. "Ten. You?"

"Eleven. Will you stay here tonight?"

He chuckled. "All you had to do was ask." Though he had no intention of leaving now, not just because it was the middle of the night, but because he wouldn't leave her until she kicked him out.

She nuzzled deeper into his chest with an incomprehensive murmur. It was only a few minutes before her soft snores tickled his skin.

Seth waited until her breathing suggested she was in a deep sleep. Then he slipped his arm out from under her and got out of bed. He found his phone as well as hers in his discarded pants. After setting his alarm to wake him up at seven, he threw both phones on the nightstand. Seven was earlier than he needed to be up to get to the set on time, but he couldn't leave until he told Heather the truth and he had no idea how much time that would take. What he hoped was that he'd tell her and she'd be fine, that they'd laugh about it even. After that, they could spend the rest of the morning fooling around or making love or whatever it was called.

That was what he hoped anyway.

But after having been left by a woman once before because of his lies, he knew that scenario might be overly optimistic.

Still, he had to believe it wasn't.

He climbed back into bed and spooned himself around Heather's sleeping form. There would be a lot on the line in the morning. Tomorrow, he could lose it all.

Tonight, though, he had everything.

Chapter Nineteen

Heather was vaguely aware of buzzing. Then movement. Then the buzzing stopped so she buried her head in her pillow and slipped back into sleep.

What felt like only seconds later, the buzzing returned. Except this time it wasn't buzzing, it was something else. It stopped before she could wake up enough to interpret the sound. Then it started again and she recognized it as her phone's ringtone.

She reached for her nightstand, searching for her cell with her eyes still closed. By the time she'd located it, the ringing had stopped. Then it started again.

Without glancing at the Caller ID, Heather knew it was Lexie. Who else would be such a pain in the ass at God knows what time of the morning? She pushed the button to answer and put the phone to her face. "What?"

"Turn on Channel Four."

"I'm sleeping." *Sleeping with Seth,* she remembered. She rolled over to cuddle with him while her annoying assistant continued to chatter on the other end of the line.

"Wake up and turn on Channel Four."

But Heather only rolled into empty bed. She opened her eyes. Yep, no Seth. She strained for a moment and realized the shower was running in the bathroom. Good, he was still there. "What time is it, anyway?"

"A little past seven." Behind Lexie's voice, Heather could hear what sounded like a television. "Now turn on the TV."

Heather didn't know if she was more annoyed with being wakened so early by Lexie or with not being wakened by Seth. Was he planning to sneak out while she still slept? He still had hours until his call time.

She sat up and rubbed her hand over her face. "Can't you just tell me about whatever it is you want me to know?" *So that I can get off the damn phone and surprise Seth in the shower?*

"Heather, get the fuck up and turn on Channel Four! That TMI show is doing a segment on you."

With a sigh, Heather stretched to rummage through her nightstand drawer for the remote. "Shows do segments on me all the time. What's so special about this one?"

"Just turn it on!"

"I am. I am." She pressed the power button and scrolled through the guide until she found Channel Four. "How do you know what they're going to say, anyway?"

"They did a lead in. It said, 'Coming up next,' blah, blah, blah and all this stuff about your family."

Someone on the crew must have leaked the interview. Maybe even on purpose to build up interest. Whatever. She expected it. "People are going to be talking about my family, Lex. I didn't think so soon, but—"

"That's not what I want you to hear. Wait, shut up." Lexie paused. "It's on now. Do you have it on?"

"Yes, I have it on." A publicity picture of her filled the television screen behind a familiar entertainment reporter. "I just have to turn up the sound." She pushed the volume button up and threw the remote on the bed next to her.

"*—tells us that Heather Wainwright gave Jenna Markham a tell-all exclusive that actually tells all,*" the interviewer was saying. "*In the upcoming interview airing on this station at the beginning of the month, the star opens up about her life growing up, her abusive parents, and about ending her long-time relationship with Collin Satchel...*"

Heather heard the shower turn off. So much for joining Seth. She sighed into the phone. "I told you I don't give a shit about this, Lex—"

"Shh!"

"But not all of Heather's secrets are heartbreaking." Heather's picture was replaced with a candid picture of her and Seth at her house from the day before, probably taken on someone's smartphone during lunch. *"Seems she has a new man in her life. Hollywood Production Designer, Seth Rafferty, is the guy on her arm and our source says the couple is a very happy couple indeed."*

Heather's brow creased. "Why did they say he was a Production Designer?"

"They said it in the lead-in too. He never told you he was a P.D.?"

"He's not a Production Designer. He's a carpenter."

"Are you sure?" Lexie asked softly.

Despite Lexie's gentle tone, Heather was getting irritated. "Of course I'm sure. He's not a P.D., Lex." She rubbed her forehead trying to think. God, she needed coffee. There was an obvious explanation for the report and she wasn't getting it because she wasn't quite awake.

The network had probably just made a mistake. That was it. "They got it wrong, Lex. In the interview. You know how the media can mess facts up."

"I looked him up, Heather. While I was calling you. He's listed on IMDb as S. Patrick Rafferty. He hasn't done any carpenter stuff for years. He's been doing P.D. work for a long time now."

Heather shook her head, confused. "But why..."

"Heather—"

She looked up at the sound of her name to see Seth standing next to the bed, hair dripping wet and a towel wrapped around his waist.

"Heather," he said again. "I can explain."

"Lexie, I'll talk to you later." Heather hung up before Lexie could respond.

Seth took a step toward her. "I was going to tell you."

"Tell me what?" She drew the sheet up over her naked breasts. For some reason, she felt the need to hide. "Did you...did you get offered a job as a P.D.?"

"No." He took another cautious step toward her. "I...I've been a Production Designer since I've met you."

Her brows furrowed. "I don't understand."

"I can explain," he said again.

"Then start explaining. Please."

Seth tightened the towel at his waist. "I haven't been honest with you, Heather." Normally, she would be beyond excited to see him standing in her bedroom wet and near naked. Now, it felt awkward. She wished he were dressed. He shifted his weight and she suspected he felt the same.

"You haven't been honest..." she prodded.

"And I'm so, so very sorry. I didn't set out to lie. You assumed I was a carpenter and you were so turned off by that and I was so proud of where I came from so I decided not to correct you. Then it snowballed and I actively had to lie to keep it up. By the time I realized I had to tell you the truth, I couldn't find the words or the right timing no matter how many times I tried."

Her mouth went dry. His monologue hadn't been that long, but Heather felt overwhelmed by the information. She couldn't be hearing what she thought she was hearing. It was a misunderstanding. Clearing her throat, she clung to what she knew as truth. "But you're a carpenter on *Girl Fight*."

"I am. I used to be a carpenter. I pulled strings with a friend to get that job. To be near you." He met her eyes. "I did it for you, don't you see?"

"No, I don't see." Although, she actually *was* beginning to see. She sat forward, pulling the sheet even higher. "So you're saying that you're not really a carpenter? That you've been a P.D. this whole time?"

"Yes."

"And you pretended to be a carpenter because you...you what?" Rage seeped into her now and showed itself in her tight voice. "You wanted to put me in my place?"

"No." He looked away. "Not exactly."

"Then you *pulled strings* to work with me? In a job you don't even do? That's not just creepy, Seth, it's sick."

"Heather—" He took another step toward her.

"Don't!" Heather scrambled out of the opposite side of the bed, taking the sheet with her. What the fuck had just happened? She'd spent the most amazing night ever with the man she loved—*loved*—and now she'd found out that their whole relationship was based on a sham.

She paced as her mind sorted through the last few weeks, piecing together holes in conversations, realizing the full extent of his lie. Was this really happening? Had she really opened up for him? "I trusted you," she said, her voice breaking. "I gave you all of me. I made myself vulnerable. For you."

"I know."

"And you lied to me!" Angry tears burned her eyes. "No, this is bigger than lied—you deceived me. You *betrayed* me. You convinced me to be honest about everything I am while you were actively lying to me? You fucked me over, Seth!"

"I'm sorry you feel that way."

"Sorry I feel that way?" As if he didn't think she had a right to feel exactly the way she was feeling. "I let you in, asshole. I don't let anyone in. I let you in and you betrayed me!"

"I understand why you're upset, but—"

"This isn't upset, Seth. This is beyond anything even close to upset. I...I can't even look at you right now." She turned

236

away from him, so furious, so hurt, she didn't know what to do with herself, with him.

"Come on, Heather." She hadn't heard him come up behind her until his arms were around her and his voice was at her ear.

A part of her—a big part of her—wanted to fall into his embrace, to let him love the pain away.

But how could he love the pain away when he was the cause? She struggled to get out of his arms, one hand still holding tightly to her sheet. "Let go of me!"

She managed to slip free of his hold, but he grabbed her by the arm and pulled her back toward him. Facing her, he clutched at her elbows. "We can work this out. Give me a chance. Give us a chance."

Heather continued to fight, putting all her resentment into the battle. Surrendering her hold on the sheet, she pounded at his naked chest. "Let me go! Let me go, you fucking asshole!" Tears poured down her cheeks, blurring her vision.

Seth held her firmly, taking her assault as though he barely felt it. "Heather, I love you. You love me."

She continued hitting him as well as she could with him restraining her. It was no use, though. He was stronger than she was and he'd hold her as long as he wanted. Exhausted and overcome with gut-wrenching sobs, she collapsed against his chest.

Seth wrapped his arms around her whispering apologies and *I love yous* that she didn't fully register. It was as if she'd put up a shield of armor and everything he said bounced off her and fell away like her tears.

She let him hold her while she cried out the worst of it. Eventually her peripheral mind realized they were both naked, Seth having lost his towel in the struggle. Wasn't there some rule about fighting naked because you can't stay angry then?

But though Seth was naked, she was still angry. Still very angry. Very angry and very hurt.

With a new rush of fury, she pushed him away. "Get your hands off of me!" she screamed.

Startled, Seth let go. When he reached for her again, she shouted, "Don't touch me! Don't you dare touch me ever again. Get out." She darted past him and gathered his clothes from the floor where he'd left them the night before. "Get out of my house." She threw his phone and clothes at him, aiming his shoes at him with force, hoping the impact would hurt. "I don't want to see you. Ever!"

Seth caught his shoes, which only fueled her rage.

"Get out!"

"Okay!" He put his hands up as if in surrender. "Okay, I'm leaving. I'm leaving."

He gathered his clothes and walked out of her room, still naked. She watched after him as long as she could before her vision clouded with a new set of tears and her voice became too choked to call him back.

This wasn't over. Seth wasn't giving up on her. He'd fucked up, big, and he'd known his deceit might lose her. But he wasn't ready to let his stupidity wreck them for good. Not after all they'd shared. Not after he knew she loved him.

Seth dressed quickly in the hallway outside Heather's room to the sound of her sobs. It took all his strength not to run back to her, take her in his arms and make her believe how sorry he was. He wanted nothing more than to soothe her through her pain, the pain that he'd caused.

But he'd come to know her well enough to know she needed time to think before she could listen to him. He'd give her that, if that was what she needed. Then he'd fight. It was the mistake he'd made with Erica—he'd let her leave. Not this time. Not with Heather.

He considered calling in sick to the set. He certainly felt sick—his head pounded and his gut twisted so tight he thought he might puke. But that wasn't professional. And he wanted to be near Heather, in case she decided she was ready to talk to him.

So after stopping by his house for a change of clothes, he drove to the studio. He flashed his ID to the security guard and parked his truck, then headed toward the set to check-in with the Assistant Director, ignoring every instinct that wanted to turn him toward Heather's trailer instead.

Time, he reminded himself. She needed time. He'd give her a day. Maybe two. If she still avoided his calls tomorrow, then he'd go to her.

So wrapped up in his regrets, Seth didn't notice Joe Piedman until he'd practically knocked into him.

"Joe. I didn't know you'd be on set today." Most of Joe's work was already done in the planning and design. He rarely showed up on the lot. It was odd.

Odder still was that he was with the asshole producer, Brandon, who had wanted to maul Seth's girlfriend when he was finished with her.

Girlfriend? Not anymore. The knot in his stomach tightened. Maybe not a good time to think about that.

Seth nodded stiffly at the producer. "Brandon."

"Seth."

Joe gave an awkward smile. "Seth, can I talk to you a minute?"

"Uh, sure." Yeah, something strange was definitely going on. The vibe was completely off.

Joe called over to the director, who was going over notes with a stand-in. "Don, we're going to use your trailer. Brandon, I got this."

Nothing good ever came from being summoned to the director's trailer with your boss, who was also your friend. Had something gone wrong with the set crew? Had Seth fucked up somehow? Again?

Once inside Don's trailer, Joe gestured for Seth to take a seat at the table. Seth sat and Joe took the seat across from him.

After a deep breath, Joe said, "Seth, this is really hard for me to do, and believe me I wish I didn't have to. Please know that this is in no way a reflection of your work." He paused.

"Just say it." Seth was eager to get the shit over with.

"We've had a request that you no longer work on this movie."

Seth ran his hands through his hair as his heart plummeted to his stomach. "Are you fucking kidding me?"

"I'm afraid not."

"There's only a week left of shoot. She couldn't deal with me for one damn week?"

"I'm sorry." Joe looked about as bad as Seth felt. Which was pretty shitty.

He knew Heather wouldn't want to see him, but he never thought she would go to those lengths to keep him away. Playing the movie star card...it was disgusting. The producers would bow to her demands. They had no choice. They couldn't do the movie without her, but him—he was nothing.

He wanted to laugh. All the time he spent proving to her that he was worth something even though he was "just a carpenter" and now she'd proved exactly the opposite.

"So you know who the request is from?"

Seth leaned his elbows on the table and covered his eyes with his hands. "Yes."

What did he expect? She was mad. She was hurt. This was the way she knew to retaliate. God, though, if she was this upset, did he even have a chance?

240

He slammed his palm on the table. "Fuck!"

Joe didn't flinch at Seth's outburst. "What happened?"

"Honestly? I fell in love."

"With an actress? That's always dangerous territory."

"Tell me about it. But I'm the one who fucked it up. Big time." He let out a gruff laugh. "I can't believe she won't even give me a chance." It was an immature move on her part, especially since it affected more than just him.

Suddenly, guilt hit him as hard as his earlier frustration. "Look, Joe, I'm sorry. I'm truly sorry. I know this puts you in a bind. I can get you a replacement by this afternoon if you need one."

"That would be really great if you could."

"It won't be a problem. Again, I'm sorry. She shouldn't have let the movie suffer because I was an idiot."

Joe shrugged. "She doesn't have a diva reputation for nothing. You know we have to keep the stars happy."

Seth bit back his desire to defend Heather. "I get it. It's fine. I'll get on that replacement. Are we done here then?"

"Except I have to give you this." Joe dug into his jacket pocket and pulled out an envelope. "Your final paycheck."

"Of course." Seth stood as he took it. "Thanks, Joe. I appreciate that you let me on the show in the first place."

"Anytime you want to be my carpenter, the job is yours."

"Ha, thanks. But I think I'm going to be happiest getting back to my old job." Seth folded up the envelope, stuffed it in his back pocket and left the trailer.

He was surprised to see Brandon waiting for him. Or disappointed. Rather than deal with him, Seth walked past him without so much as a nod.

Brandon followed him. "So you and Heather are done then?"

"Shut the fuck up, Brandon." Jesus, he had to deal with this shithead too?

"What? I'm just stating the obvious."

Seth stopped walking and spun to face the other man. "Why? So you can rub it in my face or because you're planning on making her your conquest? If it's that last thing, trust me, you don't have a chance."

Brandon's grin could be described as nothing but smarmy. "Are you sure about that? She got with you and she thought she was slumming."

"I don't have to listen to this." He turned away again.

"I know her type, Seth," Brandon called after him. "They'll spread their legs for anyone who treats them like royalty. Not only do I know I can get her in bed, but I'll bet it will be cake."

Seth spun around and grabbed Brandon by the lapels. Pinning him against the outside of some random star's trailer, Seth got in his face. "Don't you fuckin' even think about laying a hand on her, Brandon, or I swear to God, I'll make you live to regret it."

Brandon shook under Seth's grasp, and there was no mistaking the look of fear on his face. "Get your hands off me, Seth."

Seth held him a few seconds longer. Then he released him—not because he didn't think he couldn't punch the living daylights out of the asshole, but because he didn't have the energy to deal with such an insignificant prick.

Once Brandon was out of Seth's grasp, he seemed to get his balls back. "Don't think I don't have power in this town, Seth. I can fuck you over in a heartbeat. How easy will it be to get a job after I have you dragged off this set by security?"

"Don't bother. I'm leaving." He didn't need Brandon to fuck him over too. He'd already fucked himself pretty damn good on his own.

Once in his truck, Seth didn't leave right away. Instead, he waited until he saw the familiar BMW hybrid pull up. Lexie saw him almost at once and tossed him a glance that seemed to say, *hold on a minute.*

He watched as Lexie escorted Heather out of the car. Heather wore oversized sunglasses, but he knew they hid red, puffy eyes. Another wave of regret rolled through him like nausea and he was almost glad when the object of his affection had walked out of sight.

As he'd hoped, Lexie came back alone shortly after. He pushed the button for the power window to move down as she approached.

"Seth, she doesn't want to see you. I'll make sure you get anything you left in the trailer, but I can't let you in there yourself."

"I know. I was actually looking for you."

Her brow arched. "For me?"

"I figure you're the only one who can tell me what I can do to fix this."

She crossed her arms over her chest and looked absently into the distance. "I'm not sure if you can. You screwed up pretty bad."

"I know." His knuckles turned white as his hands clutched the steering wheel, even though the car wasn't on. "Does it matter at all that I...?" He swallowed. "That I honestly love her?"

Lexie cocked her head, seeming only mildly surprised by Seth's confession of love. "You know her pretty well now. What do you think?"

"I think she doesn't trust people very easily. And she trusted me."

"Yep. Your lie erased every bit of that." She nodded as though she were deciding something. "I'll tell you what—I'll do my best to persuade her to talk to you. I don't know if it will do any good, but I'll try. You can call me."

243

He let out a small sigh of relief. It was something. The best chance he had, anyway. "Thank you, Lexie."

She smiled then appeared to think better of herself. "Jesus Christ, you're going to get me fired, you know that? Why am I such a sucker for you?"

"Because you know I'm good for her."

"You do make her a better person."

It was Seth's turn to look into the distance. "She makes me a better person too."

"Well, right now it's hard to see that. It seems more like you're a total shit." She leaned onto the window frame. "So here's my advice—show her. Show her you're a better person."

Seth's forehead creased. "How?"

With a shrug, she stood upright. "You're a smart guy. You'll figure something out."

Show her. Lexie's words echoed in his ears as he watched her walk away, his mind already racing with ideas.

Chapter Twenty

Heather gazed out the window of the Trump Towers Suite overlooking Central Park, rubbing her hands up and down her arms to warm herself. It wasn't that it was cold, exactly. The weather was actually quite warm for November in New York City. Still, she felt chilled. She'd blame it on the change of climate from L.A. if she hadn't been cold there as well.

How long had it been since she'd felt warm now?

Almost three weeks. Since the day she watched Seth leave her bedroom.

She turned to the suite's thermostat and hiked the temp up to seventy-four. From across the room, she felt Lexie's eyes on her, watching her every move like a nervous hen. It seemed she'd been watching her like that for as long as Heather had felt the chill. Did she really seem that much of a mess? She knew she was inside, but thought she'd managed a pretty decent façade. Guess not.

She sighed and looked at the clock on her phone. Six hours left until check-in at the New York City 24-Hour Plays. That left hours of pretending she was fine. It was easier when she was busy. This downtime was the worst, when all she wanted to do was cry or sleep. Or cry *and* sleep.

God, how long could this heartache last? She'd only known Seth for three months. She'd been with Collin off and on for two years and didn't feel a fraction of the anguish she did now. Maybe it was because she'd been betrayed so deeply, but she suspected it was more than that. Like, maybe because Collin wasn't ever *the* guy. And Seth was.

"Do you want me to order room service?"

Heather glanced at Lexie, who was still watching her every move. "No, I'm not hungry."

"Heather, you haven't eaten all day." Someday Lexie had to explain how she'd so effectively mastered that motherly tone at her young age. "You need to eat something before the Intros meeting tonight."

"I already looked at the menu. Nothing looks good." Heather didn't need to look at the menu to know nothing looked good. That was another side effect of lost love—no appetite.

"I could order some Chinese. Or pizza. Or anything! This is New York, everything delivers."

Heather weighed her options for a moment, deciding whether it would take more energy to continue the battle or just give in and eat something. A compromise, maybe. "The only thing I want is a Diet Coke and a bag of Cheetos." Junk food. Her trainer would go ballistic.

Whatever. Who cared? She certainly didn't.

"Then I'll run out and get some. There's a store on the corner." Lexie grabbed her purse and coat from the closet, obviously elated that Heather had shown an interest in eating.

A weak surge of satisfaction filled Heather's chest. At least she'd made Lexie happy.

She flung herself on the sofa and wrapped herself in the blanket she'd snagged earlier from the suite's bedroom and watched her assistant as she buttoned her pea coat.

The concern returned to Lexie's eyes. "Are you sure you want to be doing this?"

"You're the one forcing me to eat something."

"I meant the plays."

Heather ran her hand through her hair. "Why wouldn't I? I always do the plays when I have time in my schedule." She had considered canceling, but what would be her excuse? Life went on. She had to figure out how to go on with it. Without Seth.

The thought of moving on without Seth brought a fresh wave of remorse. Which made her irritated. Which made her irritated with Lexie. "Jesus, you're so weird. I mean, months ago you were eager to sign me up without telling me and now you're being all freaky because I want to do them." It couldn't just be because she'd been moping around. Lexie was always the biggest proponent of the keep-yourself-occupied mentality. There had to be something else.

Heather sat up and glared at her friend. "What is it you aren't telling me?"

"Seth's doing the plays too."

She'd said it so quickly it took Heather a moment to register her words. When she did, she'd wished she hadn't asked. The air whooshed out of her lungs and she slumped back into the couch cushion. "Oh."

"Yeah."

It hadn't even occurred to her that Seth would be invited. Of course he would be. His addition to the plays in L.A. had brought in a lot of additional funding. If she'd had any capacity to think at all the last few weeks, she would have already realized it.

Lexie should have already realized it.

Heather shifted to give her assistant the best glare she could manage. "Why didn't you tell me before we got here?"

Lexie crossed the room and sat on the couch next to her before answering. "Because I was afraid of what you'd do. But I feel guilty. So I told you. Besides, I think you should be prepared."

A lump formed in Heather's throat that she quickly swallowed down. "I don't know why you're so concerned. I'm a professional. We can figure something out." She was an actress—those lines should have been more convincing.

"You've refused to talk to him or see him for weeks and now you're okay with it?"

Heather flung her arms halfheartedly in the air. "No, I'm not okay with it, but I don't really have a choice, do I?"

"Don't you? You didn't want to work with him anymore on *Girl Fight* and poof! He was off the film. It seems to me you have all the choices, Heather." Her tone was laced with malice.

Heather hadn't realized Lexie felt that way. They hadn't talked about it before now. Yeah, throwing Seth off the movie hadn't been one of her finer moments, but she just couldn't see him then. Not when the wounds had been fresh.

She didn't know if she could see him now either. She was still working that out in her head. One thing she knew for certain—she wouldn't get him fired from the plays. He was too important to the cause.

"*Girl Fight* was different," she explained to Lexie. "He was there for the wrong reasons. He works on the plays because he believes in them." Seth at that elementary school flashed through her mind. "He did a lot of good for other people in L.A. I wouldn't take that away from them because I got my silly little heart broken."

Her voice choked and Lexie put her arm around her in a hug.

Heather let herself fall into the embrace, relishing the warmth of human contact. She wasn't usually a hugger, but now, after so many weeks of missing Seth's touch, a hug was exactly what she needed.

When she pulled out of the hug, Heather leaned her head against Lexie's. "How do you know Seth's here, anyway?"

"He, um, told me."

Heather shot upright. "You've talked to him?"

"Maybe once or twice. Or five times." She shrugged like it was no big deal.

But it *was* a big deal and Lexie knew it. Her play-it-off tactic was not working on Heather. "Five times! Behind my back? How could you do that?"

"You refused to talk to him and he wanted to know how you were."

Heather wavered between feeling this was yet another betrayal from a loved one and an intense curiosity to discover whatever she could about her ex-lover.

Before she could figure out which emotion to go with, Lexie added softly, "I've talked to him enough to genuinely believe he cares about you."

Heather wanted to believe that. Almost did. But his lie... "Yeah, he's got a real fine way of showing it."

"So he fucked up. Have you never fucked up in your life? I want you to think long and hard about that answer before you give it."

Heather didn't have to think long and hard. She'd fucked up plenty. In fact, she was pretty sure she'd fucked up with Seth, though she didn't know how she would have played it differently.

She bit her lip, hoping to curb any emotion that might spill out when she spoke next. "How is he?" Then she held her breath while waiting for Lexie's answer.

"He's not good. He misses you. He seems to be a real mess."

She let the air out of her lungs in a shaky exhale. "Well, that's something."

"You should talk to him."

Three weeks ago, she'd vowed to never talk to him again. Two weeks ago, she'd still believed she could keep that promise. But now... She wasn't quite sure when her resolve had weakened, but now she found herself considering.

Then she stopped considering. "I just...I can't, Lex."

"You're going to be working together. Wouldn't it be a good idea to at least smooth things over?"

Smoothing things over wouldn't be necessary if she planned on avoiding him the entire twenty-four hours. But she didn't say that to Lexie.

"Since the interview's aired, you should probably decide how you're going to address questions about the two of you."

Heather closed her eyes and held her head in her hands. "I don't want to think about the interview." Her Jenna Markham special had aired earlier that week to record network ratings. So far, Heather had managed to avoid any follow-up press. Lexie had warded off most of the media by releasing a statement that Heather needed some personal time to deal with people affected by the things she'd said in her interview.

It wasn't a lie. Just most people assumed that meant her family, not Seth. Right now, the world still thought she was with the *Hollywood Production Designer*, because she hadn't bothered to tell anyone any different.

But there would be press at the end of the 24-Hour Plays. She wouldn't be able to avoid the questions then. And people would see her. And Seth. Her and Seth not together.

That was why she couldn't think about the interview. Because it inevitably led to thinking about Seth and how eventually she'd have to tell the world that they'd broken up. The thought was devastating. Because then it would be real.

"I know you don't want to think about it," Lexie said, unaware of what tormented Heather most about the interview. "But it's out there now. You can't avoid the press forever. And do you really regret saying any of those things? Even without Seth?"

"No." The only thing she regretted was that Seth wasn't in her life anymore. "I miss him, Lexie." Her voice caught. "Like, so much."

Lexie pulled her into another hug. She tucked Heather's blonde hair behind her ear and out of the way of her fresh tears. "If you think about it, it was kind of romantic. Taking a job with a pay cut in order to be near you."

"You don't think that's, like, stalkerish?"

"It could be, if the guy was a freak. But it's Seth."

"Yeah." *Seth.* God, just thinking his name made her heart beat faster. There was no one like Seth. Never would be, she was sure of it. "But he lied."

"You don't always make it easy for people to love you," Lexie said. "Can you really blame the guy for having to play games to get to see the real you?"

"Am I really that awful of a person?"

"No, sweetie. You're really not." She wiped at Heather's tears with her thumb. "But you put up a lot of extra stuff that people have to look past in order to find that out."

"I do do that, don't I?" If Seth had been honest from the beginning, there was a good chance things wouldn't have gone down between them like they did. They'd probably have had a one-night fling and that was all. By keeping the truth from her, she'd been forced to deal with things about herself that she never would have dealt with otherwise.

She'd never have been able to love him like she did. Or had. No, did. She still loved him. She couldn't deny that, even to herself.

Heather took a Kleenex from Lexie and wiped her nose. "I kind of liked myself better when I was with him."

"Me too."

She laughed. "Now you're just being mean."

"Okay, maybe I am." Lexie stood and moved back around the couch. "All right, I'm leaving for the store. You'll be okay?"

"Yep. Take your time. Enjoy the fresh air." The alone time would give her time to figure out what to do about Seth.

"You're sure?"

"Yep. Besides, I bet you're tired of being cooped up with my crazy ass."

"Bitchy ass is more like it. And I won't answer for fear of keeping my job."

Heather turned to lean her face on the back of the couch. "You always act like I'm on the verge of firing you. You know you can't get rid of me that easy, don't you?"

"Yes." Lexie sighed, her hand at the door. "But a girl can dream."

Heather laughed—her first genuine laugh in weeks, and kept chuckling after Lexie had left. It was good to feel something besides depressed. Did she feel good because she'd had a good moment with Lexie or because she was finally moving past her heartache?

Or was her better mood because she knew Seth would be at the plays?

She let herself daydream about it for a few minutes— imagined rehearsing the plays, bumping into him backstage. Would he try to talk to her? Would she want to talk to him? Would they end up making out against the wall, their bodies pressed together in all the right places?

And that was why she was afraid of working with him. Because she wanted to talk to him and touch him and kiss him and lick him as much as she wanted to never see him again. At least the never seeing him again option protected her from further heartache—but she was so hurt already, could there really be a "further"?

Maybe she should cancel her participation in the plays. Lexie would be disappointed, but—

A rapping at the door jolted her from her increasingly tormented thoughts. She jumped up, glancing at the table by the closet where she knew Lexie had left her keycard earlier. Yep, just as she suspected—the keycard was there.

She picked up the card and opened the door to hand it to her assistant. "Damn it, Lex, when are you going to remember..."

Except it wasn't Lexie.

Heather's mouth went dry and a lump caught in her throat. "Daddy." She was stunned, to say the least. When she'd seen Dean on the set of *Girl Fight*, she'd told him she was done with the handouts. That didn't mean she didn't expect to see him again, but certainly she thought her generous check bought her a couple of years reprieve.

Dean brushed past her, swinging the door open as he did.

"I didn't say you could come in."

"But you'd never turn me away."

"Yes, I would. I told you last time no more." She turned to face him, aware that the door hadn't closed completely behind him, but unwilling to take her eyes off him to shut it herself. Besides, being alone with her father was never the best option, though habit kept her from wanting their encounter to be broadcast to whoever might be in the hall.

She watched as he crossed to the windows and whistled at the view. "Nice crib," he said. "Definitely a step up from your fancy trailer."

Heather ignored his comments and adopted a defensive posture, crossing her arms over her chest. "How did you know where to find me?" It was one of the first questions she asked every time she saw him even though it didn't really matter how he found her, just that he had.

He evaded her like he invariably always did when she asked. "I always know where you are baby doll. I'm your daddy."

She cringed at his parental declaration. Was she too old to be emancipated from him? Because it wouldn't bother her much if she never saw him and his yellow-toothed grin again. "What do you want, Dean? Let's skip the bullshit this time and you just tell me."

His eyes narrowed slightly at her use of his name. It was the first time she'd called him anything but Daddy, and though she'd rather not have to call him anything at all, the departure felt good.

"Well, you see, life was going along just fine." He turned away from the view and began inspecting the minibar. "The money you gave us was helping your mama, and I even managed to find a good job." He pulled a few bottles out and stuffed them in his pocket without reading the labels.

"That's fabulous." Her tone couldn't be any drier if she tried.

"But see"—he pocketed another handful of bottles—"then some report came out where you told the world I was a bad father."

Her heart skipped a beat, but she refused to let her father know he'd affected her. "And your point is?"

He shut the fridge door and turned to pin his eyes on his daughter. "Why would you tell people lies like that?"

"Because they aren't lies." She'd wondered how her father would take her tell-all exclusive, but she'd been more concerned about her own life post-Jenna interview than his. Even with him standing in front of her, she still didn't care about his reaction. She just wanted him to go. "If that's all you came to talk about, you need to leave. Actually, you need to leave period."

"But, Heather, you don't understand the consequences of your lies." He took a couple of steps toward her. "I lost my job because of the things you been saying."

"You lost your job because you show up stoned out of your mind." *Unbelievable.* He'd never kept a job more than a few months at a time, and he was blaming this termination on her? He might not have even been fired. He might not have even had a job. He wasn't exactly the poster boy for honesty.

Which was why she was done with him—done with him the moment she'd said on national television that she'd wished he was dead. If he couldn't be dead for real, he could at least be dead to her. "Dean, I'm not doing this anymore. Seriously. You need to leave."

"I ain't leaving until I get some compensation."

"Compensation?" Her voice rose. "What about my compensation? Who's going to compensate me for all the time and money I've given to you?"

He gestured to the luxurious suite. "I think you've gotten the better end of the stick."

"I made my end of the stick myself." She was pissed now. Seriously pissed. How dare he claim what she'd busted her ass to achieve? "All of this you see here? It's mine because I earned it. I don't owe you anything. I'm not giving you anything else. Last time was the end."

"Now don't be like that, Heather. Just give me what I deserve and I'll be going." He started a slow saunter toward her that she found more than a bit creepy.

Still, she played brave. "Or what? Do you think you have something over me? The only thing I've been embarrassed about is you and you're not a secret anymore." Surprisingly, she was pissed enough to play brave convincingly.

"Don't fucking tell me you're embarrassed by me." He continued his approach, each step he took backing her up until she'd reached the wall. "It's me who's embarrassed to have a whore for a daughter—a famous whore. You think that makes me proud?"

"Get out of here!" she screamed, her fear now too strong to keep suppressed.

"It's my turn to say, or what?" He put a hand on each side of her, caging her in. His breath was foul and his voice low and snakelike. "We both know you aren't going to call security."

Now she remembered another reason she always gave Dean what he wanted—because he scared her. Legitimately scared her. She knew he wasn't above roughing her up. He could hit her. Push her around. He was skinny from drug use, but he was still strong.

Her heart pounded so loudly she was certain Dean could hear it. Or maybe that wasn't her heart, but the door.

"Excuse me, miss? Are you okay in here?"

She glanced over to see a bellhop sticking his head in the doorway. His eyes darted from Heather to Dean then back to Heather, surmising the situation. "Do you need some help?"

The Heather of three months ago would have said *no*, would have done anything to keep attention away from her and her crack-head father.

But the Heather of today was a completely different person. "Yes! Please! I do need help."

"No, she doesn't," Dean said. "We're fine here. Just a personal matter."

"We're not fine here!" Heather took advantage of Dean's distraction to duck out under his arms. She ran to the bellhop's side, wanting a person between her and the man she used to call *Daddy*. "He's here uninvited and I want him to leave."

"She's being dramatic. I'm her father."

"I want him to leave!"

The bellhop stepped inside and picked up the phone on the occasional table. "Hi, this is Wes Lang. We need a manager and security to this room, please. There's a situation."

"There's no situation." Dean turned to his daughter, eyes pleading. "Heather, come on, now."

"No, you come on!" Maybe because she felt less frightened with the bellhop with her, or maybe just because she'd finally reached her limit of Dean Hutchins's shit, Heather suddenly felt her rage welling up inside her like a geyser.

Then the geyser blew. "I am sick and tired of you manipulating me and pushing me around. You've caused me nothing but pain and humiliation my whole life—when you were supposed to care for me and love me. I'm through. Do you hear me? I'm through being ashamed. It's not my fault that you're messed up. And it's not my fault that you are a horrible excuse for a father. Just because I grew up with you doesn't mean I have to be anything like you. So I'm not enabling you anymore. I'm done. As soon as I get back to L.A., I'm filing for a restraining order, something I should have done years ago. And so help me God, if you come near me again, I will throw you in the slammer without a second thought."

"Baby doll—"

"I don't want to hear anything you have to say." She turned to the bellhop, her body shaking. "Can you get him out of here?"

"Don't bother," Dean said gruffly. "I'm leaving."

But that wasn't good enough. He couldn't just walk out on his own accord. Heather was determined to finally make a stand where her father was concerned. Laying it on him had been cathartic, but she craved more. She wanted him banned from the hotel, thrown out on his ass. Wanted photographers to take his picture and report the situation so that maybe, *just maybe*, her public would understand who he was and make it harder for him to find her again.

Wow. Wasn't that a complete one-eighty from the woman she'd been before?

Before Seth.

Thank God security arrived before she had to explain her thoughts to the baby-faced bellhop/hero in her suite. And with them was Lexie.

When Lexie saw Dean, she dropped the bag of Cheetos and the bottle of Diet Coke and ran to Heather's side. "Oh my God! Are you okay? I shouldn't have left you!"

Heather stared at the pop bottle as it rolled down the hall. "I guess I'll wait on drinking the Diet Coke."

"She's in shock," Lexie exclaimed to the hotel manager. "I think she's in shock. Heather, are you in shock?"

"I don't think so." She was still shaking from her outburst, but other than that, she felt pretty damn good. She'd stood up for herself—stood up to her father. She'd been scared as shit, but then she let herself go and now she felt invincible. Now she could do anything.

The security guard and hotel manager had Dean out of her room within minutes. Heather smiled to herself when she caught the bellhop taking a picture of the scene on his smartphone. If her father wanted what she had, why shouldn't he have the press that went with it?

After the door clicked and the lock was bolted, Lexie buzzed around with adrenaline. "I can't believe he was here! I can't believe he found you. He didn't hurt you, did he?"

"Shook me up a little, but that's all." Actually, Lexie seemed more disturbed by the event than Heather did.

"I'll get on the phone and see if I can get us a flight out of here tonight." Lexie sat down at the suite's desk and opened up her laptop. "We can forget the plays—they'll understand; stars cancel last minute all the time—and just get home."

Here it was—the perfect opportunity to get out of seeing Seth. But for some reason, when she opened her mouth to answer, what came out was, "No."

"No?"

"No, I want to stay." The thing was, Dean's appearance had showed her something fascinating about herself—she was strong. Stronger than she'd ever realized. "I'm fine. I'm more than fine. I feel great."

"Do you really want to have to deal with all this *and* Seth?" Lexie swiveled and leaned on the back of the desk chair. "You don't have to put up a brave front. It's my fault. I shouldn't have signed you up for this. Not when I knew he'd be here. It was a bad, bad idea on my part and I—"

"Yeah, I think I do." Heather interrupted. "Want to deal with this and Seth, I mean. It's not going to be easy, but I can see him. He didn't break me. Hell, if Dean didn't break me, I don't think anyone could."

Lexie paused. Then with dramatic flair, she shut her laptop. "Damn straight!"

"It's settled then. We're staying." Heather couldn't stop smiling as she curled up on the couch to eat her Cheetos and drink her Diet Coke. She was proud of her decision. It wasn't often that she felt empowered.

And working with Seth would be fine. He would be absorbed with his building and carpentry anyway. She knew him well enough to know he'd respect however she wanted things to be between them. She wouldn't have to see him or talk to him if she didn't want to.

And, hell, maybe she even wanted to.

Chapter Twenty-One

Check-in at the 24-Hour Plays went a lot smoother than it had in L.A. since Heather had Lexie to help her fill out her forms. Which was almost a bad thing. Heather was anxious and without anything to keep her occupied, her anxiety increased.

She sat on the lobby bench next to Lex, her foot swinging as she looked over her assistant's shoulder. "Put eight there. This is the eighth time I've done the plays."

"Yep." Lexie filled in the blank with the appropriate number.

"And list that I was the spokesperson last time. You can put that right there."

Lexie looked up and glared. "Do you want to fill this out yourself?"

"No, that's your job."

Turning so it was harder for Heather to see what she was writing, Lexie resumed her task. "Then go smoke a cigarette or something."

"I don't smoke."

"Maybe you need to start because you're bugging the shit out of me."

"Fine." Heather crossed her arms and put on her best pout. No one saw it, though. Lexie was buried in the forms and no one else in the lobby was paying her any attention.

For the fiftieth time that evening, Heather scanned the small crowd. The Urban Arts volunteers who were running the check-in all wore black T-shirts in order to be easily distinguishable. Heather recognized a fair number of the actors and directors. But there was one face she kept expecting that still hadn't appeared. What time was the crew supposed to arrive? Weren't they there before the actors? Where in the hell was he?

Without looking up, Lexie said, "You're looking for him."

"No, I'm not!" Of course, that was exactly what she was doing, and her quick answer proved it. She twirled a piece of hair around her finger and attempted a recovery. "Looking for who?"

Her assistant sighed. "If you want to see him, you should just go find him."

"I don't want to see anyone." There was no way in hell she was searching him out.

But she also couldn't sit anymore. It was driving her insane. Across the lobby was a familiar face. "I changed my mind. Because the person I was looking for is right over there." She stood and pointed toward the actor she knew. "And I'm going to go see him right now."

"Fine. Good riddance."

Heather rolled her eyes as she traipsed away. Was it only a few short hours ago that they'd been bonding? Now she wanted to smack Lexie. She was supposed to be her support system. Her help.

God, she needed help.

Where was Seth? Had he decided not to show? And why did she care?

The actor she knew was flipping through screens on his smartphone and didn't notice her approach.

"Howdy, stranger," she said, nudging him with her shoulder.

Micah Preston looked up at her with his famous Hollywood grin. "Hey, Heather." He put his phone in his pocket and gave her an obligatory hug.

It felt strange hugging her former costar. Awkward. Not because they weren't friendly with each other, but because they had, on occasion, been extra friendly. They'd known each other for quite a while before they'd worked together on the Colorado movie. They'd slept together a handful of times over the course of their acquaintance. But after he turned down her last hook-up proposal, things between them got weird. Hence the awkward.

An uncomfortable silence spread between them, their grins pasted on their faces. "You look good," Heather said finally.

Micah shifted. "Um, thanks."

"Don't freak out. I'm not hitting on you." She looked him over trying to remember what it was she'd seen in him. Convenience. That was it. He didn't attract her now at all. He wasn't...Seth. "You aren't my type anyway."

"Not your type?" Micah's eyes widened. "How can you say that after, you know?"

Heather laughed. "So which is it? Do you want me hitting on you or not?"

"Not." He smiled guiltily. "But you could still acknowledge all my awesomeness."

"What the heck was I thinking? Of course. You are totally overflowing with awesomeness."

"Now that's more like it."

She smiled. Had it really only been three months since she'd last seen Micah? It felt like years separated her from the person she'd been then. The awkwardness between them wasn't just that they'd seen each other naked. It was her. She was different. Was she forever tattooed by Seth now? Completely unable to relate to the life she'd had before him?

"But now I'm all curious," Micah said, interrupting her reverie. "Am I really not your type?"

"Yeah, you're really not. But it isn't you." She chuckled over her *it's not you, it's me* innuendo. "I guess I'm more aware now of what I need than I used to be."

"Well, good for you." He raised a brow. "Wait, didn't I hear you were seeing someone?" He snapped as he tried to remember. "A producer or something?"

"A Production Designer." God, she'd expected questions from the press, but not her fellow actors. She had to get a story together. A story that would likely require Seth's input.

For now, she diverted the attention off her. "You're with that camera girl, right?" Micah had been a perma-bachelor until recently when he'd fallen for the camera assistant on the movie they'd done together.

He beamed at the mention of his girlfriend. "Maddie. Yeah. She's here, actually." His eyes swept the lobby. "There," he nodded when he'd spotted Maddie. "She's one of the directors."

"That's your girlfriend? Oh fuck, she's my director." Heather hadn't connected the name when she'd gotten her assignment. "That means it doesn't matter that I'm not hitting on you—if I don't stop talking to you right now I seriously fear for what she's going to make me do on stage."

Micah rolled his eyes. "Whatever." Then he thought better of it. "I mean, Maddie will probably make you do something insane, but you can handle it."

Yeah, she probably could. She could handle a lot more than she used to think she could. Maybe that was why she'd been looking for Seth—because seeing him would be the ultimate test to her strength. She wanted to know if she could handle that.

The lights flashed in the lobby, indicating it was time for everyone to convene on the stage for introductions. Heather waved goodbye to Lexie, then followed Micah and the rest of the crowd inside, noting that there was still no sign of Seth.

Heather's intro was first. She did her regular spiel and then showed her prop. She had brought her fur-lined handcuffs from L.A., intending to use them since she hadn't gotten to last time. Then at the last minute, she'd stopped in the hotel gift shop and bought a hat with the Statue of Liberty on it. The handcuffs stayed in her purse.

The rest of the intro session dragged on. Usually, this was Heather's favorite part of the plays process, but she couldn't seem to stay focused. Was he backstage working already? Was he avoiding her? Had he decided not to do the plays after all? Was it because of her?

Finally, the meeting was over and everyone was dismissed for the night. Heather headed out to the lobby to look for Lexie. When she didn't find her, Heather pulled out her phone and called her.

"We're done. You can come get me." Heather wondered if her voice sounded as heavy as it felt.

"Oh, okay." Lexie sounded surprised. "Um, so, did you see him?"

"No," Heather snapped. She didn't want to talk about it. She was having a hell of a time figuring out why she felt disappointed about Seth's absence. She certainly didn't need to try to analyze it over the phone.

"Okay." Lexie's voice seemed puzzled. "Where are you anyway?"

"At the theater. Where else would I be?" Heather's head was starting to pound. She needed to get back to the hotel where she could commence her nightly routine of curling up in a ball and crying.

"Are you still on the stage?"

"No. Jesus, Lexie, is this twenty questions? Just come and get me already."

"Go back to the stage. I'll meet you there. On the stage. In, um, soon."

Heather hung up and let out a sound of frustration as she stuffed her phone in her purse. She wasn't in the mood for cryptic Lexie. She also wasn't in the mood for waiting in the lobby where the floor to ceiling windows had attracted a small crowd of fans eager to see which star would walk out next.

Waiting on the stage was a good idea.

Heather walked down the back hallway to the stage door. She stepped into the now empty theater and headed toward the skirt of the stage.

Except the theater wasn't empty after all. The circle of chairs that had been set up for the cast introductions remained.

And sitting in one of the chairs was Seth.

Her heart dropped into her stomach and her hands got sweaty. Maybe she wasn't strong enough to see him.

But when he stood from his chair and pinned his eyes on her, a wave of euphoria washed over her, calling goose bumps to the surface of her skin. Then she knew she could handle seeing him. She could handle it just fine.

Taking a deep breath, he spoke. "My name is Seth Rafferty."

Heather narrowed her eyes. "What are you doing?"

"My plane was late getting in so I missed introductions. So I thought I'd do mine now."

She got it immediately, that he'd planned this out—for her. That Lexie had set her up to meet him. But she played along. "Intros are for the actors, not the crew."

He smiled slightly and she melted. God, she'd missed his face.

"For one night only," he said, "it's for the crew too. Well, for one crewmember. And just for you. Now stop interrupting. Where was I? See, this is why I'm not an actor."

She put her hand over her mouth to suppress a giggle and took a step closer.

"Oh yes. I was at the beginning. My name is Seth Patrick Rafferty." He met her eyes. "And I'm a Production Designer. A good one, even. I worked hard to become one. Came out of poverty, worked every job in between to get to where I am. I'm what you call a success story."

She nodded, encouraging him to go on.

"Because I've had so much success, I wanted to give back. I offered to do the 24-Hour plays, design and construct furniture so I could give arts back to the kids who need it. It meant I'd be working carpentry again, but hey, those are my roots. I could deal with that. I'm proud of my roots."

He clapped his hands together and she could tell he was nervous. It was sort of impressive he'd made it so far through his monologue, being a crewmember and all.

"Urban Arts welcomed the proposal," he continued. "They were crazy about it, in fact. Everyone was." He narrowed his eyes. "Except this one person. She hated the idea. Loathed it. Despised—"

"She thought it was a shit idea."

"You get the picture then." He caught her eye again and she shivered. "Funny thing was, this woman, this sassy little diva— it really bothered me that she hated my idea."

She'd wondered about that before, wondered why he'd been caught up with her in the first place. "She was just a silly movie star. Why did you care?"

"Do people usually interrupt during the introductions?"

"No, but—"

"Then shush. Please." He waited until Heather closed her mouth to continue. "In answer to your question, there was something about her that made me care. Not just about whether she liked the construction idea, but about what she thought of me. Problem was she didn't like me. At all. I think she might have hated me more than she hated my carpentry plan."

"I never hated you. I wished I hated you." Her voice was barely above a whisper.

"Well, I wished I hated you too. But I didn't. Not for a minute." His words were equally soft, but strong all at the same time. In the subtext, Heather heard the depth of not-hate Seth had for her. It caught her off guard, made her lose her breath.

Seth continued, unaware of the effect he was having on her ability to bring air into her lungs. "And when I realized the reason that you, uh, disliked me—because of what I did, well, I judged you. Not only because I wanted to put you in your place, but because I thought that if there was any chance that you could like me, any chance at all, then I wanted you to like me *for me*. Not for what I did or didn't do."

He looked at a spot on the stage floor. "And I'd been burned before. My ex-girlfriend—ex-fiancée, actually—left me because of who I was."

"Ex-fiancée?" She swallowed her jealousy.

"Yes. Several years ago. She left me when she found out about my past."

"Ouch."

"Exactly. I could tell you more about her if you want. Because I won't hide anything from you anymore. But it's really a boring story and what I felt with her—well, now I know it was nothing. Nothing compared to... Well."

"Maybe you can tell me about her. Someday." *Someday.* Did she mean to give him a someday? Yeah, she did.

"Then I will. Someday. Anyway, it influenced why I did what I did. Why I lied. I know it's not an excuse..."

Heather took a step toward him. "It counts. Being hurt in the past definitely changes how we act in the present." How could she not give him that when the past had been so much of what dictated her life for so long? Dictated how she'd behaved with him. "And I was a stuck-up bitch."

"You had your reasons too."

She shook her head. "But it was wrong to judge you."

Seth took a step toward her. "See, that's just the thing. I was all pissed because I felt like you were judging me. But in reality, I judged you. I decided that you needed to learn a lesson. That you needed to change. Because you were a person who could never see beyond someone's outside to find what was inside."

He took another step toward her and Heather felt the warmth of his nearness now, felt the chill she'd endured for weeks finally disappearing with the gap between them.

Seth swallowed. "I was wrong. You could see beyond a person's outside. You did. You saw me, Heather. The real me and you...you cared for me."

"I loved you," she corrected. She couldn't let him diminish what she'd felt—what she still felt.

He smiled. "You loved me." He said the words as though they were precious and fragile. "And while I was hoping to change you, I had no idea how much you would change me. For the better."

His body twitched as though he wanted to move even closer, bridge the final distance between them. He could do it with five steps. Instead, he did it with his words. "I love you, Heather Wainwright. The only emotion I feel nearly as deeply as that one is regret. I am so sorry that I hurt you and that what I did took away the most amazing thing I've ever had in my life. If I could turn back time, I'd do it differently, I swear."

"I wouldn't." The words were out of her mouth before she could stop them. She looked away, suddenly shy in her honesty. Studying her shoes, she went on. "I mean, you hurt me. But truthfully, I don't think I'd ever have let you get close enough to hurt me if things hadn't gone down like they had."

Seth opened his mouth to say something, but she cut him off. "Look, I can't play *what if*. I don't know what would have happened. What I do know is that you changed me too. You taught me how to let go of the past. How to move on."

Her knees were shaking and her stomach fluttering with butterflies, but she knew what she had to say next. Because of him, she knew she had the strength to say it. "So, could we put this whole thing in our past and move on? Because I really don't think I can stand another minute of not being in your arms."

His brows rose in surprise. That was the last thing Heather registered before they were holding each other, their lips wrapped around one another, their tongues sliding together. She dove into his kiss, drinking the taste of him as if she'd been parched. And she had been—she'd been completely dry of his love and now that she'd rediscovered the oasis, she drank him in gulps.

She curled her fingers in his hair and tugged him closer, letting out a moan as her pelvis ground against his. God, she was happy just kissing him, being in his embrace, feeling his hands on her body. But the moisture between her thighs and the thickening bulge at her belly told her that they'd need more of each other. Soon.

"Take me to my hotel?" she asked against his mouth.

"Uh huh." He lingered a moment more in their tongue tango before he pulled away. "Wait a minute, I haven't shared my prop."

She pursed her lips. "Is it a drill?"

"No, princess. We'll save the drill for the hotel. For now, I have this."

Her brows furrowed as he reached in his jacket pocket and pulled out a three-fold paper. She took it from his outstretched hand and scanned it, only needing to see the words *DEED* and *San Gabriel Mountains* before she understood what it was. "You bought it!"

"Yeah. I figured if you were able to stop looking in the past, it was time for me to look to the future." He cupped her face in his hands, stroking her jaw with his thumbs. "Because my future is with you, Heather. At least, I hope it is."

Her throat tightened. "It is." A tear slid down her cheek. "It is."

Then they were kissing again, a sweet, slow kiss that spoke of building cabins and wedding rings and swollen bellies. A kiss that not only looked into the future, but sealed it.

After they'd made promises with their lips and shared a lifetime of dreams with the caress of their hands, they drifted apart, ready to move on—with their life, with their relationship. To the hotel.

Heather gestured toward the deed still clutched in her hand. "You know this is really too small of a prop to show up on stage. You need something more substantial. Something that can be seen from the audience."

He cocked a brow. "Do you have something in mind?"

"Let's just say I might have a pair of fur-lined handcuffs in my purse."

A sexy smile spread across his lips, burning her skin and making her thighs twitch. "Heather, can I take you back to my hotel room and handcuff you while we have wild monkey sex?"

"You mean you want to go play rough?"

"Always." He nodded toward the door, holding out his hand for her.

"Oh, tool boy," she said, putting her hand firmly in his. "You know all you ever had to do was ask."

About the Author

Laurelin Paige is a sucker for a good romance and gets giddy anytime there's kissing, much to the embarrassment of her three daughters. Her husband doesn't seem to complain, however. When she isn't reading or writing sexy stories, she's probably singing, watching *Game of Thrones* and *The Walking Dead*, or dreaming of Adam Levine. She is the author of the bestselling Fixed trilogy and is represented by Bob Diforio of D4EO Literary Agency.

It's all about the story...

Romance

HORROR

www.samhainpublishing.com

CPSIA information can be obtained at www.ICGtesting.com
Printed in the USA
BVOW02s1115171115

427457BV00004B/142/P